## "What is that?"

Dumbfounded, Burke scanned sixty-plus feet of sky-blue trimmed silver-painted steel.

"Burke, exactly what did you think I'd come here in?" Savannah asked mildly.

"I didn't. Didn't even wonder." He shook his head as if to clear it before slicing a look at the slender, fragile woman who actually navigated this monstrous machine for a living. "It's a truck.... You're a trucker."

"Right on both counts."

Not only was she not his type, Burke thought, she wasn't any type he'd ever met before! "But you're..."

"What?"

"Small and...small."

"I don't push the truck, Burke. I drive it. I assure you I have all the necessary equipment to do it competently. Still want to drive? It has ten gears, and it takes them all to get from stop to go."

"Are you kidding?" Burke tossed her the keys. "A chance to ride shotgun with a lady trucker? I wouldn't miss it."

Dear Reader,

*Spellbinders!* That's what we're striving for. The editors at Silhouette are determined to capture your imagination and win your heart with every single book we publish. Each month, six Special Editions are chosen with *you* in mind.

Our authors are our inspiration. Writers such as Nora Roberts, Tracy Sinclair, Kathleen Eagle, Carole Halston and Linda Howard—to name but a few—are masters at creating endearing characters and heartrending love stories. Their characters are everyday people—just like you and me—whose lives have been touched by love, whose dreams and desires suddenly come true!

So find a cozy, quiet place to read, and create your own special moment with a Silhouette Special Edition.

Sincerely,

The Editors
SILHOUETTE BOOKS

# MARIANNE SHOCK
## Run Away Home

Silhouette Special Edition

Published by Silhouette Books New York

America's Publisher of Contemporary Romance

To Kathryn Thompson,
for laughter in the tough times.

SILHOUETTE BOOKS
300 East 42nd St., New York, N.Y. 10017

Copyright © 1987 by Marianne Shock

ISBN: 0-373-09412-4

First Silhouette Books printing October 1987

America's Publisher of Contemporary Romance

Printed in the U.S.A.

## MARIANNE SHOCK

has always been a romantic, and her happy marriage confirmed her belief in love at first sight. The encouragement to bring this romantic spirit to print came from her parents, who had love enough for all ten of their children. Now the mother of four active children of her own, Marianne finds she is able to devote herself to family, some theater work, home decorating and, of course, her writing career. Finishing a book, she says, is a "very gratifying exhaustion."

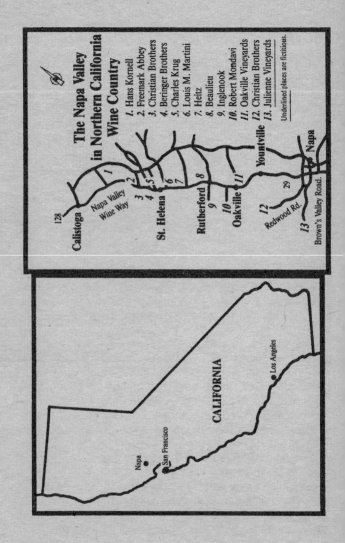

## The Napa Valley
## in Northern California
## Wine Country

1. Hans Kornell
2. Freemark Abbey
3. Christian Brothers
4. Beringer Brothers
5. Charles Krug
6. Louis M. Martini
7. Heitz
8. Beaulieu
9. Inglenook
10. Robert Mondavi
11. Oakville Vineyards
12. Christian Brothers
13. Julienne Vineyards

Underlined places are fictitious.

Calistoga
128
Napa Valley
Wine Way
St. Helena
Rutherford
Oakville
Yountville
Redwood Rd.
Napa
Brown's Valley Road.
29

CALIFORNIA

Napa
San Francisco

Los Angeles

# Chapter One

Soon. A few more minutes, a couple of miles, and she'd be there. Leaning forward, Savannah shifted through the sequence of gears.

*Soon.* The word whispered through her like a long, contented sigh. She sat back and smiled.

She'd driven through the night—ten, nearly eleven hours. The moon had vanished; the sun was still tucked below the horizon. Fatigue nagged at her muscles, but her head was clear, unclouded; anticipation kept her alert. Arrivals, whether to traffic-jammed cities or drowsy little towns, never failed to excite her. To Savannah's mind, the only thing better than the end of a journey was setting out on one.

She particularly looked forward to the end of this journey. A predawn fog covered the road, the air rushing through her open windows was soggy with it. With each mile the swirling mist thickened, blunting her headlights. She flipped on the wipers. The blades clicked rhythmically, reassuringly, but did little to improve visibility.

Eyes narrowed to keep track of the lane markings, Savannah hunched over the steering wheel. Then she heard it: a thin, high-pitched whine slicing through the engine's steady drone. She tensed instinctively, her knuckles whitening as she strained to isolate and define that single sound. Trouble, she brooded. The sort that would take repairs to put right. And expense. Possibly a layover.

Uneasiness stirred at the thought of delay. Savannah was neither frugal nor lavish with money. When costly repair bills were necessary she paid them, if grudgingly. She hadn't the same tolerance for layovers. The mere prospect of one knotted her stomach.

She was making too much of it, she argued. Hadn't she had everything from brakes to carburetor to wiper fluid thoroughly checked before setting out? Hadn't a qualified mechanic given her the thumbs-up? So, how bad could it—whatever *it* was—be?

It could run the gamut, she admitted grimly, from mildly annoying to crippling. Because, thumbs-up or no, there was a whine . . . and two thousand miles to go before her final stop in Chicago.

Wait and see, she told herself, as if she had a choice.

She once more gave her attention to the fog and to staying on the partially obscured highway bisecting the valley floor. Napa Valley. When Savannah thought of Napa, she recalled lush vineyards, ivy-covered wineries, Victorian houses and breezy summer days.

Over the years she'd been coast to coast more times than she could count. She'd seen the country's soft, its savage and its shades between. She'd traveled crop-quilted farmlands and deserts at sunset, navigated every mountain range from the perilous Rockies to the softly sloped Blue Hills. Every state, every square mile, had fascinated her. Still, she had her favorites, and California's wine region was one of them.

Now, gazing out at the ashen vapor, Savannah sighed regretfully, wishing she could at least enjoy the view this trip. But if she stayed on schedule—and, much as she hated them, Savannah was a stickler for schedules—she'd reach her destination, deliver the goods and be back on the road before sunrise. Another arrival. One more departure.

The fog grew treacherous, an impenetrable shroud glued to her windshield. Without taking her eyes off the road, she reached for the floppy hat on the seat beside her and shoved it onto her head. The fawn-colored felt was droopy with age. Its brim was wide and a bit frayed, dipping low on her brow in front and resting on the black hair spilling onto her shoulders in back. Though it was large enough to fit a grown man, it had been Savannah's since she was a small girl. While other children had braved troublesome moments by clutching tattered security blankets, Savannah had always reached for her hat.

Anxious to arrive, she accelerated. The glitch beneath the hood objected with an angry spit and snarl. Savannah breathed a curse when a guttural grind replaced the whine. Just as she decided to pull off the road, she spotted the beacons she'd been watching for. Though only a few yards ahead on her left, the gas lamps were barely visible, reduced to twin blots of smothered light.

Downshifting, she swung out in a wide turn and, with skillful precision, threaded sixty-one feet of truck and trailer through the estate's single-lane entrance. The arc of her headlights briefly illuminated a wooden signpost: Julienne Vineyards—Seventy-five Years of Fine Wines.

The private road was narrow and rutted, lacing the hillside in a series of tricky switchback turns. Straight ahead loomed the blackish shape of an enormous house. Its towers and turrets rose from the milky ground cover in ebony silhouettes; the softer, vaguer shadows of trees and shrubbery clung to its edges. Savannah grinned, fully appreciating its nocturnal cloak of menace and mystery.

One side of the formidable structure was bathed in the opal glow of floodlights. Figures milled about the yard, churning the illuminated fog. Peering through it, Savannah searched the slow-moving men for Claude Julienne.

She found him, head and shoulders above the others, puffing on the pipe habitually clamped between his teeth.

At Savannah's rumbling approach he lifted an arm in salute. Two of his employees hustled forward and, with the exuberance of signaling a 747 in from the runway, guided her eighteen-wheel Class Eight truck and semitrailer alongside the yawning doors of a storage shed.

Savannah braked and shut down. Rolling her shoulders to work the kinks out, she watched Claude stroll over. With his full head of dark hair and athletically trim torso, he looked a decade younger than his sixty years. His face was long and aristocratic, his eyes coal-black and sharp. His scowl was deliberate—"to chase away fools expecting hospitable welcome," he was fond of saying.

"Morning, Claude." Muffling a laugh, Savannah touched the brim of her hat. "Fine weather we're having."

His lips twitched to grin, but he pursed them around the pipe stem instead. So like him to be stubborn and act annoyed, she mused. When he met the laughter dancing in her slate-gray eyes, he shook his head and lost the battle with his smile. "You're late, Savannah. I wish you'd called. I was beginning to worry."

Genuinely surprised, Savannah gazed at him, wide-eyed. "You should know better, Claude. How long have I been hauling for you? Must be a year now." She retrieved her clipboard from the floor, where it had fallen, then opened the door. Her feet met the gravel with a quiet crunch. "Don't I always come through? Through sleet and snow and dead of night..." She paused, thinking that hadn't sounded right. "How's the rest of that go?"

Before he could answer, Savannah bent over to root around under her front seat.

"We always get our man?" he speculated with friendly irony.

As her hand closed on the weapon-weight flashlight she'd been feeling for, Savannah looked over her shoulder at him. Her eyes narrowed suspiciously. Getting a man for

Savannah was Claude Julienne's pet project. "You haven't been out rounding up eligibles, I hope. Haven't got one cuffed to one of your fancy parlor chairs, have you, Claude?"

"'Rounding up?' 'Cuffed?' Come, now, Savannah. I may be intrusive; I am never indiscreet."

"Mmm." Savannah recalled a time he'd have thought it unpardonably indiscreet for a vintner to pass the time of day with a trucker—one twenty-five and female, to boot! But that had changed last winter, when floods devastated the valley.

She'd come to pick up a load of Private Reserve wines and had been stranded when the first dams burst, washing out the roads. Over the next four days she, Claude and a hundred others had labored side by side, wading knee-deep through icy water, filling and stacking sandbags, shoveling mud dikes. Every waking moment, as more reservoirs overflowed, more rain fell, more snow melted down from the mountain, they'd each worked with the strength of two and the stubbornness of ten. They'd had to; to sit, to rest, was never to get up again.

And now—to show his appreciation, Savannah supposed—Claude was hell-bent to see her married. "My being single hasn't held me back so far," she pointed out.

"I've noticed." He took the clipboard and flashlight she handed him, then waited while she touched her toes, reached for the sky and ran in place. It was a routine they'd repeated on dozens of twilit mornings. "A woman alone on the highway. At night. I don't approve."

"So you've said . . . many, many times."

"You're a lovely woman, Savannah. Get a suitable job."

"I had a suitable job," she reminded him. "Flying the so-called Friendly Skies. And for two miserable years I had my 'lovely' bottom pinched by presumably 'suitable' executives. No thanks." She took back the clipboard, he kept the lamp and they strode the trailer's length to the cargo doors. "Let's see what we've got."

Over the months Savannah had delivered everything from bottles and corks to huge fermentation vats to the Julienne Winery, often traveling empty to the pickup point. Claude paid premium rates for such special services from the trucking company for which Savannah was an independent owner-operator. He also paid a pretty penny for select hauling. The bulk of Julienne wines was moved through the forty-eight states by a firm much larger than her brother's twenty-four-truck fleet. But Claude was fastidious with his reserve vintages and contracted the smaller outfit, one he could trust to handle and transport according to his precise instructions.

"What'd I bring you last time?" Savannah reached up to unlock the trailer's doors. "Lumber, wasn't it?"

"Oak slats." Flashlight burning, Claude climbed into the pitch-dark trailer. "Limousin oak, for making kegs."

"Mmm. Today we have—" Savannah narrowed her eyes on the shipping invoice "—sulfur dioxide."

Claude skimmed a bright beam across packing labels. "Here."

"Aaannd...phosphoric acid." For the next twenty minutes he located and confirmed the items she read off. "Sodium hydroxide... Gibberellic acid... Daminozide..."

When they'd finished, Claude looped an elegant signature at the bottom of the invoice.

"Interesting stuff," Savannah noted thoughtfully before tossing the clipboard through the open driver's window. "Not planning to blow up the countryside, are you, Claude?"

He smiled and, in a gesture that startled Savannah, patted her cheek. "No, no explosives. I'm only going to grow a few grapes, make a little wine."

*A few!* she marveled. *A little!* Now there was a pair of gross understatements. Across the nation Julienne wines claimed the lion's share of liquor store shelf space. British actors of knighthood status appeared in television ads, waxing eloquent as they poured a glass of Julienne Blanc.

And Claude summed it up by saying he planned to "grow a few grapes, make a little wine."

"Breakfast, Savannah?" Claude signaled the man waiting in a forklift to begin unloading. "Or are you rushing to be somewhere else by yesterday, as usual?"

"No breakfast. Coffee, if it's already perked." Savannah fell into step beside him. "And a phone. I am rushing. I'm scheduled to pick up my backhaul at nine this morning in Sacramento. Then it's on to Chicago. But first I need a mechanic. Transmission sounds funny."

"Savannah, you've already driven through the night without sleep. Promise me you won't drive all day as well."

His concern for her was genuine, and it touched Savannah. It also made her slightly uneasy. She wasn't used to people worrying whether she'd slept or that she was detained or on a deserted road at night. That Claude Julienne did, if only now and then, was as pleasing as it was perplexing. Savannah rarely allowed people to please or perplex her. Emotions made her vulnerable and, therefore, cautious.

"I'll be fine. Besides," she added, masking her discomfort with lightness, "I'd risk my license if I logged too many daily driving hours."

"Which, of course, you would never do," Claude drawled.

"Never." Savannah poked her tongue at the inside of her cheek. He knew well enough she often drove until she dropped, then slept a day away. "Unless it were an absolute emergency."

"An urgent matter."

"Life or death."

"You have them often, I suppose," he uttered with mock gravity.

She sniffed audibly. "You'd be surprised." Certain she'd laugh if their eyes met, she kept hers trained on the spray of pebbles she kicked up with each step.

"And this time?" Claude persisted.

"A standard run." Dull, her sigh seemed to say. "Nine o'clock at the loading dock; call it a day at the first rest stop."

"Good." Claude cupped her elbow as they turned a corner of the house. "Tell me, how was your drive up the coast?"

"Uneventful—oh, except for a storm. It was wonderful!"

Claude laughed softly in the gloomy dawn. "But of course it was wonderful. All your storms are."

"I do love a good firecracker downpour." She threw her head back on a laugh. "I shouldn't have enjoyed it quite so much, though. It caused the fog I hit when I turned inland. *That* set me back a bit."

"Not as much as it should have," he muttered as they climbed the dozen or so steps to an expansive terrace fronting the house. A pair of thick carved doors arched to meet in the center tower from which the rest of the fortresslike house fanned out.

Claude led Savannah into the cool, dim foyer. At the flip of a switch soft radiance showered down from a multitiered chandelier of teardrop crystal. The entrance hall was constructed entirely of pale fieldstone, with a selection of deep slate tones blended in for warmth. A massive tapestry of forest green and burnished gold boasted the Julienne family crest, which was reproduced on the label affixed to every bottle of Julienne wine. A yellow velvet wing chair and walnut telephone table were tucked beneath a sweeping staircase.

"Phone book." Claude lifted the slim directory from a drawer in the clawfooted table. "I'll arrange for coffee while you make your call."

Sinking into the soft chair, Savannah thumbed to the listing of garages and began dialing. She'd replaced the receiver a third time when Claude returned, a steaming mug in each hand.

"I struck out," she informed him. "Guess it's too early for them to be open." If she'd been on the interstate, she observed in silent irritation, she'd have had her pick of twenty-four-hour garages every thirty miles or so. Apparently Napa and its surrounding communities had little need for such services.

"So have your coffee. Rest." Claude smiled, smug and approving. "After I've supervised the unloading, we'll have breakfast. You can look for mechanics later."

Short on options, Savannah nodded and watched Claude depart.

Leaving the phone book open on her lap, she sipped the hot coffee. It was rich and strong, but it would have taken gallons of the wonderful brew to keep her eyes from drifting closed. The nag of fatigue was now a weight on her shoulders, the heaviness liquid, flowing over bone and muscle to settle in her arms. All she'd ever needed to fall asleep was a soft place to settle and relative privacy. Setting the mug aside, she folded her legs Indian-fashion and tugged her hat brim low on her forehead. She crossed her arms, tucking her hands inside the roomy rolled-back cuffs of her denim shirt. Seconds later, she slept.

Burke Julienne spun the cold water tap in the shower and gave himself a thirty-second blast of icy spray. Reaching for a bar of soap with one hand, he added hot water with the other. When steam billowed in the glass-enclosed stall, he turned his back to the pulsating water jets and let the hot pummeling have a go at the knots and stiffness.

Clearheaded if not exactly energized, Burke stepped from the tiled cubicle, pulling a fleecy burnt-orange towel from the rack. He toweled his hair dry, hitched the damp terry cloth at his waist and took stock of himself in the mirror over the sink.

Not bad, considering he felt like hell. Between jet lag, a body clock set on French time and the noises drifting through his open window from the yard below, he'd slept only in snatches. He'd expected red-rimmed eyes and the deathly complexion of a walking corpse. But a healthily

tanned, brown-eyed, brown-haired man looked back from
the glass. With a shrug, Burke reached for the can of
shaving cream on a ledge beside the sink and filled his
palm.

Lathering his jaw, he toyed with the idea of going back
to bed to catch a few more hours. To improve your mood?
he asked himself. Or to put off the inevitable? Not like you
to hide, Burke. Annoyed with himself, he wiped spots of
foam from his face, then hurled the balled-up towel at the
laundry hamper.

In the bedroom he took his time dressing, all the while
thinking back on his homecoming the day before. From
the moment he'd walked through the front door he'd
fought the sensation of walls closing in, of time running
out. Time *had* run out. His father had been uncharacter-
istically patient, allowing Burke to maneuver conversations away from the future and his plans, away from topics
weightier than the smog in Paris and the current crop of
beauties on the Riviera.

Today will Claude smile benignly if subjects are evaded?
Will he simply shrug and sigh if questions go unanswered? What in hell *are* you going to say? Burke asked
himself. And when the hell do you plan to say it?

It wasn't like Burke to be without an immediate course
of action. For thirty-one years his future had been me-
thodically charted, as much by himself as by the preor-
dainment of what he would one day inherit. Each short-
term goal had been a stepping-stone to that end. Now he
stood at an impasse, unsure how to move forward.
Damned if it didn't frustrate the hell out of him.

Burke left the bedroom, his mood a reflection of his
thoughts. The scent of freshly brewed coffee reached him
on the stairs, a sure sign his father would be waiting for
him. Like sand skimming down an hourglass, Burke felt
more time slip away.

He'd already crossed the foyer before a vague sense of
something out of place stopped him. His eyes were drawn
to the wing chair, to the pile of rags or laundry that bore

an uncanny likeness to human form. Curious, Burke scrutinized the crumpled heap. A pair of bony protrusions clearly resembled knees. The phone book seemed to be spread over a lap. He thought the scrap of doeskin capping it all might have been called a hat in better days.

Moving cautiously across the bare stone floor, he approached the chair. When the lump of materials didn't move, he crouched down. He didn't know whom or what he'd expected to find beneath the floppy hat brim—a scrawny, dirt-streaked teenager, perhaps, or a leather-skinned old man. But the face he gazed at was exquisitely, stunningly feminine. Burke treated himself to a good long stare. Thoughts of his father, the winery and the future vanished.

Her features were finely drawn and delicate. Soft, steady breaths parted her lips. Her face was classically heart-shaped, from sweeping cheekbones to small chin, her lashes long, lush and as black as the raven hair flowing from under the buff hat. Both lay in stark contrast against her porcelain skin. His gaze returned to her full, unpainted mouth before moving on. Though there was a hint of strength in the straightness and precision of bone, Burke sensed fragility. Intrigued, he let his eyes roam, deciding her durable clothes hid a wonderfully delicate body. It was the first time he'd ever considered the word *breakable* in terms of a person.

Burke didn't know how long he stared at her. Long enough to define the scent drifting from her as jasmine. Long enough to wonder if her voice would soothe or arouse. Her eyelids trembled, lashes fluttered. On a deep sigh, she opened her eyes. For a brief moment Burke gazed straight into a pair of huge, luminous gray pools. Waif to woman. The brief moment curled into a fist and connected with his gut.

Sensing a presence, Savannah fought to surface through the layers of exhaustion. She hated being stared at. Hated the weighing and measuring, the consideration and rejection. She could fall asleep in two blinks, but she woke by inches, each of them a struggle. The first lift of her lashes proved premature, and they fell down abruptly after opening. But not so fast that she hadn't seen a man's face mere inches from her own. Her second attempt fared better, though she did little more than gaze back at her one-man audience while her pupils worked to focus.

Attractive, she decided as the veils of sleep ebbed. In a look-but-don't-touch sort of way. Thirty, give or take a few. Thick sable hair swept back from a high forehead. His mouth was long and soft in a face otherwise lean and unmistakably aggressive. The eyes—she'd seen eyes like them only once before. Dark and depthless. No green or hazel flecks in the solid brown...black, she corrected. They weren't brown eyes at all, but black, and they looked quite capable of seeing past the obvious. His resemblance to Claude Julienne defied coincidence. So the son has returned, Savannah mused.

"Good morning," he said.

"'Morning," she managed in a sleep-husky murmur. She wanted badly to unwind and stretch, but the man's broad shoulders effectively boxed her into the chair. "When did you get back from Bordeaux?" She saw the surprise flicker in his eyes and explained, "Claude told me."

"Claude," he repeated thoughtfully. "I see." Though he didn't see at all. "I arrived yesterday afternoon. While you, I take it, arrived this morning?"

"Mmm." Savannah watched him visually sum her up, then try to place her. He was making a mental search of his memory bank, she decided, to see if she'd already been filed somewhere. Unaware at first that she did so, she held her breath and waited for a sign—any sign. A spark in the eyes. A tilt of the head or quirk of the mouth. Approval and disapproval expressed themselves in any of a dozen ways. In her lifetime she'd learned them all.

When her lungs ached to exhale, she came to her senses. Who was he that she cared what he thought? Annoyed with herself, Savannah blinked, raised her chin and arched one eyebrow.

Her transformation from artlessly open to icily closed nudged at Burke's memory. He'd watched it happen before, he was sure of it. His brow furrowed as he tried to grasp where or when he might have met her. But the impression was barely a flicker, gone before he could catch it.

"Do we know you?" he asked finally.

Savannah heard amusement run through his voice and bristled. "Some of us do," she replied coolly.

And to hell with everyone else? Burke wondered. "Well, for those of us who don't, who are you?"

When he smiled, fine lines fanned out from his eyes, and Savannah rethought the situation. The man had every right to be curious. Who wouldn't be upon finding a stranger asleep in his foyer? Besides, she was stiff enough from the long drive and sleeping upright; she'd only give herself a new set of kinks holding her nose in the air. With a sigh, she relaxed.

"I work for Jones Hauling," she explained. "I delivered some growth regulators and I don't know what all—stuff for the crops."

"Does that make you responsible for the racket that woke me?"

His stern, imperious scowl so resembled Claude's that Savannah found herself muffling another laugh. "Mmm, sorry."

Burke wasn't prepared for her smile. It rippled over him, as tangible a pleasure as a soft brush of fingers. He'd thought himself immune to sweet and soft. He wasn't pleased to learn otherwise. Glancing at her lap, where the phone book lay open, he read the directory heading. "Having mechanical problems?"

With a jolt Savannah sat upright. "Yes. Lord, what time is it?"

He glanced at his watch. "Three-ten. Or it is on the banks of the Seine. Seven-ten here?"

"One should be open by now," she whispered hopefully, taking her index finger down a column of listings.

"Anything I can do? Flat tire? Overheated radiator?"

"Transmission," she muttered without looking up. "I think."

Soft and sweet, Burke mused, and acquainted with transmissions. Fascinating. Not his type, but fascinating all the same.

"Burke! You're awake." Claude had slipped through the front door unnoticed by the two at the wing chair. Still sitting on his heels, Burke turned his head. "I see you've met Savannah."

Burke, Savannah thought. Claude had never mentioned him by name. It was always "Soon my son..." or "When my son returns..." So it's Burke. It suits him, she decided, tracing his profile with her eyes. A neat name, as neat and trim as his slightly damp, sinfully thick hair. Nothing fussy about a name like Burke, just as there was nothing fussy about his white French-cuffed shirt, his discreetly elegant gold watch, his immaculately creased navy slacks. A strong name, she thought, like his profile, like the long-boned hands loosely joined between his knees. A strong, unfussy, neat name. Like the man?

Then he brought his eyes back to her. "Yes, I've met Savannah."

He savored her name, she thought, rolling it over his tongue as he might a bit of chocolate. A shiver raced under her skin, unexpected, surely unwanted, though not wholly unpleasant.

"Find a garage, Savannah?" Claude asked, coming all the way into the foyer.

"A garage," she repeated. Burke stood, and Savannah's view was of summer-weight wool expertly fitted over narrow hips and lean thighs. Her pulse jumped, and she dropped her eyes. What on earth was that about? She was around men constantly. None made her blood surge. Flutter occasionally, but never surge.

"Try Jackson's," Burke suggested. He withdrew a tapered gold pen from his breast pocket and leaned over to circle a number in the book. Light winked off the slanted cuts of a monogram in the gold. A man who brands his possessions, Savannah told herself in the way of a warning. "Use my name," he suggested. "Jackson'll see you're taken care of."

Savannah breathed in the scent of him, one layer at a time. Soap, hair, skin. The whole was a musky fragrance, distinctly male. It shouldn't have been half as stirring as it was. "Thanks, I will," she murmured.

"I'm glad to see you're up early, Burke." Claude clapped a hand to his son's shoulder. "We can talk before the day intrudes. Savannah, meet us in the dining room when you're through."

Father and son departed. Savannah grabbed a cleansing breath of unscented, unmusky air. Strange that he'd unsettled her. There was a slight tremor in her hands, an airy lightness in her head. She was exhausted, Savannah reasoned, and not herself. Attractive as he was, Burke Julienne simply wasn't her type.

She passed her fingertips over her eyelids to blot out his lingering image—his neat, self-assured, impeccable image. A precise man, she thought. She knew the sort—a place for everything, and everything in its place... including people.

Straightening, Savannah shook off thoughts of him and dialed the number for Jackson's garage.

Burke filled a fragile china cup with coffee from the silver urn on the sideboard. He was alone in the formal dining room while Claude located Mrs. Weatherby to inform her there'd be a guest for breakfast.

Turning, Burke scanned the vast room, with its cathedral ceiling and polished parquet floor. First light whispered through thin sheers at the long narrow windows. The fragrance of lemon wax hung in the air, mingling with the fainter scents of tobacco smoke and perfume. He recalled drawn out dinner parties at the endless oak table, conversations invariably turning to last year's vintage, next year's harvest. Four of the room's two dozen chairs were arranged at the table, one each at head and foot, two at the middle distance facing each other. The other twenty, oval seats and high narrow backs covered in a cream-and-green striped satin, were banked at the silk-papered walls, bookending curve-legged tables that held brass buckets spilling over with fresh-cut flowers.

There were memories here. Burke heard their echoes in the silence. The low, restrained voices of business deals. The gay chatter of holiday gatherings. The quiet, comfortable sounds of a close family in happier times. The Juliennes had been that. Very close, very happy. Now Burke wondered if his relationship with his father was about to be strained past the breaking point. God knew that in the last two years they'd been through all the strain a family could take and still come out whole.

But they weren't whole, would never be whole again.

Without tasting his coffee Burke set it down to roam the room. At a window he swept back the delicate curtain. Dawn spilled over the sloped fields. The fog was dissipating, but enough remained to make a surreal picture of the view, as if he were seeing it in a dream. *His.* But not his. Claude was much too vital to retire, Burke too ambitious to be patient. Neither was figurehead material. There would be obstacles, he thought with typical frankness. Claude would pace off the boundaries. Burke would step over them.

Do we have that kind of relationship? he wondered. Is it strong enough? Is it worth risking to find out? In many ways they were alike, he and his father. In others...

Against the lightening September sky Burke saw the range of hills where he'd plant the new cuttings when they arrived. *Champagne.* The first hurdle. When Claude learned of it he would scoff, then he would dig in his heels. "Bubble wine," he would sneer. Burke had heard his father debate this issue with other vintners, adamantly supporting the European view that the United States should sign the treaty with France banning Champagne as a generic name. But whether Claude agreed or not, Burke knew this had to be Julienne Winery's next step in securing its stronghold on the American market. Their own Champagne. Not an injected sparkling wine, but a naturally fermented, softly sweet Champagne.

The first hurdle, Burke thought again. But not the last.

He glanced over his shoulder at the room, at the table where his grandfather, and before him his great-grandfather, had dined with their families for three-quarters of a century. Tradition decreed that Burke would do the same with his children. Only Burke knew that he would not.

"Has it changed?" Claude crossed the threshold and entered the room.

Burke looked over. "Some things never change."

"You looked... unsure." Claude busied himself at the sideboard, pouring coffee, adding cream. "Like a man who can't find what he's searching for."

And that, Burke thought as he turned to gaze out the window again—Claude's incredible talent for reading Burke's mind—would be Claude's most powerful weapon in the battles to come. "Tell me about Savannah." A diversion, Burke told himself. A convenient delaying tactic, nothing more.

Claude stopped in the act of pulling his chair out from the table. "Tell you what about Savannah?"

"Anything. Everything."

Claude sat, placed his cup and saucer on a monogrammed linen placemat and withdrew pipe and tobacco pouch from his pocket. "I doubt there's a living soul who knows everything about Savannah. What makes you think I would?"

Letting the curtain fall, Burke faced the room. "Most people, your close friends included, call you Julienne. I can count on my fingers those you've invited to use Claude. She does."

"Yes, now that you mention it, she does."

Amusement danced in Claude's eyes. And fondness. Burke knew his father too well to miss either. Once again he felt the nudge at his memory. Once again it escaped him.

"I can't recall asking her to," Claude said with a grin. "But then, Savannah isn't the sort to wait for invitations. She pretty much does as she pleases." Placing a flame to his pipe bowl, Claude sucked on the stem. When the packed tobacco was a glowing ember he shook out the match.

"So tell me about her." Burke took his customary seat to the right of his father. Assuming they wouldn't be served until the woman under discussion joined them, Burke lit a cigarette.

"I'm surprised you ask," Claude said casually. "I wouldn't have thought Savannah your type."

"She isn't."

Claude gave a noncommittal grunt. "Savannah," he murmured, as if lining up his thoughts. "She works for her brother, Neil Jones. He owns the new hauling firm I've contracted with. I think I wrote you about it. Anyway, the work seems right up her alley, though I don't approve of her doing it and I've told her so. Ask her where she's been lately, she'll talk your ear off. Girl loves traveling. And eating. You'd hardly know it to look at her, but she'll put away anything edible you set down in front of her. Let's see. Kids. She's a sucker for kids. And animals. Anything helpless."

Not his type, Burke thought again. He'd always been drawn to women who traveled as far as the Mediterranean to park for two weeks on a beach. They sent *haute cuisine* chefs into temperamental tantrums in deference to their figures and kept a safe distance from the sticky fingers and drooly mouths of children. Burke drew deeply on his cigarette, then gazed at his father through the blue haze of exhaled smoke.

"Is there anything she hates?" he asked with more bite than he'd intended. He was not one bit comfortable with his father's enchantment for this woman.

"I don't know." Claude shrugged convincingly. "As I said, I hardly know her. I've asked a question or two, about her family, her life. She's an artful evader. When she chooses to answer at all I doubt she's telling the truth."

Before either man could say another word, Mrs. Weatherby bustled in to lay a place setting across the table from Burke's.

"Mr. Julienne. Mr. Burke," she greeted. "You'll be hungry, Mr. Burke. You hardly touched dinner last night."

Burke shrugged and smiled an apology. "My stomach is on a different clock. It wanted bacon and eggs; you offered it rack of lamb."

Crossing plump arms, the cook thrust her chin free of its doughy folds. "It wouldn't be wanting roast beef now, would it?"

"With whipped potatoes and gravy? A slice of your hot apple pie for dessert?"

"Is that so." She sniffed. "Well, it'll have to make do with buttermilk waffles, maple syrup and a side of sausage." Aiming a challenging look at Claude, she dared him to utter the slightest whimper against the breakfast menu.

"Nothing for me, Weatherby," he said. "I've only time to finish my coffee before I meet with Ramirez."

"Yes, sir, Mr. Julienne." A conspiratorial twinkle lit her eyes. "Don't suppose three cinnamon rolls leave much room for waffles."

Claude blinked owlishly. "Which three cinnamon rolls are you referring to?"

Drawing herself up to her full five feet, the cook said, "The three pilfered from my cooling rack, as if you didn't know."

Burke laughed heartily, savoring his first real enjoyment at being home again. The sound of his laughter filled the cavernous room, and Weatherby's big soft body jiggled with her answering chuckles. "Now, there's a sound we've missed in these big empty rooms," she said before turning to waddle back to the kitchen. "Yes, sir, we'll all be perking up some now that Mr. Burke is home."

"She's missed you," Claude commented after the swinging door had ceased wagging behind the cook.

In his father's eyes Burke read the same message. The room seemed to visibly shrink around him.

"Give yourself time to adjust," Claude said quietly. "A year is a long time to be away. I know. I did my year in France, as have all Julienne sons. I was impatient to return, to apply what I'd learned. I came home full of exciting new ideas, to a father who knew only one way to make wine. *His* way."

Burke remembered his grandfather, the man he'd called Papa Jule. They'd buried Maurice Julienne in the family plot shortly after Burke's twelfth birthday. Burke had gone through his childhood a witness to the cold war sometimes waged between Claude and his own father. Yet Burke knew they'd loved and been loyal to each other to the end.

"We're going to disagree," Burke said.

"I imagine we will." Claude shrugged, implying future differences would be as easily dismissed. "We have before. We will, I suspect, for the rest of our lives."

Disheartened, Savannah pressed the phone's disconnect button. "Bring it in," Jackson had said. "Can't promise anything before Monday, but I'll surely put a man on it over the weekend." The last, Savannah knew, had been promised only after she'd fattened the Julienne name with ten tons of importance and indelicately dropped it on the man.

Scowling, she punched out an eleven-digit number and waited for the operator. "Charge to my credit card, please."

Neil answered on the second ring.

"Hi, it's Savannah."

"Something's wrong," he said immediately. "You only call in when something's gone wrong. Where are you?"

"I'm in Napa, at Julienne's. I can't make Sacramento by nine. I'm down with transmission trouble or something. Is there someone out this way who can pick up my backhaul?"

"I'll take care of it," Neil assured her. "You're okay? You get in all right? You sound upset."

"I'm okay. Long night, no sleep," she said, and twirled the phone cord around her finger. It was pointless to worry Neil. And he would worry; he always had. For heaven's sake, Savannah groused, it was ridiculous for anyone to worry. She *was* fine.

"Any idea when you'll be on the road again?"

"Monday, I hope."

"I'll set you up with a load." She heard him scrabbling for pencil and paper. "Where can I reach you?"

Good question, she thought. "I don't know. When I've booked a room, I'll call you."

"Fine. Need anything? Are you set for money?"

"I'm set, and you're sweet."

"Well, call if you think of anything. And, Savannah..." His tone changed. She smiled and awaited the advice she figured was coming. "It's time you took a weekend off. You've been going too hard for too long. I don't know what it is you're... Ah, hell. What I mean is, you're stuck there, so you might as well relax and have some fun."

*Stuck.* That was precisely how she felt. And helpless because of it. It happened now and then that a place so enchanted her that she'd stay on, discovering every nook and cranny. But forced to stay somewhere, she always felt compelled to leave. Well, there's nothing to be done about it, she told herself. And it's only for three days. If she had to be stuck somewhere, Napa, at least, was the place for it.

She threw her feet to the floor and stood. Delicious smells reached her from down the hall. Food. Suddenly she was starving.

At the soft thumps of her footsteps, Burke glanced up. She'd removed her hat and left it somewhere. Her hair was a swish of ebony, falling dime-straight to her shoulders, where the ends curved inward. She was as slender as he'd guessed earlier, but taller. She moved with an easy, measured grace that made a man want to watch the miracle of her moving naked across a candlelit bedroom.

The unmistakable internal tug caught Burke off guard. She wasn't his type, he told himself again. He wasn't drawn to women who curled up in boneless balls to nap in an acquaintance's front hall. He wasn't drawn to women because they stirred an urge to protect, an impulse to be careful. Nonetheless, a thudding heaviness below his stomach told him he was drawn to this woman.

Skimming the length of her, Burke noticed her shirt-tails clinging to her jeans mid-thigh. A man's shirt, he realized. A scene from his past flashed before his eyes: a woman slipping into his shirt after having slipped out of his bed. The intimacy of it had irritated him then. The intimacy of it irritated him now.

"How did it go?" Claude asked Savannah. He pointed to the place setting across from Burke's, where a plate of thick waffles awaited her.

"Jackson said to bring it in, but he can't promise to do anything before Monday." She sat and met Burke's eyes. "By the way, he said to tell you your car is ready. You can pick it up any time."

"Oh?" Burke slid his father a questioning glance.

"It's been sitting for a year," Claude explained. "I arranged to have it taken in and gone over. Savannah, what are your plans now?"

Savannah shrugged, cut through the stack of golden waffles and speared a forkful. "Limp it into Jackson's, then find a room somewhere."

"You have a room," Claude said. "Here."

Laughing, Savannah shook her head. "It's sweet of you, Claude, but I can't impose."

"How would you impose?" he argued. "By occupying an empty guest room? Maybe you plan to throw wild parties? Or eat us out of house and home? Though I suppose that's a possibility." Claude tossed his napkin to the table and stood. "It's settled. You'll stay. The weekend, at least."

*At most*, Savannah corrected silently. She wouldn't even consider a longer delay.

"Burke will go with you to Jackson's," Claude decided. "That way he can pick up his car and bring you back."

Savannah saw little reason to argue: staying with the Juliennes beat an impersonal motel room, hands down. Her eyes followed Claude's progress from the room. On the threshold, he stopped and turned around.

"Bring her back quickly, Burke. The child drove through the night. She needs to sleep."

*The child.* Savannah gasped softly at the endearment. How long since she'd been a child? Anyone's child? For as warm and tender was the emotion that crept into her heart, she knew how cold and cruel were the others she'd risk. This wasn't her home, she told herself firmly, nor did she want it to be. She wasn't young, helpless or in need of being cared for. And she *wasn't* Claude Julienne's child.

Watching her, Burke saw the gray eyes blur and widen with an inexplicable yearning. Then, suddenly, she closed off whatever she'd been feeling, as if it were wrong or impossible. For all the composure she strove to adopt, her eyes, when she brought them back to Burke, gave her away. He saw something there—not panic, but close. The look of someone backing off, afraid of what she wanted, yet wanting what she feared.

In that moment, Burke knew who she reminded him of. On the heels of his discovery came feelings—all of them. Despair. Joy. Fear and frustration. Anger. And the desperate, impossible wish for one more chance.

## Chapter Two

*A my*. Grief was swift and stunning. Burke struggled with the memory of his sister. Two years, but he could still see her clearly. Her stubborn mouth and clenched fists, her wide, pleading eyes. Sweet Amy. Young, confused, unhappy Amy.

Consciously erasing her image, Burke narrowed his gaze on Savannah Jones. Now, looking for the resemblance, he failed to find it. She was once again a stranger, someone he was meeting for the first time. His flash of recognition had been just that—a flash.

Still, if he'd been startled by occasional glimpses, might his father have seen them, also? And wouldn't that explain Claude's unlikely affection for this woman?

Linking his hands, Burke gazed at Savannah from over the top of them. He studied her—her face, her eyes. He watched her square her shoulders, silently defy his scrutiny and withdraw behind ice. He watched her and was completely distracted from his original intent.

"What?" Savannah asked of his lengthening stare.

Burke only hiked an eyebrow.

"You're dissecting me," she said. Looking past the obvious, she thought. "Why?"

"You have a room here?"

His tone maligned. Savannah made hers wintry. "Pardon?"

The quirk of his mouth doubted her request for clarification. "My father said you have a room here. How do you explain that?"

Her eyes dulled, becoming as flat and unrevealing as slate. "Just how do you *think* I'd explain it?"

"Oh, I can think of a few ways without much stretch of the imagination."

"I'll bet you can," Savannah said dryly. "And you should be strung up by your thumbs for every one of them. Look, I couldn't care less what you think of me, but your father deserves better than—"

"My father!" Burke interjected, then allowed himself a long, full-bodied laugh. "No, I wasn't insinuating a guest-room arrangement between you and my father. Claude Julienne with a mistress," he murmured, trying to imagine it. "Impossible. Even if his puritanical ethics allowed for liaisons, I assure you my mother would not. A very possessive woman, my mother. You, on the other hand..."

Oh, yes, Savannah thought, this is definitely a man with precise labels and neat cubbyholes for everything—especially for people. It always pleased her to find she'd been right in such matters. It especially pleased her this time.

Munching thoughtfully on a bite of syrup-soaked waffle, she smiled across the table at Burke Julienne. "I see your point. I could be a fortune-hunter, a conniving fake who'd schemed her way into the heart of an old fool—shall we make him a *doddering* old fool, possibly senile?—in the hopes he'd eventually disinherit his family and leave the whole shebang to me." Propping her chin on her palm, she slitted her eyes in evil speculation. "And if the old fool doesn't dodder off to his grave in due time, why I might become an arsonist, or a fool-strangler.''

Despite himself, Burke was enjoying her. "So." He lowered his arms to the table. "Just how is it you have a room here?"

Smiling, Savannah shrugged.

"You're not going to tell me."

"If I did, you'd know all my secrets." She sipped her coffee, her eyes laughing over the rim at him. "What is a woman if not a mystery?"

A bore, Burke thought, completely surprising himself. The women in his life had all been bright and beautiful. And bores. Three days, he mused. He'd untangled knottier mysteries in less.

"Shall we go?" he asked, glancing down at her plate. "You're finished, aren't you?"

Savannah noticed that, while she'd demolished her breakfast with predictable thoroughness, he'd hardly touched his own. Giving a satisfied sigh, she nodded. "I'm finished."

She followed Burke from the dining room, down the gallery lined with ornately framed paintings of wind-tossed seas and brooding ancestors and into the stone foyer, where she retrieved her hat from the chair arm it had been left to dangle on. Turning, she saw a flood of daylight pour through the door Burke opened.

In the east the sun had cleared the hills. Savannah crossed the wide terrace to lean on its waist-high wall and looked out on row upon row of flourishing grapevines, their greens and purples glistening in the strengthening light. The fog had dwindled to a few thin wisps snaking along the ground. The air was fresh, beginning to heat. Closing her eyes, she drew a deep breath.

And she remembered. Harvest time. Warm days and rich earth. Good times...the best times.

Burke watched her mouth curve into a wistful smile. When she opened her eyes, he saw that unspeakable yearning again. To him, she looked suddenly small and vulnerable. A fragrant summer breeze lifted her hair and sent it flying into her face. Even as he decided touching her would be a mistake his thumbs were skimming her cheeks, brushing the raven strands back. He felt the jolt of awareness, the rush of pleasure. She felt better—creamier, silkier—than he'd imagined. *When had he imagined?* With a fingertip he drew a line from her temple to her chin. He felt delicate bones, saw pale smudges beneath her eyes. Breakable, he thought again.

"We can do this later, Savannah, if you're tired."

Savannah worked to slow the sudden gallop of her pulse. She felt strangely unsteady. Too many feelings tumbled over one another; past and present skidded together. Needing an anchor, she clamped down on her hat with both hands, crushing the supple material.

"Actually—" she had to clear her throat before continuing "—I'll sleep better if I know the mechanic's already working on the trouble."

He nodded, his eyes still roaming her face, finding too many shadows of fatigue. "Let me drive?"

"That'd be nice." She dug the keys from her pocket. When she dropped them into his palm she noticed his hands and thought them amazingly graceful for a man. Flesh tanned to a rich gold, fingers long and slender. Strength and power were evident, but none of Claude's thick calluses. Of the two of them, Savannah decided Burke was the thinker, the planner.

Touching her arm, he turned her toward the steps. As they descended the smooth stones, his hand coasted up from her elbow to her shoulder. Moving, having a destination, helped her ignore his thumb resting at the back of her neck.

"What time did you tell Jackson you'd be there?" Burke asked.

"I didn't." She saw him grimace and rolled her eyes. "People don't generally make appointments to have breakdowns."

"An appointment tends to facilitate things."

"I suppose." Savannah tossed her head back to gaze at the cloudless blue sky. She lived by clocks when she had to, by impulse the rest of the time. "I never make appointments. Not even to see a doctor. If you're ill enough to need one, one'll see you. Once you're committed to being somewhere at a certain time you're forced to schedule everything else around it. If there's anything I hate, it's a schedule. I have to keep to them now and then, but I hate them all the same."

A free spirit, Burke thought. One of the world's perpetual children. It was a discovery that should have curtailed his interest. It didn't. "The world would be chaos without them. Schedules give order to life."

"Only for those imposing them," Savannah returned. "Don't you find—" But Burke was no longer beside her. She'd walked right out from under his arm. Glancing back, she found him staring at a point beyond her left shoulder.

"What is that?"

She tracked the path of his eyes with her own. "My truck."

Dumbfounded, Burke scanned sixty-plus feet of sky-blue trimmed silver-painted steel. "Truck? I've seen smaller houses!"

Because her rig was fairly standard as trailer-trucks went, Savannah began to understand why its size would amaze him. "Burke, exactly what did you think I'd come here in?"

"I didn't. Didn't even wonder." Burke strolled the vehicle's length. A minivan, he thought now. Or a pickup. *Not* a semi. He shook his head as if to clear it before slicing a look at the slender, fragile woman who actually navigated this monstrous machine for a living. "It's a truck.... You're a trucker."

"Right on both counts."

Not only was she not his type, Burke thought, she wasn't any type he'd ever met before! "But you're ..."

"What?"

"Small and . . . small."

"Five-six. Not so small."

His response to that was muttered under his breath. She missed the words but caught the drift—and the faint inflection males used when they thought a woman was messing around in a man's kettle of fish.

"I don't push the truck, Burke. I drive it. I assure you I have all the necessary equipment to do it competently." There wasn't a reaction to her occupation Savannah hadn't confronted at least once over the years. She handled them by never defending. "Still want to drive? It has ten gears, and it takes them all to get from stop to go."

"Are you kidding?" Burke tossed her the keys. Savannah neatly snatched them from midair. "A chance to ride shotgun with a lady trucker? I wouldn't miss it."

Savannah flung her hat to the dashboard and climbed onto the high seat. She watched through the windshield as Burke rounded the front end. He stopped once to gaze up at her and shake his head.

When the engine roared to life, Burke remembered his father saying he didn't approve of Savannah's job. She's a trucker, he mused. An honest-to-God, move-'em-out-boys trucker! He wondered why the discovery that she wasn't as fragile as he'd first thought her should disturb him when that very fragility hadn't sat too well with him in the first place.

Savannah navigated the snaking private road. It demanded total concentration to shift, steer, clutch and brake her way out of the vineyard. Approaching a particularly ticklish zigzag, she flashed Burke a look of utter disgust. "Shall I tell you what I think of this road's planner?"

"Be my guest," he invited with a smile.

"He should have taken two more days to sleep off the party."

"I was stone sober."

"I might have known," she muttered.

"We had a straight road until three years ago. It kept washing out. Would it help if I explained the gradient problems to you?"

"It would help if the road were straight."

She pulled onto the highway and began shifting up to speed. Burke leaned back and lit a cigarette. Blowing out a thin stream of smoke, he studied her hand on the gear stick. A deceptively delicate hand. Curled around the shift's knob her fingers looked slimmer, daintier than when they'd been folded tranquilly in her lap. He watched the muscle in her forearm flex each time she rammed into a higher gear until she attained tenth and ran with the engine wide open. Remarkable. Fascinating. A puzzle he could spend many a long, quiet evening searching out pieces for.

"Savannah."

She turned her head, her gray eyes wide and smoky. "What?"

"Nothing. Just . . . Savannah."

Her breath caught. He had a way of saying her name that made her bones dissolve.

"I like it," he said thoughtfully.

"Me, too." Occasionally people tried to shorten it to something cute like Savvy. Savannah discouraged them by turning a deaf ear. Other than her two young nephews, who barely managed a simplified Aunt Van, no one called her by anything but her full name. It was different, distinctive. There'd been times in her life when that alone had made her stand out in the crowd, reminding others that she actually existed.

"It's unusual," Burke noted. "Where does someone get a name like Savannah?"

"From Georgia. Yes, really," she vowed when he returned a bland stare. "I was named for Savannah, Georgia." Her slim shoulders rose and fell as if to say it had hardly been *her* idea. "I was born there."

"Your mother . . . sounds interesting."

"Think so?" She sniffed disdainfully. "A woman carries a baby nine months, she can't have a name ready? And you think she might be interesting?" Her dry tone questioned both Burke's and her mother's capacity to reason. "She asked the nurse, 'Where am I?' If she'd asked what day it was I'd have been called Tuesday." Suddenly she leaned into the steering wheel, her thoughts leaping elsewhere. "Hear that?"

Burke, too, leaned forward. "What?"

"That noise. Like a whistling teapot."

"Faintly." What Burke heard was the motor's thundering rumble, and he wondered how she managed to hear anything short of a wailing siren above it. "Is that your trouble?"

"Mmm." Snatching the hat from atop the dash, she rammed it onto her head. "Transmission," she murmured. "I'm sure of it."

They drove in silence awhile. Burke finished his cigarette, his mind busy with solving Savannah. He began with first impressions. Fascinating. She obviously possessed a good deal more strength than he'd originally credited her with. She stirred his protective nature, though he suspected she neither needed nor wanted protecting. And she was, by God, the softest, most feminine woman he'd ever laid eyes on.

"Who are you?" he asked impulsively.

Her smile said she was prepared to indulge him. "Savannah Jones."

"From where?"

"Savannah, Georgia."

So, it was to be a puzzle piece at a time. He'd start with the frame and work in. "Where do you live now?"

She tipped her head back in order to see him from under the droopy hat brim. Her silky black brows rose, and her lush mouth held back a smile. He'd swear she was debating whether she'd answer truthfully or hand him a line. Then, making a fist of her right hand, she rapped on the panel behind her seat. "In there."

Angling his body, Burke considered the panel. It was wood-grained and plasticized, with recessed hinges and a latch. Burke reached for the latch, then glanced at Savannah. With a nod and a sound he took for indifference, she granted permission.

The panel popped forward and slid aside on runners. Jasmine-scented air from the sleeper compartment flooded the cab. He supposed incongruous things like that would eventually stop surprising him.

A bed claimed most of the cabin, though he was amazed at how many of life's conveniences she'd managed to cram into an area that measured no more than six feet in length, width and height. The interior walls were a pale silver-gray, the blanket on her bed sky-blue. He saw a mini-size color television, a microwave oven sitting atop a small refrigerator and the selector dials for a stereo system. The roof was domed, a patchwork of windows through which sunlight flowed into the tiny cubicle.

"You do a lot of long hauls." It wasn't a question as much as a voiced discovery.

"I usually get the cross-countries."

"But where do you *live*, Savannah?"

"I told you, in there." His expression was that of a man braced for the joke's punch line. "Ah, I see. That isn't neat enough for you. I'm supposed to have a street and a city. A zip code." She paused to gauge his reaction and knew that she was dumbfounding him again. "I have a post office box in Chicago. Will that suffice? I need the state of residence to be issued my driver's license. But essentially—" she hooked a thumb over her shoulder "—that's where I live."

Burke registered her dig, but he was too surprised by her revelation to be more than mildly irritated. No home, he thought. Not even an apartment. It was incomprehensible to him. Juliennes were prepared to spill blood if that's what it took to protect and preserve their land. "Four generations," his father prefaced so many statements. Four generations of Juliennes have harvested the same vineyards. Four generations have been born in the same hours. Four generations have put their name on bottles of wine. This woman hadn't put her name on anything more permanent than a driver's license.

"Jerk." Her mutter pulled Burke's attention back. With a steady eye on her left mirror, she scowled at something he couldn't see.

As the car she'd watched climb up on her rear pulled to the left to pass, Savannah slowed. When the driver veered back into her lane, she saw four elfin faces lined up in the back window. All but the tiniest toddler raised clutched fists, yanking them twice. Granting their request, Savannah reached for an overhead cord and gave two long blasts of her air horn. The children laughed and applauded on their side of the window before the car shot off and sped away.

"Delaware plates," she muttered. "Their father is a stupid jerk. Nothing makes me madder than a lead-footed tourist risking his family's lives to get where he's going five minutes faster."

"You should practice what you preach," Burke told her and considered the score evened.

"What does that mean?"

He tapped the box prominently displayed on her dash beside a standard AM-FM radio and the CB receiver. "Isn't this a radar detector? Your basic black fuzz-buster?"

Savannah heard censure in his voice and made her own casual. "You're certainly up on the lingo, I see."

Even as he prepared to debate, Burke wondered why the hell he bothered. "But you do have this gadget in your truck so that you can cut back to a legal speed before you drive into a police car's radar range."

His tone condemned. She bristled. "Driving is my *business*. I'm familiar with the roads. I know which bridges ice up in winter and every county cowpath with a pothole. I can drive a hundred-mile stretch of curves and never cross the center line. When I don't know the road, I drive at a reasonable speed, which is often under the maximum limit." It wasn't like her to defend, not like her at all, and so she wondered why he made her want to. "It's different for me."

"So say tax-evaders and draft-dodgers."

Blood simmering, Savannah downshifted with utter disregard for her ailing transmission. "Are speed demons your pet peeve?" she tossed out with only half the disdain but twice the temper she'd intended. "Or do you get fired up about jaywalkers, too? Maybe you have an opinion on little old ladies who sneak strawberries in the supermarket."

Beneath the heat of her retort Burke heard sarcasm for what she'd decided was his intolerance. "Laws," he said in a voice humming with restraint, "are meant for everyone, Savannah. You're not above them."

Oh, so he doesn't approve, doesn't he? Well...so what! "Laws," she said with quiet frugality, "are meant for those who make them."

"Like schedules?"

"Exactly." Savannah was in the midst of making a right turn into the drive of Jackson's Garage. Because she could tell Burke hadn't finished with the subject, she decided to finish for him. She cut the wheel sharply, went over a hump in the drive, geared down to first and came to a sudden stop. Burke managed to grab the dashboard on the first jostle and hold his seat through the rest. He cursed fluently, having picked up a few colorful phrases in France, Savannah noticed.

"That was for your own good," she explained sweetly. "You were about to spout off and make yourself sound like a pompous ass."

She'd gone too far. She saw it in the jaw he clenched, in the black eyes gleaming with fury. Quickly, she opened her door and hopped from the cab. A mechanic was already coming toward her, and she trusted Burke wouldn't cause bloodshed in public. It was against the law, after all.

So he thought her unprincipled, Savannah fumed. So much the better. He had a way of making her forget her aversion to entanglements, and she considered the slight interest he'd already shown in her an invitation to what could prove to be a terribly messy tangle. Yes, it was better all around if she provoked nothing more in Burke Julienne than his annoyance.

It was another hour before she was free to leave Jackson's. Savannah signed authorization forms and gave instructions to be contacted at the Julienne Winery as soon as the mechanics worked up an estimate. Burke's car was brought around, and Savannah looked askance at the conservative dark brown Mercedes sedan. It had probably been foolish to hope for a two-seater convertible, but a long drive in the open with the wind rushing at her face would have been nice.

"I have to get a couple of things from my truck," she told Burke through the window he let down. "Pull up on the driver's side."

Packing was a chore accomplished quickly. A drawer beneath her bed held her Chicago clothes—those she wore whenever she stayed with Neil and his family. Savannah withdrew its contents, stowed them in a collapsible duffel bag and handed it out to Burke, who stood at the open sleeper-cab door. She opened a secret safe and cleared out the cash.

"Here, take this, too," she called out and angled an awkwardly shaped, unbendable item through the door.

Resting it wide-end-down on the ground, Burke held the object at arm's length. "What is this?"

Popping her head out the door, Savannah gave the instrument a quick once-over. "Isn't it obvious Burke? Honestly, for a world traveler, you've got some pretty big holes in your education. First you ask me what a truck is. Now you can't see that that's a cello?"

"Cute," he managed through gritted teeth. "I meant, why are you bringing it? What are you going to do with it?"

"What do you think I'd do with it?" She locked the sleeper compartment and turned to face him. "I'm going to prop it up in a convenient corner and use it for a clothes rack. What do you do with your cello?"

Pointless, Burke decided. It was pointless to expect a straight answer from her, even to the simplest question. Thoroughly fed up with her, he unlocked the trunk and prepared to ram the instrument into the carpeted pit.

*"Don't!"*

Her cry stopped him dead. It wasn't angry, as it might have been, but frightened. The eyes she raised from his hands were full of pleading.

"Please. It's special ... and it breaks."

He felt like a heel. A petty, temperamental heel. "Sorry." He carefully arranged the cello on top of her duffel and let the lid down. Then, with an equally gentle touch, he helped Savannah into the front seat.

Burke suspected the instrument meant more to her than something to make music on. Had it been a gift from someone special? Someone gone? Had she experienced a triumphant moment playing it? Achieved a dream? He waited until they were on the highway and skimming through the valley to ask her about it. "Where did you get the cello, Savannah?"

The car's soothing vibrations had nearly put her to sleep. Opening one eye, she smiled softly. "I stole it."

For several seconds there was only the humming of a well-insulated motor carrying them down a slick highway. Then an oath—his—and a sigh—hers. "You're not kidding, are you?"

"I'm not kidding."

She'd copped it, Burke thought angrily. But of course she had! What the hell had he expected her to say? I saved my weekly allowance when I was a kid? I bussed tables in an all-night diner? "No rules, hmm, Savannah?"

She sighed solemnly. "No rules."

Sitting straighter, she watched the gently sloped hills pass by her window. Here on the valley floor the ripening process preceded that of vines planted at higher altitudes. There were pickers in the fields, though not as many as Savannah knew there would be in another week or so. Now and then she'd see a child hurry after an adult, gleefully, proudly offering a weighty clump of grapes. After a hair-ruffling pat on the head or a kiss on the cheek, the child would watch the plump cluster be tossed onto others in the heaping gondolas.

"Sweet, hmm?" she murmured. "It's nice to see families working together. Nice when kids feel they've contributed."

Burke cut her a look. Actually he thought it barbaric that parents subjected children to hot sun and back-breaking labor.

"You don't approve," she noted quietly.

"Children belong in schools. On baseball fields."

Savannah faced the window again. When she spoke her voice shook. "It never ceases to amaze me how many people think they know where children belong."

Burke pulled into the winery drive, relieved to be home. Her scent filled the car and drove him crazy. *She* drove him crazy! Not only did she defy convention, but she defied it with relish if she thought doing so would irk him. Yet he still wanted to know how the parts of her he hadn't touched would feel in his hands. He still wanted to find all the pieces and slide them into place. He'd never felt this way before. He didn't want to feel this way now.

"Christina looks wonderful."

Burke ducked his head to see his mother watching their approach from the terrace. She did look wonderful, hardly changed in the year he'd been gone. Her slight figure was as trim as a girl's. What silver threaded her hair only enhanced the blend of blond shades. When Burke braked in front of the house, Christina descended the steps to greet them.

"Savannah, it's good to see you again." Christina reached for Savannah's hand and squeezed it in heartfelt welcome. She looked smart and elegant in lavender-blue silk. Savannah remembered her soaked and mud-caked, distributing thermoses of hot soup in the fields.

"You're looking wonderful, Christina. In fact, I was just saying so to Burke."

"I look like a mother whose son has come home after a year." Her smile glowed from her aquamarine eyes, making them look more green than blue. "But you look terrible, Savannah, exhausted. Claude explained your dilemma and said that you'd driven through the night. I've had your room prepared."

From the corner of her eyes Savannah saw Burke lifting her cello from the trunk. "Will you excuse me, Christina? I have to go save a friend."

Without further explanation, she strode to the Mercedes's tailgate and removed her instrument from Burke's grasp. Keeping his face expressionless, he showed her the flat of his palms as if promising never to touch the damn thing again.

Adept at slipping in and out of narrow places with the large, unwieldy cello, Savannah made short work of securing it under her arm and catching up with Christina. Other than offering a smile, Savannah ignored the other woman's raised eyebrows.

Christina led the way into the house and up the winding stairs. At the top of the circular staircase was a large square hall from which a web of corridors reached out. Christina opened the door to the room Savannah had stayed in once before. A suite of rooms, actually, situated in the center tower.

The bedroom was large, with a black marble fireplace set into one wall and a huge four-poster brass bed against another. From the windows one looked out over fields of unfurled greenery. Savannah sank down on the bed's white satin coverlet and gazed into a sea-foam tiled bathroom, beyond which was a dressing room. She'd set her cello in one corner. Burke had dropped her bag just inside the door and left.

Fitzhugh, a withered old woman who moved like a snail but refused to retire, silently entered the room and began Savannah's unpacking. The last time Savannah had been there, she'd tried as hard to make the shuffling woman skip fussing in this room as she had to engage her in conversation. Having failed on both counts then, she didn't bother to renew her efforts now.

"Hungry?" Christina moved a daisy in the bowl of flowers on the mantel before glancing over. "Would you like a tray before you sleep?"

"Thanks, but no." Flat on her back already, Savannah patted her stomach. "Waffles."

Satisfied with the bouquet, Christina crossed to the door. "Shall we wake you for dinner?"

"Uh-uh. You know me. I'll be a miserable crank if I don't stay down till I'm slept out. Please, Christina, don't feel you have to hostess me. I'm quite capable of taking care of myself."

"We won't disturb you, then." The door had almost closed when Christina popped her head back in. "When you do wake, Savannah, you know where to find the kitchen."

Savannah laughed and nodded.

Alone, she vacillated between crawling under the covers and pushing her tired body into the shower. She'd seen a long string of truck stops with woefully inadequate shower facilities. Calling forth every last ounce of energy, she headed for the bathroom.

Savannah woke stretching. When she didn't run out of room against cool, slick walls, she knew she wasn't in the sleeper. Eyes shut, she absorbed her surroundings, waking by inches, by impressions. Softness beneath her. Darkness around her. A breeze tickled her cheek, whispered at her ear. Her hands, spread on top of a coverlet, were sunk in satin. White satin, she remembered. A wide four-poster bed. The winery.

Turning her head on the linen pillowcase, Savannah opened her eyes. Ribbons of moonlight streamed through the windows. The scent of roses drifted in. The growl of her stomach intruded rudely on the quiet.

Shoving the quilt aside, she slipped out of bed. Barefoot, she crept across thick pile carpet to the door and peeked into the unlit hall, greeting a silence exclusive to houses where everyone slept. Unconcerned with the length of leg exposed by the cut of her silk nightshirt, she stepped out of her room.

The stairs creaked in all the familiar places. The polished mahogany banister felt like satin under her hand. The stones of the foyer floor were cool and surprisingly smooth under her feet. It was simple to find—she had only to remember how to get to the dining room, cross it to the magnificently carved swinging door at the far end and pass through a short serving hall.

Finding a wall switch, she flipped it. The burst of light after darkness stabbed painfully at her dilated pupils. Squinting, she zeroed in on the stainless steel doors of an institutional-size refrigerator. Inside, the shelves were crammed with a culinary variety fit to rival New York's finest deli.

Savannah chose randomly and with utter disregard for the eventual flavor combination. Selecting dishes as they struck her fancy, she moved them to a maple worktable. Pulling a stool out from beneath the table, she sat and began with a cream-filled chocolate eclair. The instant the buttery chocolate met her tongue she thought of Burke Julienne saying her name. It was the only time his voice wasn't perfectly pitched, his diction not precisely executed. Even angry, he'd controlled his speech...except for when he swore blue streaks.

Giggling, Savannah popped a black olive into her mouth. On the whole it had been an enjoyable morning. So why did thinking of him now disturb her? Because she was attracted, possibly infatuated—a first. And firsts were always a bit unsettling. Spreading cream cheese on a cinnamon roll, she asked herself why, of all the men in the world, she should find Burke Julienne attractive.

Because he was, and she did. It was as simple as that.

Yet he was all the things she'd run away from. Conservative and practical. Law-abiding to a fault. He was morally upright and so principled that he was practically pompous. He probably belonged to a posh country club. He had a social conscience. It had been Savannah's experience that few people did as much harm to society as those with a social conscience.

But she was attracted. And she had two more days to get through before she could get out.

Gathering up scattered orange peels and the now empty pickle jar, she took her dirty dishes to the sink. Leaving the kitchen pretty much as she'd found it, if a bit emptier, she turned out the light and backtracked through dining room, gallery, foyer, staircase and finally bedroom.

She wasn't sleepy. She'd slept eleven hours, and slept deeply. Normally she'd be on the road at this hour, singing along with Willie Nelson on the radio. Restless, she paced. She paused to run her fingers over a collection of rare books arranged on an exquisite rosewood desk. No, she'd need a light to read. There was something about being alone in a lit room at night that made her feel encapsulated by her own isolation. She dragged her hands through her hair and muttered an oath.

*Stuck.*

Then her eyes lit on the cello resting in the corner. If only she could play. That would settle her. She always felt less trapped if she could send the music. Glancing around, she considered the soundproofing quality of stone walls. If she chose a soothing melody and played softly, she probably wouldn't disturb a soul.

Working quietly, she lifted the dainty rosewood chair tucked up to the desk and moved it to face an open window. Next she let down the zipper on the soft vinyl case and withdrew the treasured instrument. It glowed in the twilight, the wood warmly polished by oil and age. Taking the horsehair bow, she sawed it on a cake of rosin.

At the chair, she arranged herself and her instrument. She set the cello's wide belly between her knees and applied the bow to the G string. It sounded a tad high, and she turned the string's peg a hair clockwise. She tuned each of the remaining three strings in turn.

Burke drifted in the oblique world between sleep and wakefulness. He thought at first that he was hearing a man softly humming. Gradually he placed the low groan as music, a faint, elusive melody. Savannah's cello. Tossing back the blankets, he slipped into the slacks he'd slipped out of earlier.

He found his way through the halls to the guest room in darkness. The music swelled in the tower hall, and he noticed that Savannah's door was slightly ajar. At his touch it swung wide on silent, well-oiled hinges.

Music poured over him. A moan of a song, haunting, shivering from the cello's belly in rich, resonant tones. Savannah sat in a spill of silver moonlight, her head tipped back so that her hair fell away from her alabaster face. She played with her eyes closed. The cut of her nightshirt revealed her bare legs and, higher, her creamy hips. He decided she was naked beneath the silk.

Dear God, she was breathtaking.

Savannah felt the tension leave her with the music. She pictured invisible notes strung together in an endless chain. She saw them fade away over the hills to the mountains beyond, sail across unseen plains and cities to finally die at the ocean's edge. Going where she could not. As she had in her youth, she sent her soul with the music and felt, for a while, free.

Riveted, Burke stood on the threshold. Her face was soft with submission, glowing with rapture. Raising her chin fractionally, she drew the bow's full length across a string, slowly, so that she and the cello gave up one long last sigh.

"Beautiful."

At first his soft baritone seemed a part of the music. Still caught in its trance, Savannah slowly turned her head. Until her eyes adjusted to the deeper shadows across the room he was only a silhouette in the doorway.

"God, that was beautiful," Burke murmured. "The music. The magic. The moonlight in your hair."

Now she saw that his chest was bare, his torso lean and rippled with muscle. His disheveled hair made him look appealingly rumpled and approachable. Feeling vulnerable and believing she'd feel less so if she stood, Savannah forced herself onto legs that were trembling at the knees. If anything, she was more vulnerable now. With one hand holding the bow, the other wrapped around the neck of her cello, she was intensely aware of how thin her nightshirt was. Of how it clung to her.

"Was there something..." Her voice trailed off. She didn't have to ask; she *knew* what he wanted. His eyes seemed to burn the message into her.

Burke took a step into the room before stopping himself. If he touched her, then what? If he kissed her, could he stop? She wasn't the sort of woman a man sampled as casually as this season's offering of wines. She'd leave her mark, like a bittersweet aftertaste.

"You're okay?" he asked lamely.

"Sure. I'm fine." *My heart has quit, I'm not breathing and if my knees don't stop quivering, I'll fall on my face in about two minutes. But I'm just fine, thanks.*

"Need anything?"

*Yes. Oh, Lord, yes!* She'd never been more aware of a man. Or that she was a woman. Turning her head slightly, she looked out the window and wished she could evaporate and follow the music. "No, I don't need anything."

Her smile was sad. Her shoulders moved, not quite a shrug. Burke knew he'd been turned down—but with kind apology, if that was any consolation. Just as well, he decided. She wasn't a woman a man could count on walking away from. She wasn't a woman a man could expect to stick around, either.

"Good night, Savannah."

"'Night."

Unable to move, Savannah watched him back out of her room and pull the door shut. She didn't relax until she heard the sound of his own door closing down the hall. When she let her muscles go, they did so with a shudder. Dear God, she'd come much too close to calling him back.

## Chapter Three

Tradition." Claude uttered the word with reverence. It hung in the air like the Amen of a benediction. "Preserving family tradition is the first obligation of Julienne men."

Beside him, in a field of thriving Zinfandel plants, Savannah arched an eyebrow. "And the Julienne women?"

She'd expected his usual reaction—a grimace or an exasperated sigh, not the brief hesitation that dulled his eyes. He fumbled clumsily at his pocket for his pipe. By the time he'd withdrawn it the cloud had passed, and his smile was a teasing grin. "Why, they give us more Julienne men, of course."

Savannah laughed deep in her throat. "Of course."

Fluid gold sunlight drenched the countryside. The air smelled of oak trees and dust. An indolent breeze stirred grape leaves and seeped through the thin muslin of Savannah's pale apricot blouse. Untidy smudges marred the knees of her white slacks from when she'd impulsively knelt in a damp field to root out a weed. Now, soaking up the day's lazy heat, she tugged her hat low on her brow to shade her eyes and smothered a yawn.

She'd been awake most of the night. It had taken that long after Burke left her for the ache to ease and the heat to drain. Dawn had been a pink light creeping through her windows before she was finally able to sleep. At nine she'd awakened to Christina's tap at her door, and then she'd spent a deliciously extravagant hour breakfasting off a tray. She'd no sooner swallowed the last mouthful of omelet when Claude announced from outside her room that it was time to dress and meet him downstairs for her tour of the vineyard.

"We are wine makers," Claude continued in the same instructive tone he'd used to explain the irrigation system, the training of vines to stakes, the benefits of handpicking versus mechanical harvesting. "And we are grape growers." They turned at row's end, skipped one and started down another. "But always, *always*, the seeds we plant and the roots we protect are those of our heritage."

As they had for hours, Claude and Savannah strolled the trenches between staked and wired plants, stopping at least once in each row to let Claude fuss at a bush.

"How will you know later which leaves are which?" Savannah asked.

"Leaves?" he repeated distractedly. "What leaves?"

Savannah poked a finger at his breast pocket. Cuttings he'd stuffed there crackled under her touch. "Those leaves. You've pinched them from every row of every field we've walked through. How will you know which is which when you do whatever it is you do with them?"

"I'll know because I'm a vintner. Would you look at a maple leaf and think it came from an oak tree?"

She grinned. "Probably."

"Pitiful," Claude lamented. "Such ignorance is pitiful. One day I'll teach you the difference between maples and oaks. For now, the Zinfandel. Pay attention."

His back was to her as he selected a leaf to demonstrate with. Savannah rose up on her toes and propped her chin on his shoulder. The hair she'd tucked behind one ear tumbled forward to spill down his shirt front.

"The Zinfandel leaf," he began in solemn, tutorial tones. "Crimped and ruffled, with three, sometimes five lobes. The veins are deep and long. The front is dark green." He turned the leaf over. "The back covered with down."

"And only the Zinfandel looks like that?"

"Only the Zinfandel. Each is unique. The canes, too." Parting vines, he exposed the plant's purplish bark. "Medium stalk, not too thick. Left to grow wild, the Zinfandel hasn't enough leaf to protect the grapes from sun blast, so we prune the plants to make the canes grow long and the foliage thick. In the spring we bind them in the middle, forcing them to grow wide on top, like an umbrella, to shade the fruit."

Claude crouched, and Savannah knelt in the moist earth beside him. With a gentleness approaching reverence, he cupped a weighty clump of deep purple grapes in his wide, callused palm. "The clusters are large, compact. This second bunch on the side is called a shoulder. Because the skin of the berries is thin, they're unsuitable as market grapes. Watch." He pinched one between thumb and finger. The grape split wide, releasing a squirt of juice. "Too thin; they crack when transported."

"Are these ready to harvest?" she asked.

He picked off a second grape. "Try it. See what you think."

The fruit broke between her teeth, filling her mouth with sweet, tangy juice. Savannah closed her eyes on a hum of pure pleasure. "They are if taste is any way to tell."

"There was a time when taste was the only way to make decisions . . . and mistakes. Now we have scopes and laboratory tests to give us sugar counts, a viticulturist to choose harvest time." Claude pushed himself to his feet with an effortful groan Savannah decided was exaggerated. "My viticulturist says Monday. Ramirez is already arranging for the pickers. We'll have three days. On the fourth we begin losing the perfect balance between sugar and acid. From those grapes we'll make jug wine.''

Following his lead, Savannah stood, also. But not before snitching another grape. Claude glanced over as she popped the fruit into her mouth, his brow furrowing in mock reproach.

''Uh-oh. Caught in the act.'' She giggled and shrugged. ''My father used to—'' Abruptly, she cut herself off. Two memories in as many days. Odd, she thought. And unwise.

''Your father?'' Claude prompted.

Savannah stuffed her hands in her pockets and studied the ground. Avoiding his question shouldn't be so difficult, she told herself. It was a subject she sidestepped easily, often. But it was getting harder to do that with Claude. He'd given her more than most just by caring; it seemed unreasonably selfish of her not to give him something as simple and undemanding as the answer to a question.

Glancing up, she smiled a bit sheepishly. ''My father used to say I could eat more cherries in half an hour than he could pick in an afternoon.''

''A child of the land,'' Claude murmured. ''I'd sensed that about you. I've seen it in your face, in your eyes.'' Separating a grape cluster from its vine, Claude placed it in Savannah's hands. ''Enjoy. Now come, it's time I had a word or two with the Cabernet Sauvignons.''

''A word or two.'' She looked askance at him, gauging whether she was supposed to take him seriously. ''With grapes?''

''Mmm, though a self-respecting raisin wouldn't claim them as kin at the moment. Shamefully scrawny. But you'll see. When they hear me praise the Pinot Noirs for being plumper than I've seen them in five seasons, my Cabernets will fatten. In two weeks, they'll be the ripest in Napa.''

Savannah swallowed a mouthful of grapes, then gave a gurgle of laughter. ''Claude, does anyone actually fall for your little-old-wine-maker-me act?''

"Everyone," he replied blandly. "I wouldn't bother otherwise."

"Not everyone," she corrected. "Not me. I think you're an astute vintner, a shrewd businessman . . . even if you do talk to a grape now and then."

They topped a hill. The view was magnificent. No wonder so many people were drawn to this place, Savannah thought. Aside from the acclaimed wineries tucked throughout the valley, the slumbering hills were home to Hollywood film directors, famous novelists and even a European title or two.

But from this vantage point every lush acre for as far as the eye could see was Julienne land. Savannah made a full revolution, taking it in. In the east, tall irrigation poles spewed arcs of silvery water. The house dominated the north horizon, a dazzling white crown atop an emerald wave. Westward, the land gradually planed out, each slope softer and smaller than the one preceding it.

"Amazing," she marveled, facing south again. "Months ago it was buried beneath a sea of muddy water. Now look at it."

"We were fortunate. It was winter, so the vines were pruned and dormant. Our losses were minimal."

"I'm glad for you, Claude."

"And I'm grateful to you, Savannah."

"No, don't be." Deliberately, she looked away, closing the subject. But he was stubborn and, catching her chin, brought her face back around.

"You've never let me thank you."

"It isn't necessary."

"You may not need to hear the words, Savannah, but I need to say them. It was *our* tragedy; you were only a bystander. Yet you worked frantically for us, as if it were your own family you struggled to help, your own home and ancestry you fought to save. That there are grapes in the fields and a crop to harvest is due in part to you. I'll never forget that."

She acknowledged his words with a nod, too close to
tears to speak. Beneath the tears other emotions moved
through her. Foreign emotions. Pride, possessiveness.
She'd had a hand in salvaging what grew here now; she'd
helped preserve a season's worth of someone's heritage. It
seemed only natural that a bit of it should belong to her.

After one more sweeping glance, Savannah squinted into
the sun and blinked her eyes dry. Before turning back to
Claude, she cleared her throat. "Now, where are these re-
calcitrant Cabernets?"

He pointed straight ahead. "They begin on the next
hill."

Savannah considered the terrain. To get from here to
there entailed staggering down one steep incline and
climbing up another. She estimated the round trip would
take her an additional half mile from the house. "Much as
I hate to admit this, Claude, I don't think I can make it. In
my line of work I spend most of my time on my behind.
We've been walking—" she glanced at her wrist for the
time "—nearly three hours."

"Pitiful," Claude muttered for the second time that
morning. "A young girl can't keep up with an old man?
Unsuitable. Then again, so is your job. Tomorrow we'll
walk again, and the day after and the day after that. By the
end of the week we'll have you in shape."

"But I'm—" *Leaving.* Savannah couldn't say it. Something about this place, this land, was taking hold. Claude
waited, his eyes wondering. "I'm getting my tour of the
winery tomorrow," she improvised.

"With Burke?"

Cursing the lie, Savannah nodded. She made a mental
note to find Burke later and invite herself on a tour, and
cursed that, too. It would have been foolish to think she'd
get through the rest of the weekend without running into
him. However, she certainly hadn't planned on seeking
him out or spending an afternoon with him. Well, she had
no one but herself to blame for this one; she'd backed
herself into this corner all on her own.

"Why didn't he take you through today?" Claude asked.

"I don't know. He must have had other plans."

"No, Burke's at the winery." Claude gave her one of his light-slowly-dawning looks. "Getting his sea legs before hopping back on board Monday."

Avoiding Claude's scrutiny, Savannah watched a flock of birds skim the sky. "Maybe he preferred being alone his first time through."

"Maybe. Or maybe you should find him and see if he has tomorrow free for you." When she opened her mouth to argue, Claude shooed her off with a wave of his hand. "Run along, find Burke. I'll go have a word with the Cabernets."

Smiling, Savannah watched Claude set off before turning to retrace the route they'd walked. Without breaking stride she bent and scooped up a handful of earth. Bringing the mound to her face, she inhaled the damp fragrance. What was it Claude had called her? A child of the land. Not in a very long time, she thought as she let the dirt trickle from her hand. But once, briefly.

Savannah feasted on the grapes as she walked. The day grew warmer, her legs more tired. Her pace was slow but steady, yet the house seemed to remain at a constant distance. Leaving the Zinfandel fields, she climbed the side of a knoll where the branches of a tall, sturdy tree spread a pool of shade. Removing her hat, she shook her hair loose.

*"Lie down in the shade, Savannah, and take your nap."*

Her mother's voice, so gentle and clear, reached her across the incredible gulf of time. She'd forgotten it. That subdued, patient voice, sometimes strained but always patient. And always just a little bit weary.

Savannah dropped to the thick carpet of grass, pried off her sneakers and wiggled her toes. Flopping onto her back, she gazed up at the lacy splash of leaves against sky. When the green and blue pattern blurred, she rolled onto her stomach, using her hat to pillow her cheek. The shadows had trapped the night's coolness, and it seeped through her clothes, refreshing on her hot skin. A fitful breeze bent the long grass and blew the hair back from her face.

*"Close your eyes, Savannah. By the time you wake, I'll have all these potatoes picked."*

The evening was clear. Not a hint of fog. Savannah sat on the terrace wall, knees to chest in the loose cradle of her arms. She watched the shadows thin and stretch, the crimson slashes of sunset gradually fade behind dusk. Crickets chirruped happily. Full-blown roses showered petals and perfume at each stir of a breeze.

It was so different from what she was used to. Whenever, wherever she decided to end her day, she was never this far from exhaust fumes. Days didn't yawn and nod off under a blanket of night. Truck stops didn't sleep. No matter what the hour, traffic came and went, a card game started or ended, breakfast was being served. She could join in or keep to herself, and she liked that. She could pack up and take off without having to answer to anyone, and she liked that, too.

Freedom. Savannah cherished hers in the way of people who'd known years of stifling confinement, rigorous regimentation and austere discipline. Now there was no one to stop her, whether it was from setting off on a long journey or just going for a walk. No one to say she couldn't eat chocolate chip cookies at ten in the morning or wear green pants with a purple blouse. No one to say she couldn't *own* green pants and a purple blouse. Savannah had been granted her freedom promptly and utterly on her seventeenth birthday. Though she hadn't had to earn it, she had long coveted it and worked very hard to protect and keep it.

An owl hooted. Savannah jerked and then laughed at herself. So different, she thought again. Straightening her legs on the wide, smooth coping and leaning back on her flattened palms, she gazed up at the star-splashed sky.

*If I ever settle down, this is the sort of place, the sort of peace, I'd settle down into.*

Before the thought could finish forming, Savannah wondered when it had begun. This morning, with the sun on her face and the taste of fruit on her tongue? Later, as she'd napped in the shade of a tree? Just now? Settling down wasn't something she contemplated, not even lightly. A home was the last thing she wanted. She had no desire, burning or latent, for permanence or possessions.

*Mine* was a label she was careful not to put on things. Experience had taught her that what she thought was hers one minute could be snatched away in the next. So why had she thought about settling down, even hypothetically?

Perhaps it was because Napa seemed to run at its own pace, the way she had always chosen to do. Yet even as she thought it, she knew the impression was false. There were routines and repeating cycles here, day to day, season to season.

Perhaps it was because a bit of warm pleasure still remained from the day. She'd enjoyed the morning with Claude, enjoyed sleeping on the grass with the breeze whispering over her. She was enjoying the evening and a quiet that was restful instead of isolating. Leaves rustled in the surrounding trees. Tiny nocturnal creatures scampered unseen in the garden eight feet below.

Perhaps it was because occasionally she wished there were a place where she belonged. Not a home, but...somewhere. A zip code. Wasn't that how she'd said it to Burke?

Burke. Just thinking his name did unsettling things to her system. Her pulse skipped, muscles tensed and she frowned.

He'd been absent from dinner, and she wondered why. Neither Claude nor Christina had volunteered information on his whereabouts, and Savannah hadn't asked. Now Claude was satisfying his penchant for whodunits with the Saturday Night Movie. Christina sat at her needlework frame beside him in the den. Weatherby was waddling about her kitchen, straightening the disorder from dinner. Fitzhugh was creeping around the second floor, turning down beds. And Burke?

Savannah supposed he was still catching up on things at the winery and preferred to stay with it. At least she hoped that was the case and that it wasn't her presence or her needling him yesterday that kept him away. She'd hate to think she'd upset someone to the point that he wasn't comfortable having dinner in his own home. Homes, she knew, as much as she renounced one for herself, were sacred places to those who had them.

According to Claude, the winery buildings were only a ten-minute walk along the flagstone path behind the house. How much interruption would Burke have suffered by stopping for dinner? Half an hour? Forty minutes? It was nine o'clock. Wouldn't he have gotten hungry by now?

Stop it, Savannah, she chided herself. He's a grown man and quite capable of taking care of himself.

Then, having made the decision to put him out of her mind, she heard his footsteps on the gravel as he rounded the side of the house. Tilting her head, she gazed across the long, shadowy porch to the steps at the far end.

His head was bowed as he climbed the stairs, his hands stuffed in his pockets. He paused on the top step and gazed out at the moon-bathed fields. Urges she had no business feeling coursed with her blood. To block them she made a conscious, critical survey of him. He was as impeccably put together as he'd been the day before. He might have worn the shirt all day, but it looked just-from-the-hanger fresh. His slacks were the fitted, beltless type, his loafers a butter-soft leather too discreet to gleam. Stuffily impeccable, she decided with a mental snort. Except for a lock of sable hair falling over his brow, as if he'd recently run his hands through it. That small untidy detail completely undid her resolve to dislike him.

Burke closed his eyes for a moment. They were hot and gritty and begged to stay shut through a long, dreamless night. Exhaustion—he was nearly numb with it. To be expected, he told himself. It was dawn of tomorrow by his body clock, and he'd doggedly wrung three days' work out of one. By rights, he should have collapsed hours ago. Even so, he smiled. The physical fatigue and mental drain felt good, gratifying, because they were the consequence of productivity.

He'd spent most of the day in his office. Sitting in his tufted leather chair behind his polished mahogany desk, he'd felt, finally, that he'd indeed come home. While he appreciated the feudal grandeur of the estate house, he was most comfortable in light, unpretentious, rooms that had been spared the hand of a decorator. Creativity, he believed, was an exercise for the brain, not something he wanted splashed on his walls.

Within the dove-gray and platinum interior of his office, and for nearly ten straight hours, Burke had worked with pen and notepad, preparing for the first confrontation with his father. He'd given substance to the abstract, made the confusing coherent. He'd anticipated Claude's questions and formulated the answers. He'd come away with a game plan. It was what he did best. In the last twelve months it was what he'd missed most.

Leaving his hands in his pockets, he arched his back, flexing to relieve the ache between his shoulder blades. A warning swam in his brain that he ought to put himself to bed before his overtaxed body dropped him where he stood. Monday night, he thought as he turned and climbed the last step to the porch. Monday night, after he was officially back on the payroll, he would tell Claude of the Champagne. Burke was beginning to look forward to the challenge. He didn't doubt his father would make it one.

He felt her with his sixth sense a split second before finding her with his eyes. Stretched out on the moonlit porch wall, she looked as cozy as a cat sunning herself on a windowsill. Head tipped to one side, she watched him with undisguised curiosity. She did that, he remembered—stared full-face at him. He'd thought of her today—much too often. And when he'd thought of her he'd pictured her looking at him just this way. No woman he'd ever known had intruded on his work, and he didn't even *know* this woman.

Her gathered, gaily colored skirt flowed down the porch wall to brush the stone floor. Her legs were crossed at the ankles, and her feet were bare. Her black satin hair falling away from her face and the cut of her crimson peasant blouse bared her shoulders. Moonlight did incredible things to her skin. Burke gazed at her a full minute without feeling time pass. The quick surge of desire that pumped through him defied his physical fatigue.

"Burke," Savannah called when she felt sparks of tension crackling in the air between them. "Just the man I needed."

Amusement touched his mouth. Just a touch, but enough that she noticed it through the shadows. "Somehow, Savannah, I'd gotten the impression you weren't the sort to need a man for anything."

"Somehow, Burke, I'd gotten the impression you weren't the sort to make snap judgments."

And so round two begins, Burke mused. "Did you? You seemed to think me rather opinionated yesterday."

"You are opinionated. I just don't think you come about your opinions quickly."

Savannah watched him stroll toward her, suddenly aware of coiled power. The same power, she recalled, that she'd sensed the day before. He could be pushed too far—to frustration, to anger. How could she have forgotten that? He might look like a neat, precise package of control, but she'd do well to watch how hard she poked at the wrappings. As he closed in, she instinctively drew her knees up to her chest again.

"So." Burke sat on the wall beside her. "You need...?"

"A tour of the winery." He was too close. If she let her toes slide forward an inch, they'd touch his thigh. She wished now she'd left her legs stretched out. "Tomorrow."

Burke considered her for a long moment. If there was logic or reason behind her request, it was beyond him to find it. "People have wanted tours," he reflected, "and they've enjoyed tours. But I can't recall anyone ever needing a tour."

The scent of musk sliced neatly through the floral evening. Savannah wished she didn't prefer it to the roses. "Well, I do. First, because it'll make an honest woman of me. And second, it's a tour of the winery or another marathon walk with your father. If you could feel my legs right now, you'd take pity and say yes. I don't know how he does it. *Miles.* We must have walked…" Her voice trailed away when his hand closed on her ankle beneath the flounced hem. "What are you doing?"

Good question, Burke mused. "Feeling your legs," he said. "Pity doesn't come to mind." Taking her in his arms did. *Why her?* Another good question.

"I spoke figuratively." Though she circled his wrist with her fingers, Savannah seemed incapable of stopping his hand from sliding ever so slowly up her calf.

"It's worked, in any case. How does twelve o'clock sound?" Her skin was petal soft against his palm. He'd known it would be. Coasting higher, his knuckles brushed the back of her thigh. Her breath caught, and her eyes widened. Her fingernails dug into his wrist. Her responses stirred a new excitement in him.

"Burke."

"Relax," he murmured.

"I was relaxed." This—*he*—made her tense, with wire-thin need. Lifting her ankle, he straightened her leg and draped it across his lap. "Now what are you doing?" But she knew. The instant he pressed at the taut tendons in her arch, she knew. With his thumb, he made deep, slow circles, and she moaned.

"Feel good?"

"Good." Bones melting, Savannah let her head fall back, her lashes drift down.

Burke massaged her foot and stared at her dream-featured face. Not beautiful in the true sense of the word, he decided. But a man wouldn't forget having seen it.

Feminine, he thought as he had the first time. Exquisitely so. Precisely what a woman should look like. Lifting her other foot and bringing that leg onto his lap, Burke looked with awakening fascination at the contrast of his deeply tanned hands on her milk-white skin. Her toenails, he noticed, were painted pale pink. When had he last bothered to look at a woman's toes, or at the color of her polish?

Taking a finger over the top of her foot, Burke digested the bits of information she'd given him. He knew now how she'd spent her day and that she didn't want to spend it the same way tomorrow. To get out of it, she'd lied to his father. And while he'd lay ten-to-one odds she lied often and without qualm, lying to Claude didn't sit well with her. A few more pieces slipped into place. Not enough yet to guess at the picture, but satisfactory progress.

When his kneading fingers once again journeyed to her calf, Savannah opened her eyes. "That was nice." Shifting and folding her legs up under her skirt, she gave him the message that it was also enough. "A good massage is hard work, and you've put in a long day already." She laughed at the sardonic quirk of his mouth and let some of the tension go. "When you go back to work, you really go back to work."

Burke let her have her distance. He needed a few miles of it himself. "A lot of business is transacted in a year."

Forcing herself to relax, Savannah let her knees fall open so that she sat cross-legged, hands curled in the drape of skirt in her lap. "You must be hungry. You worked right through dinner."

"No, I'm fine." He withdrew a pack of cigarettes and offered them. Savannah took one. Though she'd quit smoking months ago, she welcomed the activity for her hands. He flicked a gold lighter, putting it to the tip of her cigarette first. "I had a dinner date."

Savannah sputtered and released the inhaled smoke in a fit of coughs.

Alarmed, Burke shot to his feet. "You don't smoke?"

Pressing a hand to her chest, Savannah sucked a breath of clean air. "I used to," she rasped. "But even then I didn't smoke anything like this." She squinted to read a brand name on the filter paper, but the light was too dim. "What is it?"

"French. I haven't exhausted my supply yet." Confident she wasn't going to cough herself over the eight-feet drop to the flower beds, Burke relaxed—as much as was possible around her—and lowered himself to the wall again. "They take some getting used to."

Deciding she wasn't so inclined, Savannah tossed the unsmoked cigarette over the ledge. A date, she thought. Why had it surprised her? It was Saturday night. He'd been gone a year. Someone must have been left behind to wait. With her mind's eye she saw Burke escorting a slender, elegant blonde to a candlelit table. A woman of sophistication, Savannah thought, one whose laughter would be a tinkling of crystal bells, one whose eyes would extend seductive invitations and one whose arms would later deliver. It was a picture she didn't particularly like.

"It's early to end a date," she noted.

"Unless World War Two combat stories fascinate you, ninety minutes of Ed Zimmer is more than adequate." Burke watched her as he drew lazily on his cigarette. Her breathing hadn't completely returned to normal, and the rise and fall of her breasts made the muscles in his thighs tighten. "I got a fix on what he'll ask for his lots of Gamays, then called for the check."

An unreasonable elation filled Savannah. "I'm relieved. I thought my needling you yesterday might have driven you off."

Burke smiled at her suggestion. "My hide's a bit thicker than that."

"Mmm." Their eyes locked in a way they hadn't before. Savannah forcibly stemmed an urge to squirm. "You don't like me, do you, Burke?"

Her question startled him. Probably because he'd been asking himself that very thing. He didn't like the way she made him lose concentration. And he didn't like the way she made him want her more than he'd wanted the last woman in his life—or any of the others. Did that mean he didn't like *her*?

"I don't know."

She hadn't expected it to wound. But then, she hadn't expected him to matter.

"I don't like your personalized set of values, Savannah." Hurt. He saw it in her eyes, but it was too late to wish back the words. "But then, I don't think you rate mine too highly, either."

Furious with herself for letting him get to her, Savannah tossed her head back. "At least my values affect no one but me. I don't set them up as guidelines for society or make them into laws that are foisted onto others."

"Your way, nobody gets hurt—is that it?" Burke crushed his cigarette beneath his heel and pushed himself off from the wall. Not until he'd walked to the center of the porch did he step outside her jasmine-scented cloud. "I once knew someone who thought the same." He stared into the darkness but saw beyond it. "Some of the things I said to you yesterday are things I'd say to her, given the chance to live it over."

Savannah wasn't quite sure how to respond. He spoke quietly, as if to himself, but there was a depth of emotion in his voice. In actuality he'd told her very little, yet she had the uncomfortable feeling he'd shared something personal. "You loved her... this someone?"

"Yes, I loved her."

Grief. Savannah heard its ragged edge and swallowed hard. "She's gone, isn't she?"

She measured his silence by not breathing. Her lungs ached before he finally turned to face her. "My father hasn't told you of Amy?"

Mutely Savannah shook her head.

"My sister. She died two years ago." Hesitating, he questioned the wisdom of continuing. "Heroin."

Shocked, Savannah watched him walk back to where she was sitting. His features were controlled, as if he'd come to terms with it. Only his eyes gave him away.

"Heroin," he repeated as if he still found it all too confusing. "One more daring, provocative adventure for Amy."

Savannah hurt for him. This she understood, a brother-sister relationship. If anything were to happen to Neil, Savannah would lose more than a brother. She'd lose half herself. Suddenly she remembered the flicker of darkness on Claude's face when she'd asked him about Julienne women. Dear God, how terrible for all of them. "Claude's never mentioned her."

"The world was Amy's playground. Everything had to be tried once; every city had to be lived in, every man slept with. There was no definition to what she wanted, and no end. The most elegant, most extravagant debutante party one week, purple hair and leather dresses the next." Sitting down beside Savannah again, Burke leaned forward to rest his elbows on his knees and link his hands together. "She had this big silent stare. I remember that most. Her eyes pleading, yearning to be taken under someone's wing."

Acting on impulse, Savannah covered his joined hands with one of hers. Astonishment hit her with the first brush of flesh. She never reached out, never offered what could be tossed back. As she lifted her hand to snatch it back, Burke caught her fingertips and held them. But there was no gratitude in the eyes he pinned her with.

Savannah squared her shoulders and met his gaze. "The things you said to me yesterday, you meant them for her?"

"That's not what I said. I told you I'd have said them to her if I had the chance, but I meant them for you. There *are* rules, Savannah. It is *not* acceptable to break them."

She'd already reasoned that he was the wrong man for her. Now she decided she was the worst possible woman for him. "There is a huge difference between going a few miles over a speed limit and getting involved in heroin, Burke."

"Only if you're measuring how far one will go to prove the same point. It was Amy's right to do as she pleased, she would tell us. But we loved her. We felt her pain, and now we're left with the loss. She never stayed long after I'd bring her home—a few weeks, a month. And she never said goodbye when she left. There were no limits for Amy. And no rules."

*No rules.* Savannah remembered those words from Burke the day before. Even so, she failed to find anything in herself that remotely resembled the sadly lost woman he'd described. Searchers, Savannah called them. Hungry, desperate souls on a never-ending hunt for something to fill the holes, grabbing at anything to satisfy the empty longings. Savannah knew those souls, but she wasn't one of them. Because that something, she knew, simply didn't exist. Yet she'd reminded Burke of his sister. Rather than react with temper, as she was inclined, she asked herself why?

"Do I look like her?"

"No." He answered without hesitation. "She looked like our mother. She was blonde, very blonde, and her eyes were green. But you ... have her expressions. I'd hazard that you have her thoughts. I've seen them in your eyes. And there's the way my father looks at you." He smiled, some of the warmth returning. "I know my father. When it comes to striking up friendships, he is ... shall we say, selective? You'd be his first truck driver."

Well, now she knew where he'd pigeonholed Claude. "Are you implying that your father might be a snob?"

"Hell, no. I'm stating it quite bluntly. Claude Julienne is a snob."

His crack was like a match to her fuse. She yanked her hand free and leaped to her feet. From the moment Burke had arrived, her thoughts had been in chaos, her stomach in turmoil. She welcomed the chance to release it all with angry words. "And you're a pompous ass!"

"You're repeating yourself." How far can she be pushed? Burke wondered. Angry, she was glorious. She whirled in the middle of the porch. Her eyes blazed. Her chin was belligerently thrust out, and her hands were balled into fists.

"You've decided a truck driver is beneath Claude's dignity?" she raged. It mattered little to her that it was probably true, or that she'd realized it herself the first time she'd met Claude. At the moment, truth had nothing to do with anything. "The man talks to grapes, for God's sake. How selective can he be?"

A night hawk screeched. A breeze whispered through the trees. Suddenly Burke laughed, richly, heartily. "He does. He talks to his grapes. Did he actually take them to task in front of you?"

"No," she snapped. She wouldn't laugh, too, she told herself. Dammit, if she laughed, she'd lose whatever ground she'd gained. But it really was a ridiculous conversation. The first giggle slipped out, and then Savannah was laughing. "He would have," she said finally, leaning weakly against a stone pillar, "if I hadn't pooped out. Does he walk like that every day, or was I getting the first-timer's tour?"

"I thought you'd been here before?" Burke went to her. She dragged a hand through her hair, and as she let it drop to her side, he caught it. He took his thumb over her fingernails, noticing they were meticulously cared for. He wanted to find ragged edges and grease. She should look like, act like, what she was: a trucker.

Because she could barely concentrate on forming words as he traced the lines of her palm, Savannah missed the sharpening look in his eyes. "I've arrived in daylight and seen the vineyards through my windshield, but the only time I'd been out in the fields was during the floods."

"Last winter. I remember. I should have been here." He touched a nerve, and her fingers instinctively curled. "By the time word reached the Bordeaux region the news was two days old. I spent thirty minutes on the phone booking

flights, then called home.'' His fingers rested in the soft
curl of her hand. Burke discovered he liked the feeling.
''My father told me it was over and that the reports we'd
received were greatly exaggerated. I believed him. By the
time I'd learned differently, it really was over.'' He gazed
off at the fields, his eyes distant. ''But I should have been
here.''

''You couldn't have gotten in with the roads out. I was
stuck here for four days.'' The low, husky quality of her
voice startled sense into Savannah, and she eased her hand
from his grip.

''Four days,'' he murmured.

She thought at first that his chuckle was one of smug
satisfaction for having made her retreat. Then he gave her
the same amused look Claude adopted when he'd caught
her in one of her own verbal webs.

''Your room.''

She hadn't a clue what he meant. ''Pardon?''

''That explains how you came to have a room here.''

Her laughter was low and smoky. ''Clever. You're very
clever, Burke. Yes, that's how I came to have a room
here.'' She sighed dramatically. ''So now you know
everything.''

''Not everything.''

''More questions?''

''How do you taste?''

Her breath stopped, then shuddered out. ''You come
right to the point, don't you?'' And it was a lethal one.

Burke hadn't anticipated his question until he heard it
hanging in the warm evening air. Now he hadn't the patience to wait for her answer. ''It tends to facilitate things.''

He touched her—just his fingertips, just her cheek-
bone. ''No.''

A pulse hammered at the base of her throat. Burke saw
it and felt an urgent need to place his tongue there. ''No,
Savannah?'' He let his thumb drag over the pulse point
before plunging his hand into her hair.

Turning, Savannah stepped past him. Burke turned with her, so smoothly they might have been a single person moving. His hand was still tangled in her hair. "No," she repeated. "To the point." But her knees were unsteady as he curved a hand to her waist. She was going to put a stop to this, she vowed, just as soon as breath returned to her lungs. She met his dark, depthless eyes and experienced the sensation of falling, into them, all the way down.

"Burke, no." He drew her closer. "We don't even *like* each other."

He ran his hand down the length of her hair, letting the water-soft strands sift through his fingers. "Doesn't seem to keep us from wanting each other, does it?" His thumb brushed her lips, and they parted on a sigh.

She heard resentment and a touch of anger in his voice. Before she could make sense of it his mouth covered hers, softly, gently. She didn't want this, she told herself, or him. Then she was rising up on her toes and pressing into the kiss. Wanting. This. And him. She'd put a stop to this, she promised herself... just as soon as she'd had a little more of the pleasure.

Tracing her lips with his tongue, Burke drew in the creamy flavor. It had tormented him, not knowing her taste. He was a man whose livelihood, whose every goal, depended on the skill of his palate. He'd know her, understand her better, when he'd sampled every nuance of her mouth. He'd taste her and stop wondering. He'd taste her and be done with the question.

Lost in a velvet fog, Savannah felt him mold her, find and shape her over her clothes. In the wake of his touch, her skin burned. Her blood spread the heat. His lips brushed her shoulder, and she tipped her head to bare more of it for him. His tongue flicked lightly at her throat. Savannah began to sink, convinced she was melting.

Burke took her mouth again and again. Her taste was a blend of the seductive and the exciting. Skin-warmed satin. Iced champagne. And something else...an essence of...? A soft puff of night air brushed past them, and Burke re-

called a particular day in France, an afternoon tasting in
Bordeaux—and one memorable vintage. Not quite at its
peak but with tremendous potential. Immature but with a
taste of promise. This was Savannah. Her mouth gave up
heat and pleasure, but more, it imparted promise.

His next thought hit like a thunderbolt. *Innocent?* Releasing her mouth, he stared down until she opened heavy-
lidded eyes. Good God, was she innocent?

Savannah met his penetrating black eyes and thought,
*He's seen me.* She wasn't sure precisely what he'd found,
only that he'd looked deep inside her and discovered a
truth that wasn't his right to know.

Burke held her face in both hands. Gazing into her gray
eyes, he watched them lighten with flecks of silver. He'd
never wanted more desperately what he saw she wasn't
going to give.

"Let me go, Burke," she stated with more calm than she
felt.

"Go, Savannah." His low murmur and warm breath fell
softly into her mouth. "Walk away."

Not while he touched her. She couldn't when he was
touching her. Panic welled up, and Savannah flattened her
hands against his chest. "I don't want this."

"Yes, you do." Burke banked the rush and flow of need.
"You may wish you didn't, but you do."

"No. I don't want it, or you."

"I thought the same, until now." He caught her by the
back of the neck and tipped her face up. "Good night,
Savannah." He took her mouth once more, briefly,
chastely. When he left her standing on the porch staring
after him, he wondered how long he could physically en-
dure a life without sleep.

Savannah brought a halt to her pacing in the middle of
the dusky bedroom. The glowing digits of the nightstand
clock flashed 11:20 at her. Nearly two hours since she'd
come upstairs to bed. Nearly two hours since Burke's kiss.

Inside she was still churning. What the hell had happened in those brief moments? And why the hell had she let it?

Blowing out a frustrated breath, she walked to the corner and unzipped her cello, frown lines deepening with her thoughts. She attracted men. Men attracted her. But it never went beyond attraction. With short, jerky movements, she rosined her bow. There might have been a few with whom she'd felt sparks. But abandonment wasn't like her. She clearly hadn't been herself tonight. She set herself up at the window where she'd played Brahms the night before.

Instead of sending her soul with the music, this time she sent her trapped, restless feelings. Closing her eyes, she looked inward to find them, name them and send them on their way.

*Confusion.* That one was easy, familiar. She'd spent most of her life confused by one thing or another. The worst sorts of confusion were those left behind by people. One had to accept things like tornadoes swooping down out of the cloudless blue or rivers or water wiping out homes and highways. But it seemed people should have to explain themselves beyond trite phrases like "This is for the best" or "I couldn't help myself." Burke had been angry; Savannah had tasted the heat of it. If he'd wanted her a smidgen more, she thought he might have hated her for it. God, where was the sense in that? Savannah plucked confusion from the quagmire and released it.

*Excitement.* The most deadly of them all because it never stood alone. Anticipation was an integral part of excitement, and Savannah felt it now, pumping with her blood. She could hear it in her music, words instead of notes. "I can't wait. Please, I can't wait."

With excitement gone, the churning inside was calmer. Opening her eyes, she gazed at the silver orb that was the moon.

*Fear.* Of a journey down an unfamiliar road. Ventures of the heart couldn't be mapped out like a trip from Baltimore to Houston. She'd be driving blindfolded, trusting fate to keep her on the road. She didn't trust fate; it had always left her stranded.

At melody's end, Savannah dropped her head, letting her temple rest against the cello's neck. *Loneliness.* There was nothing she could do with that one. She'd spent a lifetime trying. But it wasn't something she could corral and push away. Lifting the bow, she played to soothe the ache. Softly. A warm, tender tune, like a comforting hand to hold.

A faint summer breeze lifted the curtains in Burke's bedroom. The air skimmed his bare chest, feeling several degrees cooler on his heated flesh.

He needed eight hours of sleep.

He wanted the woman down the hall.

Sprawled on his back, he blindly watched shadows shift and reform on the ceiling. Thoughtfully he touched his tongue to his top lip. The taste of Savannah lingered. Groaning, he scrubbed a hand over his face, rolled onto his stomach and decided she wasn't for him. He was past falling for mystique. He liked his women and his sex easy. Nothing with Savannah would be easy.

*Innocent.* Was it possible? Even now he could see her as she'd looked the night before, drawing the last passionate moan from her cello. Head thrown back, her face had been aglow with rapture. The rapture had dissolved into contentment. Somewhere, at some time, a man had taught her the depth of those feelings. But what about the sudden vulnerability she'd shown a few hours ago? Burke asked himself. That mixture of fear and wonder that every man and woman experiences once in a lifetime.

*Innocent?* Dammit, the woman was a homeless vagabond who blatantly scorned law, logic and social convention. How likely was it that she adhered to a strict moral code? But that reasoning was logical. Was Savannah?

*Innocent.*

It changed the rules, Burke thought. Then he laughed, a soft bark of self-mockery. Savannah had no rules—she'd said so herself. But he did, and stripping virgins of their defenses was against them.

From down the hall came the soft, mournful notes of a cello. Sad, sweet. A plea. A prayer. Burke clenched his fists against the urge to go to her. What the hell did her music cry for?

He needed that answer before he'd understand her.

He needed, he told himself, a shot of Scotch, straight, to burn away every last trace of her. In the end, he slept with the taste of her on his tongue.

## Chapter Four

Savannah sighed, stirred, drifted, dreamed.

In the dream she was five years old and one of three dozen or more children on a packed-earth playground. Bundled against the cold in woolen tights, a coat two sizes too big and her floppy felt hat, she watched a swirl of dust sprint across the desolate west Kansas prairie. She wasn't the only one to notice it, and soon the cry went up.

"One's coming!"

Activity ground to a halt. Toddlers tumbled from swings. Teens pocketed contraband dice. Jump ropes were tossed aside and marbles abandoned. Holding a collective breath, they gravitated to the chain-link fence to watch the ground-skimming cloud slow, turn and chase a dingy green station wagon in need of a muffler up the long treeless drive.

The car shuddering to a stop in the oval turn-around riveted eyes of every shape and color. Some were narrowed and resentful; a few were dulled by an institutional glaze. But most, like Savannah's, shimmered with an all-consuming hope. They watched as Mr. Glass stepped out the front door, greeted the visitors and ushered them inside. Then, as surely and silently as they'd gathered, they dispersed, drifting back to whatever game or toy they'd quit minutes ago.

"Come away, Savannah," Edna Beasley ordered. "Show's over." The woman was head of the day shift, and a forbidding sight to behold. Her features were plain, her iron-gray hair scraped into a bun. Her spindly frame cast a skeletal shadow. "Do as I say, now, and join the others."

Clinging to the fence, Savannah tipped her head back to meet Beasley's forthright stare. She blinked and waited. When the woman said nothing more, Savannah went back to gazing through the diamond-patterned mesh at the sun-faded car.

Joints cracking, Beasley crouched down. "Don't do this to yourself, child." Her voice had softened. And so, Savannah noticed when she glanced over, had her eyes. "If we get as much rain tomorrow as the weatherman predicted, it'll be days before you're let outside again to play. Why waste today standing around gawking at somebody's old wagon?" Her wispy eyebrows arched in a question that went unanswered. "Dear heart," Beasley whispered in a grave voice. "They've gone inside now, and you must forget you ever saw them."

But Savannah wouldn't. She never did. She thought of them when she lay on her bed at night in the girls' dormitory, and when Mary Louise Jankowski was given the red sweater to wear that was Savannah's favorite. She thought of them when she woke from a nightmare and there was no one to call for. She thought of them on Christmas, her birthday, the Fourth of July....

They came on Sundays, between one and three in the afternoon. They came dressed in their finest, be it vested suits and neat sheaths or patched overalls and freshly laundered housedresses. They came in pairs, husbands and wives as barren as this flat, forsaken land, where nothing broke the monotonous horizon but an occasional grain elevator and the chillingly blunt silhouette of the Country Youth Home. If, within thirty minutes of their arrival, they came to the fenced yard or, in dead of winter, to the second-floor playroom, it meant they hadn't chosen an infant from the nursery.

This day the owners of the green station wagon accompanied Mr. Glass to the playground. They were plain folk, Kansas wheat farmers who looked to be in their midthirties. Savannah felt their eyes on her, that critical, stripping study that took in every detail from sole to crown, and she quickly removed her hat. Annie, one of the older girls assigned to helping out with the youngsters, said Savannah had the prettiest hair she'd ever seen. It might help if these people saw how shiny and clean she kept it, Savannah reasoned. It couldn't hurt.

While she wasn't one of the eager children flocking to the couple, Savannah's prayers were no less fervent that she'd be chosen this time. *Please*, she entreated silently, *please, pick me*.

Then, as he would when Savannah was paid more than passing interest, Mr. Glass spoke a few quiet words to the couple. The man shrugged, and the woman's eyes moved on, reluctantly, Savannah thought.

Crushed and frustrated, she balled her hands into fists, mangling her hat. *Why?* She was the smartest in her kindergarten class; she knew the alphabet and could already add and subtract without using her fingers. She never sassed back, never wet the bed at night. She obeyed all the rules. But once Mr. Glass shared his message with the adopting couples, they ignored her.

So it came as a staggering surprise when, shortly after the visitors left the playground, Beasley fetched Savannah. Clutching the woman's dry, bony hand, Savannah walked the labyrinthine halls joining the orphanage to the administrative offices. Instead of sporting cheerfully bright murals of fairy-tale characters, the walls in this section were painted a dull beige and hung with photos of stern, pudgy-faced men. Damask drapes shut out the sun, and the pine floors were bare, the wood's natural color worn away from a wide strip down the center.

Their footsteps echoed in the corridor—and the thud of Savannah's heart in her ears. Beasley stopped before a closed door that had precise black lettering on its frosted window. Savannah didn't have to know how to read to know this was Mr. Glass's office. Her heart leaped and she trembled—with joy, with fear. Though he'd never sent for her before, she knew his doing so now meant she'd been chosen for a home. What she didn't know was what came next.

"Are you ready, Savannah?"

Suddenly terrified, Savannah pressed her back to the wall. "Will they ask me questions?"

"A few."

"Is it a test? Can you tell me the answers?"

The tall, thin woman spared Savannah one of her rare smiles. "No, child, there'll be no test." Placing a hand on Savannah's head, Beasley ruffled her hair, a farewell pat. "Good luck to you, Savannah."

Mustering courage, Savannah reached for the doorknob. For all Beasley's reminders not to wear her hat when indoors, Savannah shoved it onto her head, needing its comfort.

When she stepped over the threshold her feet seemed to sink into a floor made of quicksand. Fighting panic, she struggled to walk, to move forward. She sensed the presence of others, but a strange mist pouring over the room hid them from her eyes. The dream was dissolving, turning to vapor in her brain. Efforts to hold on to it were as futile as grabbing at fistfuls of smoke.

Savannah floated, shedding first the dream, then its memory. Her first conscious thought was of the hot sting of sunlight on her eyelids. Her second was that she was supposed to meet Burke at noon.

*I won't.* Still drifting, she rolled onto her side, burrowed deeper beneath the tufted satin and tugged a pillow over her head. *He can't make me.*

In the next moment she bolted upright, her eyes wide open. Dear God, where had those thoughts come from? No, not thoughts, she realized, feeling an anxious trip to her pulse. Words. A voice, small and petulant but with a fragile quiver to it . . . sounding like a child, a frightened, belligerent child . . . like herself once.

No! She wouldn't remember. She didn't *want* to remember. Savannah threw off the quilt, determined not to. It was a long time ago, she told herself. And it was over. Shoving all of it to the corners of her mind where it belonged, she strode purposefully to the adjoining bathroom, ran water in the shower and stripped.

The spray was needle-sharp and hot. She let it pound full force on her head. She swallowed past a curious lump in her throat and wondered why she felt an overpowering urge to weep. Sadness—just beneath her heart, like a lone, lingering note—a distant ache of sadness. But lingering from when, what? Last night? Sliding perfumed soap over her wet skin, Savannah thought of those mindless moments in Burke's arms. She thought of his mouth, its taste and texture and devastating softness. No, not last night. There were untold feelings Burke had uncovered and pulled out of her. Sadness wasn't one of them.

A dream.

As quickly as the possibility presented itself, Savannah dismissed it. She never had dreams. Or if she did, she didn't recall them. And yet . . . Her hand lathering her shoulder stilled as something nagged to be remembered. But it couldn't be grasped, and she shook her head. Turning her back to the hot spray, she gazed up through the rising steam. Mist . . . a misty room. And then it came back to her, in snatches at first. Only it hadn't been a dream but a moment from her past relived. *Oh, God. That day.* That wonderful, terrible day when the Mulroneys had chosen her to take home with them.

Savannah shut her eyes, but it didn't stop the images. She'd thought they'd take Neil, too. She'd been so young and trusting. She'd naively believed that once she explained she had a brother, anyone who'd want her would also want him. But they hadn't wanted or taken Neil. As it turned out, they hadn't wanted or kept Savannah.

Why? After all these years, why was she remembering? Why had a greedy breath of Napa's morning air unlocked her earliest memories? Why had a ripe, juicy grape and a bed of cool grass recalled people and voices and precious pieces of a shattered life? Why did thinking of Burke Julienne bare the wounds?

Damn the man for whatever power he had to take her back! Covering her face, Savannah remembered the first time she'd laid eyes on him, of how she'd held her breath and waited—no, *wished* for—his approval. He'd been the first person in a very long time to make her feel like everyone's unwanted child.

The first ever to make her feel like a woman.

It was that yearning, Savannah knew, that throbbing hunger he'd unsealed last night, that made her vulnerable. It was wanting someone that made her fear she wouldn't be wanted in return.

She was brisk with the towel as she dried herself off, and just as brisk with the silent lecture she gave herself. Here she was, twenty-five, and that other life eight years behind her, cowering under her blankets. Well, Burke Julienne wouldn't make her shrivel and shrink as the child she'd been had eventually chosen to do. He wouldn't, she vowed, make her feel unworthy and unwanted. No one was ever going to matter that much to her again.

"You'll go to the winery with him today," Savannah said to her cloudy reflection in the steamed-over mirror. She picked up a brush and yanked it through her snarled, wet hair, stiff bristles raking over her scalp. "You'll go and see how wine is made. You'll be fascinated and enjoy it. You'll be *fine*. And tomorrow..." Tossing the brush down, she leaned into the mirror so that she was eye-to-eye with herself. "Tomorrow you'll get the hell out of here."

She changed her mind a dozen times as she pulled slacks and a blouse from her dwindling wardrobe, a dozen more times as she applied makeup to hide the strain and shadows. Why was she risking an afternoon in Burke's company? She clearly wasn't herself when she was with him. Savannah didn't trust strangers, least of all when she found she'd become one to herself. So what was she trying to prove? And to whom? That she wouldn't cower and quail? To herself? She already knew that.

She was still unresolved when she swiped her hat from the dainty rosewood desk. Muttering and scowling, she threw open the bedroom door and found herself nose-to-chin with Burke. He stood on the threshold blocking her way, one hand poised to knock. Savannah skimmed his length quickly, freshly annoyed that his faultless appearance was starting to appeal to her.

"Don't you have shirts in any color but white?"

"Prickly this morning, aren't you?" His voice was warm and unruffled. "What's the matter, Savannah, didn't sleep well?"

"I slept just fine thanks." Not if her life depended on it would she admit otherwise.

His smile was slow and unbearably sexy. "Five blue, three gray, three beige, six stripes in a variety of colors, one yellow—pale yellow—one pink." Casually, as if it were a gesture both of them were used to, he brushed the ends of her hair back, his fingertips whispering over her skin. "A dozen white."

Dear God, Savannah thought over the shiver of his touch, the man knew how many of each color shirt he owned. She added organized to her list of his imperfections. "Pink, hmm? I didn't figure you for a guy who'd wear pink shirts."

"Only one. And only with a charcoal-gray suit that has a faint maroon stripe in the fabric. And never in the office."

She laughed because he started to first. She liked that if he had to be so damn proper and practical, he could at least laugh at himself for it. But, dammit, she'd be on much steadier ground if she didn't like him at all!

He dropped a shoulder to the doorjamb and crossed his arms. "I'd just decided it was time to dump you out of bed. You're late." His eyes left her to scan the room, coming to rest on the nightstand. "What happened to your clock?"

Savannah glanced back at the blank oval face and remembered how the glowing numbers had counted her sleepless minutes. "I pulled the plug." She brushed past him and moved toward the stairs, donning her hat as she went. "Why? What time is it?"

"Twelve-thirty. Our date was for noon."

He was three steps behind her on the stairs. Without stopping, Savannah glanced over her shoulder. "It wasn't a date."

"No? What was it, then?"

She cast about for an appropriate word, one with a more functional, less personal ring to it. "An appointment."

"I thought you never made appointments."

"I'm making an exception for you."

"I'm flattered."

She scowled at him. He infuriated her by smiling back. "Don't be. I only make exceptions for people who thoroughly frustrate me."

When she faced front again, Burke let the frown come. The delicate lace of her lingerie was evident through her sheer ecru blouse, heightening her fragility—and his fascination. Her hips were narrow, her bottom softly curved. Both begged the stroke of a hand. She jammed her hands into her pockets, straining yellow linen, and his stomach clenched as it had when she'd opened her door, stirring air faintly tinged with her scent. When she'd looked him up and down, he'd had the satisfaction of seeing her pupils dilate. He was, Burke had decided in that instant, going to have Savannah Jones—for a day or for longer, he couldn't say, but for a lover, he was sure.

As he watched the smooth rhythm of her long, model-slim legs, Burke's frown deepened. The decision, irrevocable as far as he was concerned, refused to settle comfortably beside the other goals he'd set for himself. Why would a man who preferred method over madness, pleasure over passion, consciously choose to rattle his orderly life? Choose, hell, Burke silently cursed. He'd no more chosen than he'd decided. Realized was more like it. Realized and accepted. Given time, he might even make sense of it.

Savannah wanted distance; he would give her distance. One of the files he'd spent time with the previous day had contained freight invoices for the past year. The Julienne Winery contracted with Jones Hauling on the average of twice a month. With rare exception, Savannah's signature appeared on the sign-off sheet. She'd be back, Burke told himself. In fact, she'd probably be back in a few weeks to pick up a shipment of Premium Reserve wines due in New York by the end of the month.

In the meantime, Burke had those other goals to pursue, other demands on his energy. He needed to adjust and settle back in. He needed a clear head and keen concentration for the game of wits and will he and his father had yet to play. Savannah would be a distraction.

He was a man who planned. She was a woman he hadn't planned on. She wanted distance. He wanted time. Burke had the patience and determination to give them both what they wanted.

In the foyer, Savannah veered off to the front door. She was nearly there when Burke stalled her with a hand on her arm.

"Wouldn't you like breakfast first? I understand food works wonders on a bad temper." He only smiled when she glared at him.

His scent, woodsy and masculine, tugged at her senses. Savannah suspected it was as much that, as breakfast she refused with the shake of her head. "No, I'm not hungry."

"You're sure? We have plenty of time."

It hardly thrilled her to realize she'd lost her appetite. She never had before. Nor did she want to theorize on where it might have gone. Or why. "I should know if I'm hungry. I said I wasn't."

"Suit yourself."

Reaching over her shoulder, Burke pushed the door open. With a hand at the small of her back, he guided her through. "You might at least pretend to be nice to someone who's giving up his Sunday for you," he chastised without a shred of subtlety.

"If you have other plans—"

"I don't."

"Then you aren't giving anything up, are you?"

Annoyance spurred Burke's temper. He took her by the shoulders, inches from telling her she was being insufferably arrogant, if not downright rude. But as she stared back, with that silent challenge she was so good at, Burke saw the underlying strain. Her eyes were huge and haunted, her face too pale. He sensed an emotional thinness about her and decided, without much satisfaction, that she'd slept no better than he had. Swallowing the verbal abuse, he let his eyes move up from her face.

Savannah stood frozen, riveted by the power of his black, black eyes. He'd done it again—looked inside and found what he had no right to see. Before she realized his intent, he'd whisked her hat off and tossed it through the open door. Well aimed, it settled neatly on the wing chair's cushion.

"Let's leave that here."

It wasn't going at all as she'd planned, Savannah thought, and she wondered when she'd lost the upper hand...assuming she'd ever had it. As they crossed the terrace she smelled the tangy scent of rain in the air. Looking out, she saw leaden clouds on the horizon. When she was near Burke, Savannah reflected as they walked away from the house, her emotions were like that: sun and storm in the same sky.

Emotions. They were hers to control, she reminded herself. Hers to unloose or lock up. It was her choice to be miserable or make do. If she was going to spend a few hours with Burke—and apparently she was—she'd just as soon do it feeling sunny as stormy.

Shaking her hair back, she sneaked a glance at him. Few flesh-and-blood women would anticipate a day in his company with less than gushing enthusiasm. He was, quite simply, sexy as hell. She was, she admitted, the first to poke needles in places she knew made him jump. Maybe if she stopped fencing, he would, too, and they could spend a relatively harmless day together.

"I've been rude," she said as they walked along the snaking flagstone path, passing through profusely wild gardens bursting with color and perfume. "I'm sorry."

Burke cocked his head and smiled. He didn't think she apologized often. "Are you always so difficult, Savannah?"

*She's such a difficult child. Always has been.*

It had been said often of her, usually within earshot. Even at five she'd understood they meant her to hear them, hoping she'd be shamed into submission. It had had the opposite effect, however. Secretly, she had been proud of herself, of her strength to stand against them.

Now she shrugged and glanced at Burke. "Yes, I've always been difficult."

"Then I shouldn't take it personally."

"Yes, you probably should." She couldn't help the smile or that it expanded to a grin all on its own. "Though you probably won't."

The winery entrance came as a delightful surprise. Like Alice's rabbit hole to Wonderland, a door that had no business being there appeared in the side of a stony hill. If the path hadn't dead-ended at the slab of wide, hand-hewn planks, she'd never have noticed it. A pair of tall bushes, thick with delicate white buds, helped conceal the whimsical passage.

"I love it." Savannah laughed with pleasure and began to relax. "Strange place for a door, though. Is the winery *inside* the hill?"

"Only the family uses this entrance." Burke inserted a heavy brass key into the long, narrow lock. "This is a maintenance door of sorts. Opens on one of the tunnels where the gondolas run, exits on the far side where the winery backs up to the hillside. There's an assortment of buildings there, a parking lot, the tourist center."

Inside the air was dank and several degrees cooler. Unshaded lightbulbs were staggered the length of twisting, stone-walled tunnel. A railed walkway paralleled a trench laid with track on which the gondolas traveled, transporting grapes from the fields to the crushing rooms.

"The valleys are a honeycomb of tunnels." Burke shut the door firmly. Savannah heard its echo repeat in the cave's unseen nether regions and wondered if Burke and his sister had played hide-and-seek here, frightening each other silly. She and Neil would have. "Coolies, Chinese slave labor, dug tunnels from the rock by day and were hidden from the authorities in them by night."

Savannah clucked her tongue reproachfully. "The Julienne Winery used underground slave labor?"

"Officially, no. My grandfather swore to his dying day that we didn't. According to him, the Julienne tunnels were dug during Prohibition." Burke shrugged while his mouth struggled with a grin. "He was the sort of man who wouldn't have his family name muddied with being party to slave labor in the past. However, he considered bootlegging an honorable profession, one he'd never have taken up if the government hadn't forced his hand."

"I think I'd have liked your grandfather," Savannah said.

The actual winery, she discovered, was a conglomeration of rooms feeding into other rooms, an anachronism of new buildings tacked onto old. Each had its own special

scent, its own distinct mood. There was dust in the air and
wine-tinted sweat on the walls of the original brick rooms
where Julienne's red wines were still fermented in massive
redwood barrels. There was white light and the faint hint
of antiseptic in the newer industrialized plants.

And there were, she learned, more Julienne grapes, land
and buildings in other towns, other valleys. Fifty million
gallons of wine fermented at a time; one hundred thousand cases of bottles were packed a day. To Savannah,
who'd considered buying a truck a daunting commitment, being responsible for all this was unfathomable.

"We don't crush on Sundays." Burke slipped comfortably into the canned spiel he'd recited four times a day, six
days a week, during the summers of his youth. Savannah
studied the paddle blades of a mechanism that, when op-
erating, both removed stems and crushed grapes. "Opening the berries," Burke explained, "without breaking the
seeds."

She learned something of wine making from Burke's
running commentary. But she learned more of his family,
of the goals of each generation and the practices of each
new Julienne patriarch simply by walking through arches
and doors and stepping into the changes each had
wrought.

Now, looking about a vast room dominated by shiny
stainless steel vats, a few of which she'd delivered to Julienne's herself, Savannah grimaced. Moments ago they'd
been in a room where black grapes had bubbled, hot and
violent. She thought how cool and clinical the fermenting
of white wines was in comparison. On a wall computer-
ized monitors blinked, and printers spat out readings of
times and temperatures.

Computer-made wine, Savannah thought disdainfully.
Where was the romance in that? Wine making should drip
with romance. "I prefer the dungeons," she told Burke,
referring to the original buildings they'd passed through.

"Typical tourist." He tapped her on the nose, then let
his finger drift across her cheek. He touched her often,

Savannah noticed, to stress a point, to move her along when she lingered, or for no other reason than to let flesh skim over flesh. She told herself she wished he wouldn't, but she had yet to say or do anything to discourage him.

"My father and I kick around the idea of expanding the newer portions, closing some of the old. But the tour groups don't want realism; they prefer antiquated and mold."

"And Claude? What does he prefer?"

Burke smiled. "Claude has a decided weakness for vintage mold."

"But you..." She glanced again at the progressive, streamlined equipment. "You prefer this."

In her last word Burke heard disdain. "I appreciate advancement, Savannah. And I make full use of technology." He opened a door and led her into a windowless, white-tiled hall with thick, soundproofing carpet. "Modernization saves time and money, not to mention gallons of wine. Because of it we are competitive in the marketplace, a giant in the industry instead of a struggling boutique winery." He opened another door and stepped aside. Savannah smelled the dust and felt the sweat before crossing the threshold. "But I prefer this."

Eyes adjusting to the gloom, Savannah recognized a cellar. Unlike the enormous aging room he'd shown her earlier, where as many as two million bottles of wine could mature at one time, this exclusive little cave held the air of intimacy often associated with bedrooms or chapels.

To either side of a narrow aisle, corked and dusty bottles and small oaken casks lay cradled on their sides. The walls were brick, the floor stone. Dust motes swirled in the soft light. Beneath the spigot of each cask a dark wine stain dyed the gray stone. At the far end, a beveled bay window made room for a sturdy, unvarnished table, two captain's chairs and a sunbeam spearing through the muddy sky. Wineglasses, suspended by their stems, hung upside down from a rack in the low ceiling over the table.

"I thought we'd already been to the tasting room," Savannah said.

"The public tasting room," Burke clarified. He was at her back, so close that his words were puffs of warm breath on her cheek. "This is Julienne's private cellar."

Savannah walked down the aisle, trailing her hand over the aged woods. He was a romantic, she thought with a sinking feeling. Deep down in his scrupulous, pragmatic soul beat the heart of a romantic. It was a discovery she'd rather not have made. He was hard enough to resist without romanticism clouding her objectivity.

At the table, she pulled out a chair and sat. When she glanced at Burke he was slanted to a cask, arms folded at his chest and a satisfied look on his face. He'd been reading her mind again.

"You'd decided I was sterile, hadn't you?"

"Clinical," Savannah corrected. "There's a difference."

"Which is?"

"Sterile is cold, heartless. You aren't that." She studied him thoughtfully. "Clinical is...precise. You *are* that." He didn't flinch or grimace at her blunt analysis. Rather, he nodded slightly as if he agreed with her. "To you, things are black or white, right or wrong, good or bad."

"I'm intolerant?"

"You're..." *Yes, you're intolerant.* "Precise."

Straightening, Burke slipped two glasses free and set them on the scrubbed tabletop. "And to you things are gray—until you decide what color to paint them."

It was the most accurate description of herself Savannah had ever heard. He might have intended it as criticism, but, settling back in her chair, she took it as the highest compliment.

Turning away, Burke involved himself in choosing a wine. As he skimmed and considered the labels on one bottle after another, Savannah watched him, the way he moved, turned, walked. Efficient, no energy wasted. Still, there was a rangy looseness to his body that made it a pleasure to see in motion. His hands, withdrawing and returning bottles to their cubbyholes, were sure and elegant. They had been that sure when they'd touched her, she remembered. And they had made her feel elegant. Her heart began to thud a bit too hard. He wasn't always steady and cool-headed, she mused. In anger, even in laughter, he seemed always to hold something in reserve. But in passion he was a raging fire, quick to flash and consume. Her hands trembled with remembering; her stomach jumped.

Burke decided on a Cabernet Sauvignon to start. Uncorking the bottle, he tipped it over Savannah's glass and poured the fragrant ruby wine. Filling his own glass, he glanced across the table. Was the color of her eyes suddenly a darker shade of smoke? Or was it a trick of the dimmer light here? "Do you know how to taste wine?"

Savannah shook her head. "Only the TV version."

"Let me show you the sensual version." She arched one eyebrow at his choice of words. "Wine tasting is an experience of and for the senses," he suggested. His voice was seductive and mesmerizing and so low that Savannah automatically leaned closer.

"Start with your eyes. Anticipation begins with the first look." Hers, Burke noticed with satisfaction, were on his face as she blinked slowly. "Hold your glass to the light, and clear everything else from your mind. Concentrate only on what you see. Look for clarity and brilliance. Look also for a quality that isn't as easily named—call it a promise, that what you are about to taste will be exquisite, voluptuous."

Mirroring Burke, Savannah held her glass up to the window. She saw that her hand trembled and tightened her fingers on the slender stem to steady it. Against the light the crimson wine shimmered, like a piece of stained glass twirling in the sun. "This is what it's all about, isn't it?" Her voice was husky—with the anticipation Burke had mentioned? "Brilliant liquids in crystal glasses."

"It's about more, Savannah, much more." Keeping his eyes on her, he lowered his glass. "The nose is next." With an imperceptible jiggle, he made the wine shiver so that light danced on its surface. He passed the slim goblet under his nose, and Savannah did the same.

"Take a deep, slow sniff," he murmured. "Do you smell grapes? Or do you smell the wine's age? Aroma or bouquet?"

"Which is better?"

"Bouquet. Its age. The fragrance shouldn't be old or musty but woody, penetrating. Connoisseurs will sniff a wine many times, thinking first of a scent and then searching for it." Burke watched her eyelids drift lower with each pass of her glass. Outside, the clouds moved closer and the light dimmed, but what was left of it touched her skin and made it translucent.

"I smell a fruit," Savannah murmured. She had yet to take her first sip, but her senses were already reeling, her head light. She could taste the wine's scent in her throat. "Like black-currant jelly. And something else, something..." She opened her eyes suddenly. "Bell peppers."

Startled, Burke sat back a bit. "Yes. How the hell did you recognize it?"

*We used to pick them.* In Michigan, she remembered. If we didn't pick cherries, we picked bell peppers. Distracted by the memory, Savannah let her gaze drift to the window, and beyond. "Some things you never forget."

She was smiling when she brought her eyes back to him, but for a heartbeat he'd lost her to another place, another time. With a jolt, Burke realized he resented having lost even that little bit of her. To draw her all the way back, he concentrated on the wine and on reweaving the spell. "A good varietal Cabernet has a complex aromatic blend. Fruity, pungent. Some say they detect bell peppers, others argue for green olives."

Savannah shook her head. "It's bell peppers."

"Bell peppers." He smiled and reached across the table. Touching her wrist, he nudged her glass toward her mouth. Her pulse scrambled beneath his fingertips. "Now, finally, you taste."

"I don't know." His fingers were still on her pulse. It seemed all the stimulation her senses required to turn muzzy and fuddled. "Just sniffing has made me feel strangely intoxicated."

"Prepared," Burke countered, then watched as she sipped. "Don't swallow. Hold the wine in your mouth, let it flow and fill, under your tongue, to the back of your throat. Is it sweet or dry? Does it burn?"

His voice... Savannah easily imagined his velvet voice leading her through other sensual pleasures.

"Is it full-bodied, like cream on your tongue? Or is it light, like a sip of rainwater? Has the promise been fulfilled? Swallow, and wait for the aftertaste. It should be a pleasant echo of the wine."

Flavors exploded on Savannah's tongue. The wine slid warmly, smoothly down her throat. Its essence rushed to her brain, spilled into her veins. After a moment her vision cleared, and she focused on Burke. "Is it always like this? Every mouthful?"

"It can be."

Savannah glanced at the deep red liquid, looking so innocuous in its glass. "I could become dangerously addicted."

"Americans are just now learning what the French have known for generations. You don't save your best wine for entertaining the boss; you enjoy it with a beautiful woman on a summer afternoon." Burke took the first sip of his own wine and enjoyed the beautiful woman.

"Is that what you spent a year in France learning?" Sliding her shoes off under the table, Savannah curled comfortably in her chair, cradling her wineglass in both hands.

"That's one way to put it. You only learn to make California wines in California. The States far surpass France in technology and research." Savannah tipped her head and watched the way his eyes lightened to the color of melted chocolate when he talked of wines and wine making. "Artistry is something else, and the skill of European countries..." The subject excited him, opened him, softened him. Drew Savannah in. He used his hands to speak, not in wild, waving gestures but with quiet emphasis. He touched his forefinger to his mouth when he searched for just the right word. He clasped his hands and gazed over them when he wanted to make a point. "In France you appreciate the tradition of wine making. With the French, the Italians, the Germans, it isn't a career, but a life."

"Tradition," Savannah said. "Tradition is important to Juliennes."

"It's important to all families."

"Not necessarily."

"What's important to the Joneses?" Burke asked. He saw the slight firmness touch her mouth, the thinnest of hard glazes touch her eyes.

"Trucking," Savannah tossed off. "Now that you're back, what will you do? What *do* you do here?" He offered the bottle, and Savannah held out her glass for him to pour.

"I'm an enologist."

"Ah, of course. Say no more." She gave a laugh that was soft and relaxed. She felt soft, she realized. And, perhaps, too relaxed.

"An enologist is a wine maker." Scraping his chair over stone, he rose and crossed to the wine racks.

"Like your father."

"No, my father is a vintner—a man who owns a winery and so makes wine." He found the Petit Sirah vintage he wanted and returned to the table. "Enology is a science; it requires a degree."

Yes, Savannah mused, a degree. Burke wouldn't leave his future to tradition and family recipes. He'd consult the experts, get the facts, do it by the book. At the sound of a cork giving, Savannah noticed the new bottle for the first time. "What are you doing? We've barely put a dent in the Cabernet!"

"This is a wine tasting, Savannah—many wines. A traditional end to any self-respecting tour."

Glancing around the cellar, she gave a shrug. "I don't suppose 'Waste not, want not' would carry much weight." He brought down two fresh glasses and poured the soft rosé. "So." Settling back again, she smothered a yawn. "What do you do here, Burke? Tromp around in the fields like Claude?"

"No. The grapes are Claude's domain. I leave it to him to worry about the weather not cooperating and crops failing; early harvest, late maturity; small berries, hard berries, cracked berries. My domain is the winery. He leaves it to me to worry that we'll overload the presses if his grapes all come ripe at the same time, or that we'll forecast and plant for white wines but the taste of the buying public will shift to reds. I negotiate contracts—labor, purchases, marketing."

"Sounds as if all the two of you do is worry," Savannah remarked. "Do you like your work?"

"Yes, I like my work." There was, had never been, anything else he would rather do. While he had indeed been born to his position, it was one he had chosen for himself, as well. "I make wines to toast brides on their wedding days, christen babies, celebrate a man's coming of age, a woman's becoming a mother. It's a gratifying way to spend my life."

"Yeah." Savannah sighed. "I guess it is."

The sky outside continued to darken. Burke added candles to the table, and the scent of melting wax joined that of wine. A bottle of Grenache was opened. Savannah lost track of time. "The Julienne roots Claude speaks of," she said as the walls reflected flickering candlelight and the slate-dark windows reflected the two of them at the table. "Don't they sometimes feel like chains to you? Do you ever think about breaking free and getting out of here?"

"Breaking free, yes. Getting out, no." *Amy.* They'd been chains to Amy, Burke remembered. Getting out had been her dream and her goal all of her life. "I plan to build a house," he went on, shifting his thoughts. "That's about as much breaking free as I need."

"Where?"

"A piece of land my grandfather left me, not far from here. It has a stand of oak trees and a view of the winery." She was the first person he'd told. He asked himself why. "Claude doesn't know yet."

"Uh-oh."

"Yeah. Uh-oh."

"What will he say?"

"Nothing that can change my mind." Burke met her eyes and felt as if a fist had connected with his stomach. She looked utterly open and unguarded. He knew it was the wine and that to take advantage was underhanded, but he wondered if she was loose enough to let go of more pieces to the puzzle. Before, he'd wanted them to solve the mystery. Now he wanted them to discover why she was one. "Do you like your work, Savannah?"

"Sure. I'm not in the habit of doing things I don't want to do."

It was an honest answer, he decided, and he forged ahead. "Why do you drive a truck?"

Savannah smiled a bit lopsidedly. "Because I'm a trucker."

"There are other jobs. Wasn't there something else you wanted to be once?" He stretched his legs out to one side of the table and crossed them at the ankles. "I can't quite picture you at fifteen, on the threshold of womanhood, dreaming of the day you'd own your own eighteen-wheeler."

Leaning forward, she rested her elbows on the table and cupped her chin on one palm. "I can't recall ever wanting a particular career, exactly. I just wanted out."

Burke's eyes sharpened. *Out.* But he'd known that about her, hadn't he? The first day. Last night. He tried telling himself that at fifteen every girl—and every boy, for that matter—wanted out of wherever they found themselves. He wasn't convinced. Like Amy, he thought, Savannah was driven to run.

"Neil drove trucks," Savannah went on. "So, when I was twenty-one, he taught me. *Tradition*. We were team drivers before he married." She drained her glass, and Burke opened another bottle. A White Riesling this time. "I stewed for a couple of years."

"About what?"

With her glass poised halfway to her mouth, Savannah gave a wonderful, unrestrained burst of giggles. "No, *stewed*." Pointing a finger at the ceiling, she made circling gestures. "In the sky. Flight attendant." She laughed again at his misinterpretation, then took a healthy gulp of wine. "I quit after two years. I felt locked up in a plane." She yawned suddenly, then shook her head to clear it. "Anyway, I'd thought I'd see the world. But you need about twenty years' seniority before they send you there. All I saw was the Dallas Fort Worth Airport at one end and Houston Intercontinental at the other."

Reaching across the table, Burke moved her wineglass away. She didn't seem to notice. He might be underhanded, but he wasn't without compassion for the state her head would be in the next morning. "Did your father drive trucks?"

Her eyebrows drew together in a slow frown. "When did you open the fourth bottle?" Not one of them was more than half finished, but she was feeling every ounce she'd consumed. She hadn't eaten, she remembered, nor slept a full night in three days. And she wasn't much of a drinker to begin with. Not only did it leave her fuzzy the next day, but she'd also thought it an unwise pastime for someone who was alone as much as she was. She wasn't drunk, she decided, but she was incredibly sleepy all of a sudden. "Why don't I remember the fourth bottle?"

Burke chuckled and stood. "Come on, Savannah. Time someone put you to bed before you pass out."

"No, I'm fine...really." Lifted from her chair by his gentle but firm hand, she got to her feet without resisting. "Maybe I'm not so fine." The room tilted, and she grabbed the table to stay upright.

Burke steadied her with an arm around her waist and blew out the candles.

"Shoes," she mumbled. She felt for them under the table with her toes. One kept skidding away from her. For some reason, she thought this absurdly funny. Burke bent to retrieve the shoe and placed it on her foot. As he stood up, Savannah went down. Half expecting it, he caught her in his arms.

Savannah jolted awake as she was swung up against Burke's chest. Looking over his shoulder as he moved toward the door, she thought how cozy the table and two chairs looked. "What about all that delicious wine?" she murmured. "Those bottles still have wine in them."

"I'll send someone down from the house for them." She fit his arms well, Burke thought. Her skin was soft where it touched his, her ribs fragile beneath his hand. She nestled against his shoulder as he stepped outside, giving a small sigh in her sleep. As he carried her toward the house, with the skies threatening to open at any second, he wondered what the hell he was letting himself in for.

She's too damn delicate, he thought testily. And vulnerable. Mishandled, she'd break, and he'd have been the one to break her. Even as he argued against wanting her, his need to have her grew. The first splashes of rain plopped onto his shoulders and fell into Savannah's face, waking her. He glanced down, and his mouth curved.

She lifted her head to look around as he rushed to the porch's protection. Her groan was one of utter embarrassment. "I didn't pass out."

"Mm-hmm."

"Just a nap." Beneath her cheek, his heart thudded. Through the shirt damp with rain his body was warm. "Put me down, Burke. I can walk."

"Never mind. You hardly weigh anything, and we're almost there." He shouldered his way through the front door just as the rain swelled to a downpour. As he climbed the stairs her scent drifted up from her hair, stronger for being misted by rain. He felt her eyes on him. She stirred, and he held her tighter.

A low, comfortable roll of thunder moved across the sky as he entered her bedroom. When he set her on her feet at the side of her bed, he left his hands at her waist, and Savannah left hers on his shoulders.

"It was a wonderful tour," she murmured, finding she was suddenly fascinated with the shape of his mouth.

"You may not think so in the morning." He sensed what was coming. When she put a questing finger to his bottom lip, he was sure of it.

"Savannah, you're about two and a half sheets to the wind, and—"

"I'm not drunk," she whispered.

"You are, and—"

"Do you suppose you can taste a mouth the way you taste wine?"

Burke groaned. "Savannah—"

"What is it I should look for? A promise..." She skimmed the outer edges of his mouth, marveling at how soft he felt on her fingers. "That the taste will be exquisite... voluptuous."

Could she pronounce those words if she were drunk? Burke asked himself. Would she even have remembered them? He could rationalize the situation from eight different sides, he decided, and it still wouldn't improve her balance. She might not be totally soused, but she was several drinks past tipsy.

"The scent," she murmured, her eyelids lowering to half-mast. "A deep, slow sniff." The tip of her nose touched his neck just below his ear. The tiny contact shot through his body. He tightened his hold on her waist. Pliant, she bent toward him. Her hair was a light caress on his cheek as she moved her head, searching and finding all the fragrances she knew to be his. Burke figured he had less than seconds to get out of her bedroom. If he didn't leave now, he wouldn't for hours.

"Then, finally, you taste." Her lips skimmed his jaw, thrilling to the faintest rasp of beard. She was only dimly aware that Burke was slowly backing her up. He laid her gently on the bed, her hands at the back of his neck bringing him down with her. "And hold it in your mouth..."

"Savannah." Her lips were already on his, brushing lightly back and forth. He kept body contact to a minimum, leaning over her but with his hands pressed to the bed at her sides and his arms rigid. He thought if he felt the touch of her breasts, her thighs, he would be lost. He nearly was when her tongue touched his bottom lip, then darted out to taste him again.

"Letting it fill you..."

"Mmm..." He released the sound into her mouth as she opened and took his. Burke was beyond knowing or caring whether he groaned with regret or submission. He knew only that she seemed to pull it out of him. He had never been kissed so fully, so completely. Her tongue searched languorously and savored at length. Her involvement with his mouth was absolute, passionate. He'd never been one for long seductions, but he thought now that, when he took Savannah, she would be a woman he would linger over.

But the time to take Savannah was not now. If virgins had been against his rules last night, sloshed virgins were against his rules today.

Easing his mouth free, he gazed down at her. She smiled contentedly, her mouth swollen and damp, her eyes cloudy and closing. Her hair was a spill of ink on the snowy pillow. Longing for her, aching for her, he watched her sigh and slip away into sleep. For a while he stayed just like that, bent over and watching her. Then he slid her shoes off and pulled the quilt over her.

At the door he looked back once. No, he thought, he hadn't planned on this woman at all.

## Chapter Five

Burke swept a glance over fields awash with late-morning sunlight and teeming with leather-skinned, dark-haired pickers. Pensive, he lit a cigarette. White smoke curled in the still air before dissipating. The heat had baked the moisture of yesterday's rain from the earth, and the scent of dust was strong.

For some time he leisurely smoked his cigarette. The longer the silence stretched, the more fidgety the short-tempered man to his left grew. Finally, Burke spoke. "How many illegals have you got out there?"

Alberto Ramirez bit off a pungent curse. "I don't hire illegals."

"You've seen that each has a green card? You've run a check on their social security numbers?" As Burke watched, the man's face filled with silent fury.

"Where is Julienne?" Alberto demanded. "Twenty years I work with Julienne; he doesn't ask such questions."

"Today you work with me, and I do ask such questions." That many? Burke thought, and he canvassed the vineyards again. He didn't like the contentious man who unloaded human beings from pickup trucks like cattle purchased by the head. Ramirez was of medium height, his thick body hard and muscular. He sported a gold eyetooth and a stingily thin mustache. Though Burke had never witnessed the man in an arrogant or tyrannical act, he saw the way the workers shuffled, shied and gave him wide berth.

"INS agents are going to be crawling all over us," Burke reminded him. "Immigration allows twenty-four hours to verify the social security numbers." He shifted his attention to the straight, wide rows, further infuriating Ramirez by not meeting his eyes. "Tomorrow morning you show me a list of valid numbers or I'll put my own men in charge of checking them out. If Julienne's is fined for illegal aliens, Alberto, I'll personally make your life miserable."

"Without me, Mr. Burke Julienne," Ramirez sneered, "half this valley would rot and run to vinegar. There are ways around everything, even you. Watch how you speak to me—I don't threaten."

Deep in his pocket, Burke's hand balled into a fist. The unpleasant truth of the matter was that Ramirez would be an impolitic enemy to make. A dearth of pickers, a harvest-time strike—both of which the man could arrange overnight—struck terror in the hearts of vintners. Burke took a last drag on his cigarette, then flicked it away. As he tracked the smoldering butt to see where it landed he glimpsed the delicate shoulders and fragile face. Taking two steps forward, he narrowed his eyes. "What the hell..."

Immediately on guard, Ramirez looked in the same direction. Laborers, faceless beneath wide-brimmed hats or because their heads were bent to their work, sidled down the field rows. One had stopped to toss her head back and smile at the sky, her face pale and unlined. Another rank oath issued from Ramirez.

"She's not mine," he snapped. "She didn't come in with my people." Eyes afire, Ramirez hitched up his pants by his thumbs. "But I'll sure as hell get rid of her."

Burke's hand landed on the man's shoulder with brutal strength. "You'll stay away from her. I'll take care of this one myself."

"She's not mine, I tell you," he insisted angrily to Burke's departing back.

Savannah reveled in the sun's warmth on her face, smiled, then went back to cutting clusters of Zinfandel grapes from their vines. The vague throb between her temples was gone—an aspirin and two cups of coffee had done the trick. That she hadn't awakened with a raging hangover and rebellious stomach she chalked up to dumb luck. And thirteen hours' sleep, she added.

Sweat gathered between her shoulders and rolled down her back. It felt good—hot sun and hard work. So good, in fact, her irritation with Jackson was nearly forgotten. She'd called him first thing that morning, only to be told that the man who'd worked on her truck over the weekend wouldn't be in until ten o'clock. While on the phone she'd stood at a window watching the invasion of pickers into the Zinfandel fields. Intrigued, and with hours to fill, she'd wandered out to watch. Now she was one of them, steadily clearing vines and filling gondolas.

A man wearing a dark suit entered her peripheral vision, and Savannah turned her head. Burke, looking impossibly right in the fields wearing a gray three-piece suit, strode down the row toward her. With a jolt, she sensed something new about him. This was a different man from the one she'd traded quips with in her truck cab. A different man still from the one she'd shared wine with in an intimate cave. This man was powerful, master of all that surrounded them. He drew every eye, even as his own not once wavered from hers. This man knew where he was going—at the moment and in the future—and precisely how to get there.

No one should be that sure about anything, Savannah thought. She could almost resent him for it, envy him for whatever he'd had in his life that allowed him to relax in his security. And then he was close enough that she noticed his pink shirt. She grinned and wondered if he realized he'd broken his rule about never wearing it to the office . . . and if he'd thought of her that morning when he slipped it from its hanger.

Burke was ten yards away when the woman sitting on the ground near Savannah's feet let out a surprised whimper. Sobering, Savannah placed a hand on the young woman's thin shoulder. "Don't you worry about him, Nina. This is one man I can handle."

*Handle?* Savannah nearly laughed out loud at herself. If she'd handled him any better last night, she'd have handled him right out of his clothes and into her bed.

"Just what do you think you're doing here?" Burke demanded, ignoring, for the moment, the woman huddled between them on the ground. Savannah wore the same jeans and denim shirt of the day he'd found her asleep in the foyer. Today her shirttails were tied beneath her breasts, exposing a band of delicate white midriff he imagined would feel like velvet to his fingers. A streak of dirt lined her cheek. A coat of fine dust covered the rest of her. Her sleeves were rolled back to her elbows, and her hands were stained with grape juice.

Savannah was patient through his survey, half expecting him to say such work was beneath her. Judging by the expression on his face, it was the conclusion he seemed to have reached.

"I'm picking grapes. And have you noticed, Burke, how often you ask obvious questions?" She removed her hat, wiped her brow on her sleeve and put the hat back on. "By the way, that guy you've got lording it over these people is a real pushy bastard." She saw him glance down then at the woman looking up through huge dark eyes, at the infant squirming in her lap and at Savannah's hand on her frail shoulder offering strength. "This is Nina. Her baby is sick. She hid him in a sling under her shawl." It suddenly dawned on Savannah that the few dollars Ramirez would eventually dole out to Nina would have to come first from Burke. "If you pitch her out of here—"

"Just a minute," Burke ground out, still edgy from his encounter with Alberto. "Just a minute. I'm not going to pitch her or anyone else out of here. Not for the moment, at least. And if her baby is sick, this is the *last* place she should have brought him."

Nina, alarm growing in her wide eyes, began to struggle up from the ground, babbling apologies to the angry people thrusting their chins at each other.

"Stay there, Nina," Savannah ordered, her hand on the woman's shoulder pushing her back down to the ground. "No one's going to bully you out of here." Her eyes narrowed on Burke. "If she doesn't work, she can't get food and medicine for her son. Do you have any idea how many of the women in this field have babies on their backs or stashed inside their shawls?"

"Yes, I do."

Something in his voice took the heat out of her. He really does, Savannah thought. And he despises it.

They both became aware in the same moment that their testiness had nothing to do with the topic under discussion, but rather with how often they'd come together and parted, each time leaving more between them unresolved.

"Well." Savannah sighed. "I was keeping Nina's quota up while she nursed her baby."

Because he'd waited long enough to touch her, Burke put his thumb to the smear of dirt on her face and traced it down her cheek. "Is this how you plan to spend the day? Relief-picking for nursing mothers?"

There was no disdain in his voice. No sarcasm or ridicule. Savannah detected genuine curiosity in his first question and the hint of futility in his second, as if she were trying to patch a severed artery with a Band-Aid. "No, actually, I'm supposed to—what time is it?"

Shaking his head, Burke glanced at his watch. "Eleven-forty."

"In France or California?" She arched one eyebrow to a haughty angle, but her mouth curved with a smile.

"California."

"Shoot. I'd lost track. I told Jackson I'd call back at ten."

"Come on, I'll give you a lift to the house."

Stooping, Savannah looked into Nina's eyes. She's not even my age, Savannah thought, yet she looks older and wearier by years. "I'm leaving, Nina."

"*Sí*, I understand."

"Take care of slugger there. And remember what I told you: feverfew—it has a yellow center and spiky white petals. You'll find it along the roadside, but pick it from deep in the field; there'll be too much lead from exhaust fumes on those close to the highway. Boil two tablespoons of the plant in a cup of water, then let it steep for an hour. When it's cooled, feed it to the baby. It'll take his fever down. Red clover tea for his cough."

"*Sí*. Feverfew and red clover. *Gracias*."

Savannah lifted the baby into her arms while Nina adjusted her blouse. Standing back, Burke watched Savannah's face soften as she gazed down at the big-eyed bundle. Words didn't exist to describe what he felt when she buried her nose at the baby's neck and nuzzled the soft skin.

Reluctant to give him up, Savannah helped settle the infant into his makeshift cotton sling, then smiled at Nina before turning away. She appreciated Burke's hand resting on her shoulder as she walked away.

Stupid to feel sad, Savannah told herself. She'd been waiting days for her truck to be fixed, impatient to be gone. She *wanted* to be on her way again. Right? So why did she feel she was leaving friends behind? Why this tug to return to the field and bend her back to a job for no more reward than filth and fatigue at the end of the day?

"Where did you learn roadside medicine?" Burke asked as they left the row and turned toward the crude access road. The roofless jeep he'd driven from the winery out to the fields was angled alongside Ramirez's slat-sided truck.

Savannah glanced over at him. "Same place you learned wine recipes, I suppose. A family tradition."

They walked a few more steps in silence. Then Burke took her by her shoulders and made her face him. "I can't help these people. You see that, don't you. There are hundreds of them in this valley. There'll be hundreds more in the Julienne fields alone over the next three months. They're all poor, most are hungry and too many of them sick. I can't fix all of them, Savannah."

Throughout his passionate speech, Savannah's gaze had been locked on him. "I know that, Burke."

He looked into her eyes and saw understanding. Did he want that from her? Did he deserve it? Breathing on oath, he pulled her to his side, and they walked the rest of the way to the road.

Ramirez was waiting for them, feet planted apart, arms crossed, ready to defend if the need arose. Savannah's dislike of the man was violent in its coldness. She'd known so many like him.

"See the woman in the orange and green shawl?" Burke demanded of Ramirez. "She has a baby with her. I want her left alone. Is that clear, Alberto?"

"They're not supposed to bring children," Ramirez argued.

"I don't give a damn. I mean what I say. Leave her be. And if she shows up again tomorrow, see that she's given work."

After Savannah had settled beside Burke in the jeep, she turned to him. "Thank you. I know it goes against your grain to pave the way for her to bring a baby into the fields."

Rather than acknowledge her, Burke let the silence yawn. To the marrow of his bones he believed he'd done neither mother nor child any favors. When the house was visible, he glanced at Savannah to find her studying him.

"How's your head?" he asked. "Why aren't you nursing a migraine under a cold compress?"

She shrugged. "I needed the sleep. Pull around back. I'm a mess; I'll go in through the kitchen."

At the rear entrance, he braked the jeep. "You're still leaving today?"

For a long moment she didn't say anything but simply stared at him. "I kissed you last night, didn't I?"

Burke's stomach clenched at the question. If she apologizes, he thought, if she tries to excuse her behavior or says one word of regret, I'll shake her silly. "Yes, you did."

She moved her head thoughtfully, digesting. "How unusual for me," she murmured.

Burke reached across the seats, sliding a hand behind her head. He turned her mouth up as he leaned closer. "I owe you one."

"No." Savannah drew back but could go no farther than the door. "You shouldn't. I'm . . . dirty. I'll mess up your suit."

He chuckled as his lips graced her temple. "I don't give a damn about the suit, Savannah."

"You ought to...practically speaking." His teeth nipped at her earlobe. "It looks expensive..." He nibbled his way from her ear to her mouth. Savannah was melting, sliding down in her seat. "It'll have to go to the cleaners."

"Then don't touch me if it worries you so."

He covered her mouth with his mouth, her body with his body. She felt the scrape of his teeth and the touch of his tongue, and she moaned. She still held her arms out to keep the field dust from rubbing off on him. Burke bent her closer. Her hands closed into fists as his tangled in her hair. She didn't know a kiss could last so long, take so much out of her or pour so much back in.

*Make it last.* And Burke plundered deeper. *Take enough to savor until she returns.* God, he could spend hours losing himself in her. Her heart thudded against his chest. Her muscles quivered. He wanted her heart racing and her muscles fluid. He wanted her. But before he filled her body, he wanted to fill her mind and soul. When he took her, he wanted to have it all.

The sun beat down on them. The wind shifted. And still his mouth moved on hers. Their first kiss had come as a surprise; half her concentration had been on putting an end to it. Their second kiss was barely an impression. But this kiss—this kiss stirred parts of Savannah she hadn't known existed. Shivering thrills raced up her spine; simmering heat pulsed with her blood. This kiss was an intimate, exquisite joining of man and woman. A prelude...a promise.

When it was over, Savannah didn't budge an inch. Pressed into the corner, she panted as if she'd just run the Boston Marathon. He, she noticed, had leaned back into his own seat, looking so damned composed he might not have been breathing at all.

He didn't breathe. Couldn't. Burke held himself absolutely still. If he relaxed enough to take in air, he would find himself reaching for her again, sliding her the rest of the way down on the seat and taking her here, now.

Pulling herself together, Savannah recovered her hat from the floor, where it had fallen sometime during the embrace, and then opened the Jeep's door. She climbed out, leaving her hands on the door after pushing it shut. "Well...I guess this is goodbye. It was nice meeting you."

Savannah stepped back as he shifted into first. *It was nice meeting you.* Had she really said that?

Burke smiled. "Yeah, nice meeting you, too."

She waited until he'd driven off before moving toward the house. It took that long for her knees to solidify and her brain to remember what she was supposed to do next.

"What do you mean two weeks?"

"Two, maybe three," Jackson repeated.

Staggered, Savannah dragged a hand through her hair and fought an urge to throw the phone at the wall. Around her, the kitchen was bedlam. Weatherby was huffing and muttering about trying to cook in Grand Central Station. Fitzhugh shuffled, collecting towels and dish rags for the laundress. Weatherby's son, Frank, arrived with tomatoes and cucumbers freshly plucked from the small garden at the side of the house and began unloading them on the counter where his mother was stemming strawberries. Christina and a caterer were talking about traffic flow and hot dishes in preparation for a party the Juliennes were hosting at the end of the week. The caterer's assistants kept moving around with an incredible talent for transplanting themselves to spots where they'd be in somebody else's way.

"I can't wait two weeks." Savannah shut her eyes and counted to ten. When she opened them again, Christina was watching her. "You'll have to fix it sooner."

"Listen, lady, I've just told you the parts aren't available."

"It's a transmission. A *transmission*, for God's sake." Knowing anger and impatience would solve nothing, Savannah calmed herself with a long breath. "I'm sure if you call around you'll find somebody who has one."

"It's not the transmission," Jackson countered in the exasperated voice of someone weary of repeating himself. "*That* I could fix by lunch and send you on your way by dinner. The differential is another matter. You need a new ring and pinion gears. We don't stock 'em. Nobody does. Manufacturer says two to three weeks to deliver. I've called around and everybody says the same: 'We ain't got 'em.'"

Savannah hissed a frustrated sigh and wished for a cigarette. "All right. Do the work. I'll...I'll... Do the work."

"Savannah?" Christina left her caterer and touched Savannah's shoulder. "Bad news, dear?"

Savannah pinched the bridge of her nose between thumb and forefinger and leaned back against a counter. The morning's headache was returning. "Two weeks," she muttered. She wouldn't even *think* of three. Dropping her hand, she looked at Christina. "That was Jackson. My truck needs extensive repairs. Some of the parts won't be available for a couple of weeks."

"Mrs. Fitzhugh," Christina called over her shoulder as the stooped woman played a patient game of sidestep with one of the caterer's assistants, trying to get past him. "Mrs. Fitzhugh, have you stripped the linen in the guest room?"

She gave an abrupt nod of her head. "Sheets and towels."

"Remake the bed, please. Savannah will be staying on."

"I'll take towels up now." She ripped a glance over Savannah, apparently disapproving of what she confronted. "Needs a bath."

"Christina, I can't stay here." Savannah smiled her appreciation. "I never expected to."

"But we'd love to have you. And don't you dare suggest moving into a hotel. I won't hear of it."

"It's going to be two weeks," Savannah pointed out. "I can't barge in on your family for that long."

Christina touched Savannah's wrist. Her green eyes grew soft and wistful. "Since we lost Amy, I've missed having a young woman in the house. You know then, and you needn't look surprised. Though Claude and Burke won't speak of her, I do. She was my daughter, and as unfortunate as her life was those last years, I miss her."

But Burke *had* spoken of Amy, Savannah thought. For the first time? That might explain the anger she'd sensed in him, the feeling he hadn't yet come to grips with it.

"I miss a fresh young girl to have lunch with, shop with," Christina went on. "I love my men, but..." Her laugh finished the sentence and lightened the mood. Savannah smiled.

"I'll... Let me think about it." But Savannah knew what would happen if she agreed. Frustration would knot her stomach. By nightfall she'd be pacing. "I've never been one to stay very long in the same place."

Weatherby, fed up with the crowd in her kitchen, slapped the hand of one of the caterer's assistants when he plucked a strawberry from the dish she was preparing. In a snit, the caterer rushed to his man's defense, a reaction Frank didn't take at all well. With a sigh, Christina gave Savannah's hand a last squeeze before attending to the small war breaking out. "I hope you'll stay, Savannah."

Needing a quieter place to think, Savannah stepped out the back door. She popped her hat onto her head, stuffed her hands in her pockets and set off to walk with no particular destination in mind. At first she followed the flagstone walk that led to the winery. When she neared the hillside door, she left the path for the wild flowers and high grass.

Here she stopped a moment and took in the view. Neat, parallel rows of grapevines climbed up and spilled over the rolling land. She moved toward them, wrestling with thoughts that refused to gel into conclusions. Normally there wouldn't have been a decision to make. Savannah simply didn't, couldn't, stay two weeks in one place. Particularly a place this removed from the hustle and bustle of humanity. Then she felt the draw again.

What is it? she asked herself. Letting it take her, she headed down a hill and into a thriving field. The scents of earth, leaves and sap swirled around her. She stopped to fondle a cluster of grapes that were more red than purple. They felt like jewels in her hand, soft, warm jewels. What was their name? How did they grow, and when would they be harvested? She wanted to know. She wanted to hear Claude's voice explain their development and idiosyncrasies.

Releasing the grapes, she walked on. She had two weeks to fill. What were her alternatives? Jackson didn't have only her truck strewn about his garage, he had her home. Sitting down on a boulder, Savannah listed her options.

She could use the time to take a sightseeing vacation. She'd been to San Francisco so often that it held little appeal. Los Angeles was out—one overcrowded city was the same as the next overcrowded city. Seattle. She did love Seattle. The mountains were close. Instead of dashing off to pack her bag, she leaned back so the sun touched her face.

Next?

She could fly back to Chicago and stay with Neil and Terry, then return to Napa when the truck was fixed. Except that it wasn't as convenient for them to take her in as it used to be. Their little two-bedroom house turned upside-down when Savannah stayed a mere weekend. And while Neil wouldn't hesitate to turn his *life* upside-down to accommodate Savannah, she doubted Terry would survive two weeks of her sister-in-law sleeping hours opposite the family, spoiling the boys every chance she had and growing increasingly bad tempered when the layoff began to wear on her nerves.

Next?

She could stay here. God, why did she want to? Why did waking in the tower guest room feel so right? Why did she picture herself rising with the sun and setting off for the fields to pick grapes and raise blisters? Why did she *long* to stay here?

Something echoed in the breeze. Stiffening, Savannah strained to listen... and remember.

Burke saw her from the path. At a distance she was a small figure, but even so he could see that her head was bent, her face buried in her hands. Savannah with her shoulders rounded in despair? It didn't feel right. She didn't look up as he neared, though a slight tensing of her body told him she knew he was standing there.

Dropping to sit on his heels, Burke gave it a few seconds. When she did nothing more than sniffle behind her hands, he gently removed her hat. She lifted her head but wouldn't meet his eyes. Hers were damp with unshed tears.

"My dad played the harmonica," she said, as if answering a question he'd asked. "I just now thought of that. I'd curl up on my mother's lap, and he'd play. I'd fall asleep listening. For a long time after I'd lost them, I'd lie in bed hearing that music in my head and feeling those arms around me.''

Pain for her was swift. Her tears welled, huge, glimmering drops resting on her lashes. Burke reached for her, framing her face with both hands. His palms were pressed to her cheeks as the tears spilled over.

''Baby, I'm so sorry.'' He touched his lips to her forehead. A sob tore from her, just one, then she quickly brought herself under control, her whole body stiffening with the effort. ''When did you lose them, Savannah?''

She pulled his hands away from her face but let him hold her cold fingers between his palms. ''When I was five.''

''How?''

She blinked, then rolled her eyes up to prevent a fresh flood of tears. He watched her reach for composure and don it like a mantle. She looked past him, her face settling into blank, frigid lines. ''I lost them.'' Her shoulders rose and fell. ''Some kids lose a tooth when they're five, some lose a bike. I lost my parents.''

## Chapter Six

Burke sipped from the wide-mouthed snifter, savoring the velvet perfection of smoothly aged brandy. The scents in the walnut-paneled library were of cherry tobacco and lemon oil. Books filled the four walls of shelves. A plain, plush carpet in sandy beige covered the floor. The sofa and chairs were upholstered in burnt-red leather, and the tables had been chosen for their red-grained mahogany. Christina's influence was evident in the scattering of needlepoint throw pillows and a collection of porcelain-framed photos on the mantel. But this was Claude's room, his sanctum.

It was a room in which Burke had always relaxed comfortably. Tonight he lounged in a fireside easy chair, his midsection taut with anticipation and impatience.

"No!" The flat of Claude's hand met his desk top with a reverberating smack. Because Burke had expected his father's response to be loud and abrupt, he managed not to flinch. "You'll call them and stop the shipment," Claude ordered. "Julienne's will not produce Cham-

pagne. We will not consider it.'' For emphasis, he sliced
the air with his right hand. "We will not *discuss* it."

"Julienne's didn't purchase the cuttings,'' Burke reminded him. "I did. My money, my cuttings. The shipment has already left France. It arrives in San Francisco
the middle of next week.''

Claude rose behind his desk, the fingertips of both
hands spread and resting on its polished surface. The
night-blackened window at his back provided a rearview
reflection of his rigid stance. "Then you have misspent a
great deal of money, Burke.'' But his eyes narrowed in
contemplation of that fact.

He knows me well, Burke thought. He's thinking that I
never squander money, that I don't gamble on long shots
or foolishly leap before I look. He knows I've always been
pragmatic, foresighted. And yet, Burke mused, Savannah
would be both a long shot and a foolish leap.

Realizing his thoughts had strayed, he frowned. How
was it that a woman he'd met three days ago and with
whom he had shared two slightly ridiculous arguments and
a few passionate kisses could distract him from a business
confrontation six months in the making? She wasn't anything like the women he was usually attracted to. She
wasn't easy to talk to or understand. She wasn't even easy
to be with at times. Still, he found himself anticipating his
next chance to explore her many layers for another discovery.

She'd pulled herself together quickly after this afternoon's revelation. Nothing more about her past had been
forthcoming. Nor her immediate future, he reflected wryly.
It wasn't until Burke had entered the dining room much
later in the day that he'd discovered Savannah planned to
stay on at the winery. His first reaction had been pleasure.
His second had been disquiet—because the pleasure had
been too swift and instinctive. Because the attraction based
initially on the novelty of her and the chemistry between
them was becoming complicated by emotions. And because today he had glimpsed her vulnerabilities. It shook

him to realize his urge to protect her had evolved into a self-appointed obligation to keep her from being hurt...even by himself.

What had happened to her after she'd lost her parents? he wondered. Who had become her guardians? Had she gone to relatives? Grandparents? An aunt and uncle and a passel of cousins? Her brother? Not likely, Burke decided. Unless Neil had eighteen or twenty years on Savannah, he'd have been too young. Frown deepening, Burke idly swirled his brandy. He should, he knew, be concentrating on business, but his thoughts stubbornly stayed on Savannah.

She'd lost her parents at a tender, impressionable age. Burke recalled the trauma of Amy's death. He'd been an adult. He'd had maturity and acuity to help him through the devastation. But even with age and experience on his side, there'd been that thick pool of grief to struggle out of, along with frustration for the senselessness of it and anger at the pain. It was difficult for him to imagine what the loss of *parents* did to a child—to her sense of security, her willingness or ability to trust, hope, love wholeheartedly.

*Love.* Burke shook his head. Where had that word come from? Rash even to think it. Savannah wasn't in love with him; she was only just starting to *like* him. And he... There were other ways to explain what he felt for Savannah. Compassion. Fascination. Obsession. After all, he hardly knew the woman. Then a strangled gasp pulled Burke's attention back to the moment and to the matter at hand.

Weakly, as if his knees were giving way, Claude sank slowly back to his chair. Harnessing his mental focus, Burke studied his father's stricken expression and decided Claude had finished appraising the situation and had arrived at the correct conclusion.

"Who have you talked to?" Disbelief made a raspy whisper of Claude's voice.

"Pisarro."

Claude flinched. When he again looked at his son he gazed through the eyes of a man betrayed. Luigi Pisarro was a friend, one of the few who addressed Claude by his given name. If Burke had any regrets, they were for the end of a lifelong friendship. But it had been Luigi who had made the first approach, months before Burke had left for France. Regardless of the outcome of tonight's negotiations, Claude would eventually have to have been told about it.

"He has a position available and acreage for lease," Burke explained. "I'm only interested in the acreage. The soil is ideal for my purposes, nearly identical to that of our fifties lots."

"You would leave Julienne's." It was not a question but a bitterly voiced accusation.

"Only if I had to. I'm a wine maker, as you are...as all the Julienne men before me have been. If I can't make the wines of my choosing here, then I'll make them elsewhere."

"For Pisarro."

"No. My own label. I realize that won't sit well with you, but it is preferable to joining the competition. Wouldn't you agree?" Burke allowed his father time to answer but received only a silent stare. "Talk in the valleys will make less of a Julienne striking off on his own than they will of a Julienne joining another house. It can appear an amicable parting, if neither of us comments."

"You believe that?" Claude gave a short, mirthless laugh. "You honestly think the bastards won't sink their teeth into this and spit it out at every dinner table from Napa to Del Norte? Everyone in the industry knows what I think of American Champagnes. Not only will they talk, they will laugh." Expelling another cynical snort, Claude retrieved his cold pipe from an ashtray, where it had been left to die out. After tapping it clean he began packing it with tobacco. A distant clock struck the hour. A woman in heels crossed a wooden floor somewhere else in the house.

"Tell me the rest," Claude said without looking up from his pipe. "There's more."

So he saw that, too, Burke mused. But he'd already decided this was not the time to announce he wouldn't continue making his home with his parents. It would only enrage his father, bringing tonight's discussion to an abrupt, bitter end. Burke had nothing to gain by it and too much to lose. He would have his Champagnes; he wanted them without having to leave Julienne's.

"I believe I've covered the subject," Burke said.

After a moment, his father nodded. "There's more. But that is another surprise, for another day, hmm?" Claude took his time lighting his pipe. "The grapes?"

"Chardonnay."

His father's eyes narrowed, challenged. "How badly do you want your Champagne and Julienne's, too?"

Burke's anticipation shot up to elation. Prematurely, perhaps, but he sensed Claude would capitulate if he would compromise. "You shouldn't have to ask."

"You want to grow these grapes—these Chardonnays for Champagne," his father drawled. "On lots fifty-one through fifty-eight. You propose to lease this land from us, and you stipulate that the grapes will be supervised and harvested—if, indeed, it ever comes to that—by your own labor force." Claude set his jaw and lifted his chin. Burke understood that his father had just outlined the terms he would ultimately agree to. "For now there will be no conversion of our buildings to ferment or riddle Champagne. No construction of new buildings, either."

What he was being offered, Burke realized, was acreage on which to grow grapes—nothing more.

"Your first harvest is four years away." Claude stood, a sign that negotiations were drawing to a close. "The land will be leased to you for four years. The option to renew will be subject to my approval. If I refuse, Julienne's will purchase the yield at a fair market price and compensate you for your investment. You will need to keep impeccable books." A wry smile pulled at Claude's mouth. "But of course you always do."

Burke's own mouth curved—not a smile but a grimace. "And if you don't renew the lease, my Chardonnays will be crushed into table wines."

Claude shrugged, as if to say that eventuality was a very real possibility and that he thought he'd made that possibility clear. "You have four years to convince me Julienne's should produce Champagne." He walked to the door, glancing back at Burke from the threshold. "Will you risk your grapes to your powers of persuasion? Remember, I'm a stubborn old man. I won't be easy."

Claude left, closing the door behind him. Four years. Burke knocked back the rest of his brandy, oblivious now to its excellence. Four years of uncertainty.

"The cagey bastard strung me up by my own rope." Very slowly Burke smiled. Then the smile gave way to a soft laugh at himself. Hadn't he known Claude would make this a challenge? And hadn't he anticipated meeting that challenge? Yes, he mused, we're going to disagree. But we're going to come through just fine.

Savannah sat in the foyer wing chair, the phone clamped between her ear and shoulder. At the other end of the line the receiver lay on a kitchen counter in Chicago. Her sister-in-law had answered and caught Savannah up on her nephews before going off to call Neil. Waiting, Savannah listened to the background racket of after-dinner madness and thought back on the subdued meal of five or six courses—she'd lost count—she'd shared with the Juliennes.

In both sight and sound, dining with the Claude Juliennes was worlds apart from dining with the Neil Joneses. Yet the sense of kinship, of a family coming together at the end of the day to share their experiences in the outside world and strengthen the bond that made them an indivisible unit, was the same in both households. The subtle balance of shared intimacies and respected privacies that was the bond's very fiber was a phenomenon that fascinated Savannah. The bond itself, however, threatened more than it appealed.

An ear-shattering squeal sang through the lines, nearly as piercing on her end as it had to be there in that little kitchen. Savannah smiled when she heard Neil's deep-chested voice call his sons to order. Then he was on the line.

"Back in business, little sister?"

"'Fraid not. I'll be out of commission for a few weeks. It wasn't the trans, after all, but the differential."

"Ouch! That'll take some time, all right. Want Terry to make your reservations to fly back? What's your closest airport? No, hold on a sec. This is perfect—"

"Neil—"

But he cut her off. "Anderson's in Biloxi, losing a race with a deadline. He called in looking for a team driver. Let's see . . . if we fly you to . . ."

As Neil planned routes for both her and Jimmy Anderson that would put them in precisely the same place at approximately the same time tomorrow, Savannah traced the fluting on the telephone table. This is it, she thought. Her alternative. Not a more interesting or intriguing place to sit out the delay, but a responsibility. Wary as she was of commitments, she'd developed a strong sense of duty toward her job. It was through her work that she maintained her freedom.

Now, for the first time ever, her work and her freedom were in conflict. It was a unique position for Savannah to find herself in, and an unsettling admission to make. If she chose to stay in Napa, she must have a powerful reason—one that transcended the power of duty.

*Burke.* His name shot through her brain. His image quickly followed. Savannah remembered him entering the dining room that evening, his smile of surprise warming to one of pleasure, and that warm pleasure seeming to penetrate her skin. He'd removed his suit jacket, hanging it over the back of his chair with the casual disregard of long-standing habit. When he'd loosened his tie and unbuttoned his collar, she'd found herself foolishly fascinated with watching his fingers work.

She wasn't indifferent to him. She wasn't above daydreaming about him, either. Yet, it hadn't been Burke who'd drawn her to the fields that morning or Burke who'd stirred her to tears that afternoon. It had been her past, her parents, her life before it had been shattered. She didn't know why being at the winery and walking the vineyards had triggered twenty-year-old memories; she knew only that she was compelled to explore them, discover them again before they became too faded to recapture.

But if she were to be completely honest with herself, she'd have to admit that Burke was part of the reason she wanted to stay on a while longer. How much a part? Savannah asked herself. So much that she'd be smarter to leave?

"Can you get along without me this time, Neil?" It was a question she wouldn't have asked three days ago. Neil's silence underscored that fact. "I'd planned to stay here," she explained. "You said I'd been going too hard for too long. I've decided you're right."

"Hell, if that's the case, no problem. Where will you be?"

"With the Juliennes."

Savannah was treated to another long silence before Neil demanded, "Why?"

His curtness startled her. Instinctively she responded in kind. "What do you mean, why?"

"I mean why? A simple question. Since when do you spend two weeks with strangers?"

"They aren't strangers. I stayed here before, during the flood. You know that. And since when do I have to explain myself to you?" Why was she snapping at Neil? At anyone else questioning her behavior, yes, but never her brother. Regretting her harsh words, Savannah expelled her irritation with a slow breath. "Neil," she said, quieter, calmer, "I like it here. It reminds me of when we were kids. It's harvest time. Crops are coming ripe, pickers are in the fields. Remember how it was, Neil?"

"Yeah, I remember." Bitterness laced his voice. "Do you?"

At a loss, Savannah struggled with his strangely abrupt attitude. Whom or what was he angry at? And why was she beginning to feel defensive? Maybe he'd misunderstood her. Neil had hated farming, the long days of drudgery, the back-breaking labor. But it hadn't been the work she'd meant to remind him of, but of who they'd been all those years ago.

"Tonight at the dinner table," she began haltingly, "the talk was of the weather, the day's yield, which fields to harvest tomorrow, next week. The Juliennes are good people, Neil—a family, like we were in the good times."

"We didn't have good times, Savannah." He'd never spoken to her so bluntly, so coldly. Or had he? "There were *never* good times. We didn't sit around a fancy oak or teak or whatever sort of table those people have. We didn't have bountiful meals and civilized chats about the days' events. We sat on a rusty car bumper eating stale sandwiches or somebody's leftover table scraps—when we ate at all."

A rocket of emotions speared through Savannah. Hurt. Anger. Betrayal. He's wanted to say this for some time, she realized. It was what he'd tried to say on the phone just a few days ago. "Stop, Neil. I shouldn't have brought it up. I should have—"

"No, you stop, Savannah. For God's sake, stop and take off those rose-colored glasses. To hear you tell it, you'd think we used to live on a balmy tropical island, if not in God's very own private paradise. You hated the orphanage—I know that. But, dammit, sis, the State of Kansas did more for us than our parents ever bothered to do. We were hungry, dirty and ignorant when we landed on their doorstep. We'd never had a home, a bed or a decent meal."

*That isn't true*, Savannah cried inwardly. "Why are you doing this, Neil?" Tears were just below the surface. She inhaled through her nose to keep them from rising.

"Because I love you, Savannah, and I'm worried by what's been happening to you recently." He sighed, sounding weary and discouraged. "Because I've always kept my trap shut when you'd start on the good old days, but now it's time you took the past out of that velvet-lined box of yours and gave it a good hard look. It's no diamond—it hardly passes for paste. And I'm doing this because you've got to get this thing worked out, Savannah, so you can stop running away from it. Can you do that? Can you get it worked out?"

"There's nothing to work out," she whispered.

"Dammit, Savannah! You're going to find yourself at the edge of the earth one day, with the past still right there behind you. Where the hell do you think you'll run to then?"

When Burke left the library he saw a splash of colors vault from the chair at the far end of the gallery. "Savannah?"

Whirling, she gazed down the long hall, looking like a startled deer peering down the barrel of a hunter's rifle. Her eyes were wide, her face a startlingly pale contrast to the scarlet peasant blouse and rainbow-hued skirt. He knew a split-second before she bolted that she would. She hit the front door at a run.

"Savannah!"

Without a destination in mind, Savannah ran, fleeing as if the wind at her back was on fire. She'd almost, *almost*, turned and headed the other way, straight into Burke's arms. For one strengthless moment she'd imagined laying her head on his shoulder and letting everything spill out. But some instincts were bone-deep, and Savannah's need to fall apart in private was one of them. Words were backed up in her throat. Tears pushed to be free. She had to find a place quickly where she could be alone and allow the eruption.

From the porch, Burke canvassed the grounds. The moon was full, the sky clear. He looked for a splash of flame streaking through the soft, silvery night. But the countryside was quiet. He swore with frustration as an unnerving panic crawled through his chest. How far could she go in thirty seconds? Where the hell was she? And then he spotted her, huddled on a patch of grass beneath an oak tree, just beyond the gardens. She sat with her legs pulled into her chest, her forehead bowed to her knees, a figure of misery and defeat.

Sensing she'd want to get the worst of it over without an audience, Burke tucked his hands into his pockets and walked slowly. He had no way of knowing how much of its course her emotions had run in the time it took him to cover the distance. When he walked up behind her her sobs were jagged and wrenching. Heartache and anger. He heard both and wondered what the hell could have happened. And what the hell made him think *he'd* know how to handle it?

Feeling a tenderness new to him, Burke dropped to the grass and gently eased Savannah onto his lap. She curled into his embrace, pressing her cheek to his shoulder and wrapping her arms around his neck. She managed to stem the tears long enough to say, "Leave me alone, Burke."

He almost laughed because, even as the words left her mouth, she was tightening her hold on him. "Sure, I'll leave you alone. Later, I'll leave you alone." He rested his chin on the top of her head. So damned determined never to weaken, he thought, never to lean on or need. He smoothed her hair, again and again until she no longer wept. Shifting her in his arms, he reached into his pocket.

"Here, blow."

Opening her eyes, Savannah considered the snowy linen handkerchief he offered, with its starched creases and Burke's monogram in one corner. Sniffing, she shook her head. "I'll make a mess of it."

Burke smiled and mopped her cheeks. "Come on, blow. Fitzhugh will send it to the wash regardless. Why waste good soap?"

Taking the hanky, Savannah laughed and sobbed at the same time, making a hiccuping sound. Then she allowed Burke to cradle her again. His heart gave a steady, comforting beat beneath her ear. She felt its infinitesimal pulse against her cheek. It had never felt so good to be held, to be wrapped up in another's arms and to leave being strong to someone else. She wasn't a physical woman; she didn't hug acquaintances or embrace friends. If descended upon by more gregarious people, she endured them with wooden stiffness. But at this moment something deep inside her craved Burke's warm, hard body, needed his gentle support.

Drained. She'd never felt so drained. Or embarrassed. "I never cry," she said into Burke's vest, which was now soaked with her tears. "You probably won't believe this, catching me at it twice in one day, but it's something I religiously avoid. I don't think I've cried in twenty years."

"I believe you. It sounded like twenty years' worth." He tipped her face up. Her mouth was swollen, as if a man had spent hours ravaging it. Her lashes were heavy with tears; her nose was red. But, God, she was beautiful. Emotions glimmered in her eyes, raw and eloquent. They reached inside and touched him as he couldn't remember having been touched before.

"What happened, Savannah? At dinner you were laughing with my father, making plans for a shopping spree with my mother. An hour later, you're falling apart."

Her first instinct was to shrug off the question. But that wouldn't satisfy him, she was sure. She hadn't the stamina to resist if he pushed. So she gave him a little and hoped he wouldn't press for more.

"I called Neil," she said. "We argued."

Anger and resentment rose up in Burke. Would it always be like this with her? Whatever she gave, would it be only a fraction of what she kept submerged? With some effort, he forced his feelings down. This was his problem, not hers. Three days ago—hell, yesterday—she'd have dodged the question altogether. That tonight she'd hesitated only a moment before giving an honest if succinct answer had to be a positive step in the right direction.

And what direction was that? Burke asked himself. Later, he decided. That was a question for later. "Talk to me, Savannah." He brushed the hair back from her face, letting his palms curve to the sides of her neck. "It isn't idle curiosity. I care. You hurt, and I care."

She wanted to. Something hard and heavy in the pit of her stomach wanted to crack open and give up a burden. But it wasn't as simple as putting thoughts into words and stringing words into sentences. "Could we walk?" she asked on impulse. She realized immediately how restless she felt, how desperate she was to move, go, get untrapped from the envelope of his warmth and scent.

His mouth formed a grim line. His hands fell away as she rose.

"I need to walk." Savannah saw disappointment in the black eyes she gazed into. She backed away from it as he stood. "Look, you don't have to come with me. You stumbled onto an hysterical woman, and you've been very kind. I've imposed enough."

"Imposed." He was on her before she could draw her next breath, hauling her by her upper arms onto her toes. "*Kind?* I didn't 'stumble onto' you, sweetheart." Angrily drawled, the endearment was an insult. "I came after you. I was concerned, dammit. I wanted to help. Don't you know the difference between common courtesy and genuine caring?"

"No."

Her soft, sad reply stopped him. It had triple the shock value of a slap in the face. Burke was suddenly aware he'd been shaking her and that her skin was a bloodless white where his fingers dug in. "Well, now you do." He released her shoulders and stepped back. "Genuine caring

is when someone bigger than you are shoves you around.''
He held out a hand, asking forgiveness.

Savannah sighed raggedly. She refused to meet his eyes
and stared straight ahead—at his mouth. She pictured it
lowering to brush across her own, imagined it pressed
against hers, very hard and very hot. It was safer, she decided, to meet his gaze.

''I'm sorry, truly sorry, Burke, for what I said and for
not answering you when you were kind—*caring*—enough
to ask. But I...'' Looking away, she dragged a hand
through her hair, then made a fist that she shook at the air.
''But I don't know *how*.''

Burke recognized her defiant gesture as frustration at
having a weakness; he also saw it as proof of her underlying strength. She'd begun her recovery. He couldn't help
admiring a woman who could look so fragile and have a
core of steel. ''Come on.'' He captured her clenched hand,
gently opening her fingers. ''Let's walk. And maybe, along
the way, we'll talk.'' Placing their hands palm to palm, he
laced their fingers, half dragging her the first few yards.
''Have you seen the stables?''

''Stables? No, I didn't know you had any.'' Falling in
beside him, Savannah decided to take it one step at a time.

''It's a hike. A mile by car, about half that the short way
through the fields. Up to it?''

''Yeah. Right now I think I could walk ten miles.
Twenty.''

*Or run?* Burke wondered. Instinctively, he pulled her
closer. Their hips bumped together lightly as they strolled
the uneven ground of an unplanted acre. High grass
parted, making a soft swishing sound in the quiet night.

''Are there horses?'' Savannah asked.

He looked over at her and laughed. ''Isn't that my
question?'' Savannah liked what laughter did to his face
and wondered why he didn't do it more often. He was almost a different man when the sharp planes were offset by
creases in his cheeks. ''Of course there are horses. What
would *you* put in your stables?''

She smiled, beginning to relax. "Oh, mules, maybe. Or donkeys. A cow if I had one and also had a stable but didn't have a barn. Firewood if it was January and I lived in Montana and the stable was close enough to the house. A car if I didn't have—"

"All right, smart ass. So you're quicker with a comeback." As they neared a stand of oaks Burke steered them to the left and toward a vineyard. "Tell me about Neil." It was a start, he thought. Where to start with Savannah was something he was beginning to get the hang of. "How old is he?"

A step at a time, Savannah reminded herself. "Thirty-one."

Burke subtracted Savannah's age. That would have made Neil eleven when they'd lost their parents. Too young to have been appointed her guardian. "What does he look like? Anything like you?"

"Yes, like me." They skirted a wood, close enough that the earth beneath their feet was spongy with a layer of last fall's leaves. The fertile, fecund scent stirred up by the trampling was rich and pungent for having lain so long undisturbed. "His build is bigger all around than mine. He's taller, stockier, like our dad. But we have the same coloring—our mother's."

Though she'd been the one to mention her parents, Burke thought it too soon to ask specific questions about them. He felt her relaxing and loosened his grip, slipping his thumb inside the pocket of their palms. "What did you and Neil argue about?"

"My staying here."

"He doesn't want you to?"

"Oh, he doesn't care where I am or what I do." She gave an impatient sigh and shook her head. "No, that isn't right. He *does* care. He's always cared. What I mean is that Neil's never tried to push his priorities on me. He may not like what I'm doing, but he leaves me alone to do it."

Someone ought to *stop* leaving her alone, Burke thought. "Until tonight. Why?"

Savannah replayed the phone call in her mind, but it didn't become any clearer. "I don't know why." They left the shadows and entered a vineyard. The moon illuminated the countryside, as light as night could be. Grapes glimmered, visible specimens on the vines. Savannah plucked one and savored it. A nightbird sang from a distant nest, and she became aware of time passing, of Burke waiting. His patience, she thought wryly, would bring him quicker results than perseverance had ever brought her.

"I was telling Neil how much the grape harvest reminded me of our past, of our life when we were still a family. He said things I've never heard him say before. I suddenly realized how much he must have hated our parents." Her voice had begun to waver, and Savannah stopped abruptly, determined not to cry again.

"Savannah?" Burke murmured.

"I'm okay," she said and cleared her throat before going on. "It was a shock. Neil and I have avoided talking about the years before we lost our folks. It wasn't as if we'd ever agreed not to speak of them; it was just a subject that caused strain. I'd always thought his reason was the same as mine—that it was too painful to reminisce about the good times. Good times," she repeated quietly. "I called them that tonight. You know what Neil said to me?"

Burke understood she didn't expect a response from him. He didn't want anything, not even the sound of his voice, to interfere with her sudden willingness to talk.

"He said, 'We didn't have good times, Savannah. There were *never* good times.' The hate...my God, the hate in his voice was so strong...."

And then she was telling him everything. It poured from her, words tumbling over words, thoughts running into thoughts. It occurred to Burke that because she'd always kept it locked in, she'd never mentally edited it into any semblance of order.

"We were poor by anyone's standards," she said without the slightest hint of apology or self-pity. "Our parents were migrant farmhands, and so there was never much money. But it couldn't have been as bad as Neil made it sound. They worked the Georgia, Louisiana, Michigan triangle, so of course we never had a home or real beds. But I don't remember being hungry. We were never hungry, dammit!''

Her parents had been members of the migrant work force. Of all that spilled out of her, this had the strongest impact on Burke. It explained so much: the peace he'd sensed in her this morning in the fields, her passionate defense of Nina, the gypsy blood that kept her on the road, the ease with which she shunned having a home.

"We always had enough to eat." Fresh strains of anger vibrated her voice. "We always had clothes on our backs." Realizing there were new tears on her face, Savannah yanked Burke's handkerchief from her skirt pocket. When she dashed it across her cheeks it was with annoyance at herself for having shed more tears. "And we were *not* ignorant."

Burke thought he had a fairly accurate impression of the argument between Savannah and her brother. Yet she hadn't related a single derogatory remark against her mother or father. "Is it really your parents he hated, Savannah? Or was it the life?"

"It was a *good* life," she countered earnestly. She stopped, pulling her hand free and shoving both into her deep skirt pockets. "We were always outdoors, in the sunshine. We ran barefoot in the rain while other kids were cooped up in stuffy playrooms or damp basements. We were together, the four of us. If my parents were picking a cabbage field, then we did, too. And don't give me that patronizing scowl that condemns child labor, Burke. Neil and I never *had* to pick in the fields. We *wanted* to. It's perfectly natural for kids to want to go to work with their parents and give a hand with a chore. We just did it every day."

She mounted her defense with a passion Burke had never before seen in her, and the passion stirred him. Focused on one man, she could wipe the memory clean of his ever having known another woman.

Tipping her head back, Savannah gazed at the stars, so sharp and clear. How many skies like this one had she slept under then? How many velvet nights had been her blanket? But it had been the sun she'd loved best. The heat and sweat and good, clean earth on her hands.

"No one could make me feel as important as my dad," she murmured, losing her way in the memories now. "I'd pick cabbages nearly half my size just so he'd laugh for me. He'd ruffle my hair or throw me up in the air and tell me what a big girl I was."

Burke watched her as she wandered through the past. Why, if the memory was such a pleasant one, had her brows knit in a frown of confusion? What had her father done to make her look bewildered and hurt? Die? Maybe. Hadn't Burke blamed Amy for her death? Hadn't he seen it as an unforgivable wound she'd inflicted on her family? He drew his fingertip over the silky rumpled arch of one of her eyebrows. Letting his fingers move to her ear, he tucked her hair back. His touch brought her eyes back to him.

"And we were free," she said reverently. "More than anything else, we were free. To go to the beach on a sunny day, to the zoo when we had a couple of extra dollars, to leave a town and never go back if we didn't like it." Suddenly spent of words, Savannah sighed and tipped her head to one side. She looked, Burke thought, as if she were asking him how Neil could possibly have found such a life less than perfect.

"It sounds..." *Hell, it sounds wretched.* "You were five, Savannah. Neil was eleven."

Her expression went from dreamy to furious. "What has that got to do with anything?" Whirling, she strode away. She could see the outline of the stables against the pearl-gray sky. She could already smell fresh hay and horse-flesh. She didn't need him to show her the way. She certainly didn't need him to make inane statements after she'd poured her heart out to him.

"Do you want to understand Neil?" Burke shouted at her back. "Or do you simply want to resent him because he doesn't agree with you?"

Her head snapped around, and her eyes glittered hotly. "You're not being fair."

"You are?" Burke countered. She didn't answer but swung her head back around and set off again. Burke followed. His pace was slower so that, by the time he caught up with her, she was already at a stall door tentatively stroking the muzzle of a chestnut mare. Eyes trained on her slim back, Burke saw her stiffen as he approached.

When his hands closed around her arms from behind, Savannah fought hard against an involuntary need to lean back against him. "I don't resent Neil," she said without turning. "But I don't understand him, either."

Burke touched his lips to her hair. The scent of her overpowered those of the stables. "He might have needed more than the sun on his face and the wind in his hair, Savannah. Think about it. It was his life until he was eleven. Did he go to school? And if he did, did he stay in the same one longer than a few months? Did he have friends, or didn't he bother because he'd only have to leave them behind?"

Was he reaching her? Burke wondered. Which were the right words? "You were young; it was a romp. But the transient life is a hard one, and Neil was old enough to remember that. A migrant's life . . . well, it's the life you saw for Nina and her son today." He turned her to face him. "What happened to the two of you after you'd lost your parents?"

Her dark-smoke eyes silvered. Her chin lifted fractionally. "It was just me and Neil, then."

The open door had shut. Savannah wondered how much more of Burke had gotten inside before it closed.

Burke couldn't throw off the unsettling certainty that there was more. Her first five years had come as a shock to him, but he sensed it was only the tip of the iceberg that seemed to encase Savannah at times. It wasn't his sin, he told himself as she turned back to the horse and he walked a short distance away to lean on a rail. Whatever had happened to her, he'd had no responsibility for her life during those years. Yet he ached for her, for what she'd never had and for what she'd lost and for whatever she'd been put through afterward.

Hearing his lighter snap open, Savannah glanced over. She'd discovered there was something strangely sensual in watching him light a cigarette. Maybe because his hands took on a particular grace when cupped around a flickering flame. Maybe because the smoke he exhaled had swirled through his mouth and was intimately mixed with his breath. Or maybe because of the way his cheeks hollowed when he drew on the filter.

Wrapped up in her fantasies, it was a moment before Savannah realized he was watching her. She tore her eyes from his and looked at the horse, which was enough at ease with her to rest its head on her shoulder.

"Who rides?" she asked, hoping to defuse the sexually charged air with trivialities.

"No one." Funny, Burke thought, but he could have sworn she'd just stripped him naked and taken a good long look at him. Liked what she saw, too. "Amy used to. My mother, but since . . . but not in the last two years. Frank Weatherby tends to them, turns them out, sees they get a good run daily."

"How many are there?" A second horse, curious at the sound of voices, had just thrust its head from the stall to Savannah's left. There were six stalls in all.

"Three. That's Morning Sun you're petting. And that one next to her is her daughter. The stallion will deign to make an appearance momentarily, though he'll hold out for you to coax him. The other stalls are for storing hay and equipment. One's a tack room."

Savannah turned to give attention to the other horse. "Amy must have liked animals."

"No, not particularly." His response made her frown, and Burke remembered his father saying Savannah loved animals. Animals, kids and anything helpless. Maybe if he broke a leg, came down with the flu. Realizing he was actually considering disablement, Burke nearly laughed out loud.

"Why three horses if she didn't like them?"

"She liked riding. Winning, actually." Burke said this without rancor. That had been Amy, the way he'd always known her. "She liked the blue ribbons and the gold cups and being the focus of everyone's eyes while she was in the ring." He paused to take a last drag on his cigarette before crushing it under his heel. "Frank was her groom; he went to the shows with her. He tacked them up and brushed them down. Amy just rode them."

"How old was she?"

"She would have turned thirty last month."

They'd have been close growing up, Savannah thought. Only a year between them. "You can talk about her," she said thoughtfully, almost to herself. "It's painful for you, but you're able to say her name and remember her. I'd gotten the impression from your mother that you didn't, that no one did."

Leaning farther back on the rail, Burke crossed his arms at his chest. "We may be a lot like you and Neil in that respect. Among ourselves, we become strained. Trying to blame someone else. Trying *not* to blame each other. Amy was sweet in a helpless sort of way. She was also very demanding. Was she spoiled, or had she simply been born selfish? And if she was spoiled, then which of us spoiled her? We were big on finding her wherever in the world she'd lose herself. Big on bringing her back home again. Was that a mistake? Would she have stopped running if we'd stopped chasing? Would she have come home on her own if we'd left her alone and the door open?"

Savannah heard less anger in his voice than there'd been the first time. But there was still confusion. Maybe we weren't meant to understand others but only ourselves.

The stallion chose that moment to throw his head and neck over the open top half of the stall's Dutch door. He was huge and frightened Savannah, who backed right up into Burke's arms.

"Good God! I thought he was going to take a piece out of me!"

"He's a lamb," Burke said when he stopped chuckling. "A large lamb, but quite gentle for a stallion. Go ahead and touch him. He won't snap."

"No, thanks. I'll take your word for it." Her hands were splayed over his chest. Savannah looked at them, then at the rich gray fabric of his vest and the silky sheen of his tie. A vein throbbed in his neck. The square cut of his chin was bold and blunt so that again the softness of his mouth fascinated her. Telling herself it wouldn't be wise to let him kiss her, that she was too vulnerable, Savannah watched his mouth lower to hers.

She felt the whisper of his lips and closed her eyes. She felt the pleasures of his touch, the soft sizzles and hot thuds, and smoothed her hands over his shoulders. She felt his mouth open and his tongue seek a response from her, and she helplessly stepped into his embrace.

Had anyone ever handled her so carefully? Held her so dearly? Had she ever felt so real and lovely and precious? Dear God, it was frightening to know she could be overcome. Terrifying to realize she *chose* to risk rejection. Yet she wouldn't, couldn't, put a stop to this moment.

Burke was tender with her. His arms remained loose. His hands ran gently down her back, lingered coming up her sides and over the swell of her breasts, leisurely threaded into her hair. He held her, and yet he didn't, and he knew she stayed freely pressed against him. Her scent stirred; her warmth soothed. Her taste had the allure of something rare and the headiness of something rich.

"I want you, Savannah." He watched her lashes lift over passion-drugged eyes.

"I know." This time she didn't throw up walls or hide behind evasions. Not only would it have been pointless, but it would have been unfair to both of them. When she drew back it was in panic, because she wasn't sure she could resist him. "I've been wanted before." Her voice was steadier than her nerves. "I believed if people wanted me, it meant they felt something for me. Not true. I learned the hard way it meant nothing of the sort, only that they were interested enough to give me a try. I'd already begun to feel, sometimes to love, when I discovered I hadn't satisfied."

He caressed her cheek with his fingertips. "You already satisfy me."

He couldn't have known what those words would do to her. *She* hadn't known. Hope—a belief she'd thought dead—flickered to life. She rushed to smother it. "I'm not required to satisfy you."

The ice from her seared him. Hurt him. *Damn her.* He hadn't deserved that. Burke was tempted to take her down where she stood and show her just how much she might enjoy satisfying him. Only the pain of past betrayals in her eyes stopped him. He had no wish to see them beneath him.

"So no one gets a chance, Savannah? Alone for the rest of your life?"

Why did it sound abhorrent when put into words? "I'm missing something," she murmured. With the fingers of her right hand she rubbed a spot near her left elbow, as if testing a wound just discovered. "I believe Amy was missing something. She ran at everything, trying to fill the holes. I've been running away so I wouldn't have to see them. If I . . ." She faltered, her new-found insight beginning to blur. "If I try to substitute you for what's missing, I'll be doing it Amy's way. I don't think that's the answer."

"What is?" Frustration and sympathy warred within Burke. "Self-denial?"

Exhausted, confused, Savannah shook her head, a gesture of uncertainty. "For some reason, this place—the winery, the vineyards—has stirred memories. I hadn't

forgotten, but I'd locked them away. Neil's asked me to
take them out of my velvet-lined box and look at them
again. I'm going to. Maybe, I can find what's missing . . . maybe not.''

*If I'm not careful, I'm going to fall for her.* It hit Burke
suddenly that it was already too late for caution and that
he ought to prepare himself for the landing. Talk about
risk! He was taking a leap at a long shot, and she was telling him she ran away under pressure. A wrong move from
him and she'd be packed and on the road before midnight. Physically, she was his. But if he claimed her now,
he'd lose his one chance of having the rest of her, the best
of her.

Savannah gave a sigh, the breath leaving her harsh and
shaky.

Burke heard it and ached for her. Pity, he decided,
would get neither of them anywhere. Because he needed to
touch her, he kept the contact playful and ruffled her hair.
''Been a hell of a night, huh?''

''Yeah.'' It was such an appropriate understatement,
Savannah laughed. ''One hell of a night.''

Curving a casual arm around her waist, Burke turned
her back toward the house. Maybe if he leaped from the
roof and broke both legs. Then he remembered there'd
been a fourth thing she loved. ''How do you feel about
homemade ice cream?''

''Weatherby churns her own?'' She could eat a gallon all
by herself, Savannah thought. ''I'll bet it's strawberry.''

''If we raid the fridge, we'll find out.''

''Raid Weatherby's fridge?'' She sent him a look of
mock astonishment. ''I think my presence may be cor-
rupting you, Burke. Who knows, by next week I might
have you going thirty in a twenty-five-mile-an-hour zone.''

Keeping his eyes on last month's market report, Burke
pressed the intercom button. ''Yes, Cynthia.''

''Message came in that Ramirez wants to see you immediately. He's out in the—''

"I know where he is. Does the message say what it's about?"

"A woman. You're supposed to know which one. 'Her again' is how he put it."

"Nina?" Annoyed, Burke scrubbed a hand over his face.

"Didn't give a name."

"All right. Thanks." Burke lit a cigarette and considered the report. He remembered the thin, timid woman of yesterday. Now what? And why? Hell, she hadn't looked like a troublemaker. Whatever it was, it could probably wait. He took up the portfolio, scanning the page for where he'd left off. But he'd lost his concentration. He couldn't shake the feeling that he'd made a promise of sorts to Savannah. Suppose the problem involved Nina's baby?

"Damn." Rising, Burke threw down the unfinished report and stubbed out the unfinished cigarette. Seven minutes later he braked the Jeep next to Ramirez's truck.

There was fire and belligerence in the man's eyes when Burke strode up the road toward him. "That woman's back," Alberto growled.

"Mmm, Nina something or other."

"No, not her. The other one." Ramirez pointed, but Burke knew whom he'd see before he picked her out on the row. Savannah was working alongside Nina. She wore her snug, soft jeans and a black bandeau top that bared shoulders and arms and more skin than a man should have to keep his hands off of. Her denim shirt was tied at her waist by its sleeves. It was Nina who noticed Burke and pointed him out to Savannah. She looked up, then lifted her hat to wave at him.

After a moment, Burke waved back.

"You tell me to stay away from her, I stay away," Ramirez reminded him. "But she's not mine. What is she doing out there?"

Looking for missing pieces, Burke thought. For her past, her people and maybe for herself. Without sparing

Ramirez a glance, Burke turned and started walking toward the Jeep.

"Hey! What about her?"

Burke looked over his shoulder. "What about her?"

"I don't hire her; I don't pay her," Ramirez warned.

"I don't think she expects to get paid. If she does, send her to me."

"What if she comes back tomorrow?"

At the Jeep, Burke glanced at Savannah once more. A private smile curved his mouth before he looked at Ramirez. "She'll probably be too sunburned to come back tomorrow."

## Chapter Seven

Y our secretary doesn't approve of me."

Burke finished signing a letter, one of a substantial stack, before sitting back to run his gold pen through his fingers. "My secretary," he said to Savannah, who was perched on the edge of his desk, idly swinging one leg, "doesn't approve of visitors blowing right past her. She prefers announcing them. Makes her feel needed."

Savannah shrugged, too busy looking over Burke's office to be properly contrite. It was a surprise. Light and airy when she'd expected dark and overwhelming. The whisper of importance when she'd envisioned heavy-handed authority.

Sunlight flowed through a sliding glass door that gave out onto a meticulously cared for garden. Pearl-colored walls were hung with quiet watercolors of wine bottles bearing Julienne labels. There were tints of blues and grays in the deep wall-to-wall carpet and again in the two-cushioned sofa. A cluster of grapes cut from green grained marble rested on a glass-topped table, the color as fragile as the stone was strong.

Burke's mahogany desk, the only dark object in sight, sat in the middle of the room rather than against a wall. Effective, Savannah decided, a subliminal suggestion that the man who sat here was at the center of all that took place.

Burke slipped the pen into his inside jacket pocket and watched Savannah digest his surroundings. She considered every inch of every surface, her brows slightly drawn together over gray eyes edging to silver. She worried her bottom lip between her teeth in a way that made him intensely aware of her mouth.

As her gaze moved over his office, so his moved over her body. She had a look he'd never been drawn to in a woman but that had always appealed to him in other aspects of his life: the slim, clean lines found only in what was very fragile or very strong; the subtle curves and faint hollows promising sweetness and secrets. She wore her picking clothes, as Burke thought of the faded jeans, denim shirt and black bandeau. The shirt was tied at her waist. Her clinging elastic top dispensed with imagination. Her hair was caught up in a ponytail so that her shoulders and arms were bared and, after three days in the fields, lightly honeyed by the sun.

Burke had been wrong about the sunburn and wrong about her not returning to the vineyard. She was out at the crack of every dawn and was a thorn in Ramirez's side until the sun set. When the heat peaked in the midday hours and the grapes were too easily bruised, the pickers took a break to nap in the shade, and Savannah joined Claude on his walks.

She put in long days, Burke mused. Long, physical days. That alone would explain the changes in her at night. She no longer prowled or played the cello. There was a quietness about her even when she wasn't silent. But her calm, Burke knew, went no deeper than the surface. When she didn't know he watched her, he saw turmoil in her eyes, now and again that waifish little-girl-lost look.

How long was it going to take her to find what she looked for? he wondered. Recently, it had occurred to Burke that she might not find it here. That she might go looking elsewhere.

It wasn't a comfortable thought. But little that had to do with Savannah was comfortable. He remembered that he hadn't had a decent night's sleep since he'd met her, or a woman in longer—how comfortable could he expect to be?

But he knew he was wrestling with more than physical discomfort. He couldn't plan or predict with her. He couldn't soothe her or seduce her or stop wanting to do both. Her refusals to lean on or need exasperated him even as he admired her determination and strength.

He couldn't get her out of his mind or into his bed. Yet she'd managed to get under his skin and into a corner of his heart.

And he loved her. Love, Burke mused. Things didn't get more uncomfortable, chaotic or complicated than that.

"I hadn't expected an outer office," Savannah explained once she finished her visual tour. "*Or* Ms. Universe. She isn't the sort of secretary I'd pictured for you."

"No? What did you imagine?"

Savannah shrugged carelessly. "Someone older, less glamorous. Stuffier, I guess. Women like Ms....?"

"Quince. Cynthia Quince."

"Women like Ms. Quince are usually on the covers of magazines instead of behind desks." Her voice cooled considerably. She hadn't cared for the woman's attempt to keep Savannah from Burke's inner sanctum. "Is she any good at what she does?"

Burke arched one eyebrow. "She's *very* good. Are you jealous, Savannah, or stereotyping?"

"Jealous? Of course not." But she wondered the same herself. "She wears a wedding ring. You're not the type to fool around with another man's wife. You have monograms on everything."

Burke didn't bother to unravel her logic; he thought he saw her point. "Then you're stereotyping. A ludicrous practice for a lady truck driver, don't you think?"

"The height of absurdity." She grinned, and he responded with a smile that was warm and faintly wicked. It made Savannah want to slide his jacket off and loosen his tie. "Tell me." She lifted the top from a crystal bowl shaped like an apple and scooped out a handful of M&M candies. "In addition to phoning and filing, does Quince keep your candy dish full, build fires on cold days, weed the garden?"

"Yes to the first two, no to the third." Burke picked up the hat Savannah had tossed onto his desk when she'd walked in, turning it over in his hands. A man's hat. He glanced again at the denim sleeves looped at her waist. A man's shirt. Where did she get her masculine clothes? Did she shop in men's departments? Or had they been left behind at the end of an affair? Too often Burke recalled the pain of betrayal he'd seen in her eyes.

Put there by a man? Not necessarily, he told himself. But possible. Probable. As he had when he'd realized she wasn't as fragile as he'd originally thought, he wondered why discovering she might not be a virgin should disturb him, when that very innocence hadn't sat too well with him in the first place. It was unrealistic to want or expect a woman of twenty-five to be sexually untouched. Yet he felt a cold fury for the man who might have touched Savannah and left her scarred. Innocence . . . innocence should be lost to a grand passion, to a lover worthy of the gift.

As Savannah helped herself to a second scoop of candies, Burke rose, dropping her hat to the seat as he left it. He saw her tense as he circled his desk. She still did that. In this she hadn't changed; her first response to Burke was one of prey to hunter. He lifted her hand from her thigh, pressing his lips to her palm. She gave a soft sigh, then tipped her face up for his kiss. This was new.

She was enticingly smooth, like sinking into a still pond on a hot summer day. She tasted of chocolate. Burke prolonged the kiss, languidly searching until he found the deeper, intimate flavor that was her own. His hands rested on her bare shoulders. His thumbs traced the elegant line of her throat. After a moment he let them glide over her collarbone and down the insides of her arms. Like the sigh of silk, skin whispered over skin. Finding her hands, he laced their fingers.

Humming contentedly, Savannah nestled her head in the hollow where his neck sloped to meet shoulder.

"Have you had lovers, Savannah?"

Startled, she drew back and blinked at him. "From M&Ms to lovers. How did a logical mind like yours make that journey?"

"It wasn't quite that direct."

She popped three more candies into her mouth. "It was *very* direct."

He shrugged. "I've waited ten minutes for you to tell me why you've come to my office. You haven't gotten around to your subject, so I introduced my own. Have you, Savannah? Had lovers?"

"Some subject." Freeing her hands, she slid off the desk. At the wall of glass she stared out at a cluster of purple pansies. "Suppose I'd asked you if you've had lovers?"

"I'd tell you I have."

"Bravo. Are you looking for a pat on the back?" She shot him a skeptical glance over her shoulder. "You're not planning to tell me about them, are you?"

He smiled. Not a man, he decided. Her skirting around an answer wasn't to protect a wound; rather, she'd simply found the question uncomfortable. "Are you on your way to the fields?" he asked, satisfied enough to change the subject.

"I'd planned to." Some of the light went out of her eyes. "I'm not sure now." Burke sensed the turmoil. Was picking losing some of its appeal? He realized she had no other roots to explore. Her curiosity about the community of migrants was akin to that about a flock of thrice-removed relatives who were otherwise strangers. He seriously doubted she'd find her past or herself among them.

Now, watching her, Burke saw her rub her thumb up and down her forefinger. He wasn't used to nervous gestures from her. Restless, but never nervous. The internal battle she waged was turning on her. Why? he wondered. Were the memories she'd cherished for a lifetime becoming tarnished? And if they were, what would the point have been? What good would it have done her?

Heaving a sigh, Savannah turned back to the window. "I'm tired of playing hide-and-seek with Ramirez. You ought to do something about him, Burke. He gets away with far more than he has a right to."

"Such as?"

"The way he...he..." She growled her frustration. "*Looks* at people."

"They aren't all like him, Savannah. As in any walk of life, there's the good and the bad. I can't jeopardize a harvest because a man glares."

"No, I suppose not," she muttered. Only it wasn't Ramirez that bothered Savannah. She'd gotten his number right off the bat. He was a phony, a spineless coward masquerading as a blustering bully. More than anyone else, Alberto Ramirez understood his own insignificance.

No, it wasn't Ramirez responsible for her disquiet. It was what she'd discovered in the fields, about the people who worked them, about the families. She wasn't a stupid woman; she'd never deluded herself into believing the life of a migrant was equivalent to plucking peaches in paradise. But the injustices were getting to her. And the children. Some of the children broke her heart.

Lately, when Nina quailed before Ramirez's arrogant glare, it wasn't the overseer Savannah wanted to rail at, but Nina. "Stand up straight," Savannah wanted to shout at her. "Think highly of yourself, even if you're the only one who does." Savannah realized laborers couldn't retaliate without risking their jobs, but, God, did Nina have to shrink and shuffle? What was her son going to learn of his own self-worth if he grew up watching his mother lick dust to ward off a browbeating?

It had been simple at first for Savannah to rationalize, to say Nina was the victim, that contempt begat shame and the meek begat the meek. It didn't wash anymore. As a child and with no one for example, Savannah had opted for dignity. How, she asked herself now, would she have played her part in last Monday's scene with Nina and Burke if it were to happen today? Her loyalties, she discovered, were shifting.

Yesterday Savannah had watched Nina stuff bunches of grapes into her baby's sack. She remembered her mother doing the same, loading Savannah and Neil down with whatever crop they were picking. It was done. Everyone knew and accepted that it was done. Yet Savannah had watched those grapes disappear under the rough cotton and thought of them as Burke's property. She'd multiplied that bunch times the workers in the valley, times the days they'd be there, and it wasn't insignificant. And it wasn't fair to Claude or Burke.

Good Lord, Savannah thought, more confused than ever, next I'll be harassing little old ladies for snitching strawberries in the supermarket.

When Burke's arms came around her from behind, Savannah started. The carpet had muffled his footsteps, and he'd surprised her. When he pulled her close, she gave resistance a brief thought, then leaned back against him.

Here was another confusion. She wanted him, more than in the physical sense. She wanted the experience of him, the pleasure and thrills and newness of him. At night, as she lay in her bed and gazed out the window, she found herself anticipating unbridled passion with the same impatient craving with which she used to anticipate her freedom. How would he feel? Where would he take her? She didn't think he'd be a disciplined lover. He wouldn't be tidy and methodical about it. Unguided, she thought, ungoverned. The journey fast and furious.

"Savannah." He still said her name in a way that swept lucid thought from her mind. "Want to talk it out?"

Shaking her head, she turned and wrapped her arms around his neck. She was falling for him. God help her, she was falling for him and doing nothing to stop it. "Kiss me."

Burke felt the wash of a sweet, pure emotion. She'd asked so simply, without the obvious battle between mind and body. The next test to his control would be to give her no more than she was ready to need. Having only some of her, Burke thought, could very well be more agonizing a torture than having none of her at all.

Savannah watched the way the sun sharpened the planes of his face, the way his eyes darkened with desire. Slowly, inch by inch, he brought his mouth to hers. She never took her eyes from his. Not even when he turned her head back and forth so that their lips skimmed and teased. She felt a skittering trip in her pulse and a quick sizzle run down her spine. She loved the feel of him: the thickness of his hair in her hands, the heat of his flesh seeping through layers of clothes to warm her, the hard, lean power of his muscles under her palms.

It was easier this time to let the pleasures take and consume her, to let more of the passion rise and bubble. Soon this wouldn't be enough. Soon she'd have to decide whether she'd let him into her life or get out of his.

"Now," Burke said when the kiss was over. "Tell me why you've come to my office."

"A favor, of course." She grimaced and pushed back stray wisps of hair with an unsteady hand. "I always seem to be taking advantage of someone around here."

"So take advantage." He put a fingertip to her temple where her pulse raced. "I have a sofa. There's always the floor."

She laughed, but there was a tremble in the husky sound. "I wanted to ask if you'd drive me to Jackson's."

The moment she mentioned the garage, Burke tensed. She was leaving. This was goodbye. And he didn't know how to stop her, hold her.

"I need clothes, shoes," she went on, oblivious to his sudden stillness. "My own shampoo. And then there's the refrigerator to think about." She wrinkled her nose.

Burke managed to recover before doing something stupid, like shaking her until her teeth rattled. Relief was sapping. And dangerous when it could strip him so completely, so quickly. He couldn't afford to overturn his conviction that leaving was eventually what Savannah was bound to do. It was time, he decided as he walked back to his desk, to stop wondering about Savannah's feelings and start worrying about his own.

Hands in pockets, he gazed down as if thoughtfully contemplating the letters waiting for his signature. He might have been blind for all he took in of the words. "When did you want to go?"

"The sooner the better. You may recall that I'm performing tonight?" Her wry tone held him responsible for a recital she was not looking forward to.

"My parents did the arm twisting," he reminded her. "I only mentioned that you were an accomplished cellist."

"I am not an accomplished cellist," Savannah said of his second statement after conceding his first with a snort. It *had* been Christina who'd overheard Burke asking Savannah why she hadn't played recently, Claude who'd pressed her to give them an after-dinner recital. As long as she was lining up guilty parties, she supposed she'd have to add herself for letting them talk her into it.

"I'm not any sort of cellist except by technicality," she qualified. "I'm someone who plays a cello, period. Not with any great talent, I might add. Well." She sighed and shrugged. "I've made my disclaimers and warned them it could be a fiasco. God knows the last time I played for an audience. Not since high school, I'm sure."

When Burke remained silent, Savannah glanced over. Seemingly absorbed in a piece of correspondence, he took his hands from his pockets and prepared to sit.

"Don't!" She leaped forward to stop him, but was too late.

Burke felt her hat flatten beneath his weight. Holding back a grin he extracted the misshapen felt, which to his mind looked no more battered than usual. He was coming to despise the bedraggled old thing, anyway.

"Now look what you've done," she muttered.

"Looks about the same to me, Savannah." He handed it over, then retrieved his pen from his pocket.

Savannah punched out the crown and straightened the brim. Giving a satisfied nod, she perched on his desk again. "Can we go now?"

"Just as soon as I've signed these letters for Cynthia."

"Want me to forge some of them for you?"

Torn between exasperation and amusement, Burke rolled his eyes. "Forgery?"

She smiled smugly and nodded. "I'm quite good after a practice run or two."

This is what's known as one of life's most embarrassing moments, Savannah reflected wryly. If she'd had the slightest inkling exactly how uncomfortable she would be, she'd have sworn on a stack of Mozart scores that she didn't own or play a cello, regardless of what anyone might have seen or heard to the contrary. Unfortunately, she hadn't thought of it in time, and now they were waiting for her to begin.

She rosined her bow—again. She resisted the urge to tune the strings; she'd already put them through the irritating ritual twice. Straightening into position, she applied her bow—and saw them: Claude and Christina, smiling expectantly in the twin brocade chairs; Burke, shoulder to the jamb at the living room's arched threshold. Savannah's fingers went numb on the strings. Her spine melted, dropping her into a slump.

Damn. She couldn't play with them ogling her as if she were on the verge of performing a miracle before their very eyes. Clearly, desperate measures were called for, and she set aside the cello and moved her chair to an open window.

"Fresh air," she said to Claude's questioning expression. "Weird, hmm? But we artists are such an eccentric lot. Me, I need fresh air when I play."

The moment she faced the sky and breathed the soft-scented evening she found what she'd groped for seconds ago. The mood, the magic. From them sprang the music. Without consciously choosing a piece to play, she drew the bow and released a rich, pure note. Then another, until the air in the vast, velvet-draped room was saturated with the emotional movement and humming passion exclusive to the deep-throated cello. She needed only to be fractionally present in order to command her fingers and arm. The rest of her was caught up in the spell.

Burke was caught, and he knew it. Her music moved him, seduced him. Here were her emotions, reaching out and wrapping him in the passionate embrace her arms still denied him.

Watching her, he thought back to the first night. She'd looked then very much as she did now, her face tipped to the moon, her eyes closed. Uninhibited, welcoming the rapture. Her mouth curved as the music lifted her to another plane. Her lips parted to take in a small, surprised gasp when a flourish of notes raced up the scale to hang for a breathless moment. She seemed completely unaware of being the creator of the very music to which she responded.

She wore a thin silk blouse of emerald-green silk. Its snug cuffs accentuated her delicate wrists; its neck sash elongated her graceful throat. Burke let himself imagine tugging on the silk tie and watching the bow fall apart. He pictured himself undoing each button, visualized the silk drifting away from her satin skin.

When desire edged from pleasant to painful, Burke decided to listen without looking. Without moving a muscle, he shifted his gaze to see how his parents were responding. His mother sat with her head tilted and her eyes closed. As Burke watched she moved her left hand to find and cover Claude's right. Burke glanced next at his father. He shouldn't have been surprised to meet with Claude's bold stare. The incisive black eyes shot to Savannah and then back to Burke. Claude lifted an eyebrow, half discovery, half question.

He knows, Burke thought. He knows that she completely undoes me.

Finished, Savannah bowed to appreciative applause from her small audience. Though it had gone surprisingly well, she was relieved to be done with the obligation.

"Lovely, Savannah," Claude said, rising. "You should audition for a seat with the Symphony. Now, that'd be a suitable job, hmm?"

Laughing, Savannah reached for the wineglass she'd brought with her from the dinner table. "Suitable, yes. Think they'd let me play with my back to the audience?"

Stepping forward, Christina pressed her cheek to Savannah's. "Beautiful. It so relaxed me that I'm going straight up to bed. Claude?" Arms linked, they left the room, saying good-night to Burke on the threshold. "See you in the morning, Savannah," Christina called back. "Bright and early."

"Tomorrow?" Burke asked as he entered the room.

"Shopping," Savannah explained. She curled up at one end of a royal-blue sofa, its velvet shiny with dignified age. "So that I can be suitably turned out at your welcome-home party on Saturday. A real beads and black tie bash, I hear."

Idly, Burke ran a fingertip down a string of the propped up cello, then glanced over at Savannah. "What was all that business with the window?"

"I'm not sure." She shrugged, laughing softly at herself. "It certainly caught *me* by surprise."

"But that's how I saw you playing the first night. At an open window."

"Mmm." She nodded. "Habit, I guess. It's how I always played at the orphanage."

Orphanage. Another piece to the puzzle. Several pieces, Burke amended. Though the probability had already occurred to him, hearing it confirmed placed an ache in his chest.

Carrying his own wineglass, he joined her on the sofa. He stretched his arm across the back cushions and touched the ends of her hair. What was the next question? he wondered. Tell me about the orphanage? No. Too direct. It would be like asking her to tell him about the pain.

"Tell me about the window." He knew it was the right question when she propped an elbow on the back of the sofa next to his arm and rested her temple against her palm.

"The window," she murmured. "Well, it was a rectangle, with twelve small panes—six on the top half and six on the bottom, four going down, three going across. I know; I sat at it a lot. It had wood sashes painted institutional green, and it stuck whenever it rained. Beyond it, there was nothing. A great big overwhelming view of nothing."

His fingertips slipped under her hair, seeking the soft, warm skin at the back of her neck. It pleased him to see her instinctively shift closer to his light touch. "And where was this overwhelming view of nothing?"

"Kansas." She tilted her head, and her expression went from thoughtful to inquisitive. "Have you ever been to Kansas?"

"No."

Savannah felt a stab of disappointment. They had so little in common—almost nothing. They were as different from each other as France was from Kansas. "Unless you have a thing for wheat, miles and miles of wheat, skip Kansas—at least the part of Kansas I was in."

How had she wound up in Kansas? Burke wondered. Born in Georgia. Farming in Louisiana and Michigan.

Kansas wasn't even a state they'd have passed through. "Then why look out the window?"

"I didn't look. I closed my eyes." She chuckled and sipped from her glass.

"Don't do that." His fingers tightened on her hair. Savannah felt the quick tug at her scalp, and her smile faltered. "Don't evade. If you don't want to answer a question, say so. But don't play games."

He was right, she thought. When she was cornered she didn't whack at the barriers but wore them down. Answer but don't answer until eventually people tired of the effort and went away. "I didn't sit at the window to look out," she said. "I sat there to send the music. Whenever I thought I'd go mad from being locked up in that place, I played at the window. I reached in for the feelings and pushed them out. I pictured how far the notes traveled before dying away. Sometimes I could get that music all the way to the beaches of either ocean.

"I'd sail over the Rocky Mountains and the Grand Canyon, seeing them as I remembered them from pictures in books. Usually I'd lose the music on the desert. Sometimes I'd clear the redwood forests and make it to the Golden Gate Bridge. Or I'd go east. To Kentucky, Tennessee. They were easier because I'd been there. On a really tough day I could get to New York City."

On a tough day, Burke silently repeated. Not on a good day but a tough one. When there was so much bottled up it would take a concert performance to release it all. It explained the prowling, the restlessness. "You haven't played in five days." He trailed a finger over her brow, down her nose.

"I haven't felt caged in five days." She turned her head slightly, inviting his fingertips to brush over her lips. "What did you do as a kid to get rid of frustrations?"

"Punching bag." His childhood frustrations paled in comparison. "My father has a workout room. Weights, rowing machine, the works. If he thought I was itching to give something or someone a good pounding, he sent me there. Eventually I went on my own." What used to make him boil? Burke asked himself. An undeserved punishment. Being called Burke the Jerk. Insignificant things, he thought now, though they hadn't seemed small at the time. "You stole the cello from the orphanage?"

"No, from the public school system." She glanced over her shoulder at the instrument once despised but now beloved. "It still has PROPERTY OF THE PUBLIC SCHOOL SYSTEM etched on the bottom."

Tell me about the loneliness, Burke wanted to say. Tell me about the hurt. "Tell me about the cello," he said instead.

Savannah settled more comfortably in the corner of the sofa. The cello, she thought. What was there to say? "I didn't want it," she began, then laughed dryly. "I remember that quite clearly. Kids at the orphanage were bussed to the public school in town. The academic program might have been mediocre, but the music program was excellent, thanks to a local patron of the arts. A wealthy man, philanthropic, no heirs. He financed the whole thing. Donated instruments. Set up a fund to maintain them. Subsidized the salary of a wonderful instructor. We weren't given a choice in junior high—we had to take an instrument. It was optional in high school. As seventh graders, we filled in forms listing three choices in order of preference. I asked for the violin, the flute or the clarinet." Her eyes iced over. "I got the cello."

Some of the old anger returned. Savannah set her wineglass down and rose to pace. Placing his glass beside hers, Burke also rose. If he went to her as he wanted to, if he got in the way of her wandering, she'd run. And so he crossed to the window where she had played, not for the air or the view but because that was where she'd left her cello. And there, he knew, was where she'd eventually come to rest.

"None of the town girls wanted the cello," she said. "It wasn't easy to carry or feminine to play." She paused beside a tall vase, fussing at the flowers without seeing their shapes or colors. When she looked at Burke from over the tops of them, her eyes glittered angrily. "Well, I didn't want the damn cello, either!" She gave a short, disdainful snort. "But they foisted it off on me. I lugged that elephant on and off the school bus for six years, junior high and high school. I got my skinny legs around its fat belly, feeling awkward as a goose, while all the other girls sat tall and elegant, whistling on their flutes or with their violins and violas tucked neatly under their chins."

Shifting her gaze from Burke to the cello, Savannah pushed out a long sigh. "It's so stupid to be angry after all these years. So useless and wasteful."

"Human," Burke pointed out. He watched her graceful, leggy glide as she left the flowers and found it difficult to imagine her skinny and awkward. She stopped next to handle a Steuben candlestick. She tossed it from hand to hand with a negligence that would have made his mother's heart drop into her shoes. "There is a freedom beyond the physical, Savannah. Emotions, even the stupid, useless, wasteful ones, need to be unstrapped now and then."

"I guess that's what I'm doing, finally." Returning the candlestick, she worked her way back to the cello. "I was released from the orphanage at seventeen. My birthday was in April, seven weeks before school closed for the summer, but I wasn't sticking around to finish. I'd waited twelve years for that day. I was free, and I was leaving. I packed the few things that were mine and left the cello on top of my stripped bed in the dormitory." With her fingertips, she lovingly traced the cello's smooth scroll. "I got all the way to the front door. But I couldn't leave without it; it was part of me by then. They'd pushed it on me when I didn't want it, and that made it mine. I went back for it. No one stopped me. I guess they'd all forgotten it wasn't mine."

She looked up and into his eyes then. Burke hadn't expected to see the smile, the shine of laughter in her eyes. "I thought Neil was going to pitch a fit when he saw me coming down the road with it tucked under my arm. Said he didn't have enough room for me and it, too, that I'd have to make a choice.'' Without her usual hesitation, she slid her arms around Burke's waist. Resting her head on his shoulder, she gazed out at the terraced gardens at the back of the house. ''When I put the cello on the front seat, and he realized I was prepared to walk the thirty-five miles to town, he shoved a few things over and made room for both of us.''

Though he wouldn't know Neil Jones if he passed him on the street, Burke thanked God the man had been around for Savannah. ''Is that when Neil took you on as his partner?''

''No.'' She tipped her head back and gave a wry smile. ''That's when Neil made me finish high school.''

''Smart guy.''

''Mmm, sweet, too. I gave him a hard time at first.''

Burke smiled and ran a hand down her back, stroking her from neck to hips. Giving people a hard time was her most frustrating, most enjoyable quality. ''What made you change your mind?''

''Seeing the way he lived. And learning why. He'd rented a room for me at the same boarding house. We got heat when the sun shone and hot water from the teakettle. And the food! I swear the woman who ran the place didn't know squash from cucumber. But he'd lived there six years, putting every spare nickel in the bank so I could be a flight attendant like I'd always wanted. I owed him for that,'' she murmured. ''When he wanted to open his own trucking firm, I was finally able to pay him back.''

''How did he take it when you quit the airlines?''

''He understood. If living at the orphanage was like being confined to prison, being cooped up in a plane all day was like being locked in a cell. My driving with him was supposed to be temporary. I was going to decide my future while I helped him raise his seed money. We doubled his mileage, traded off who got the cab bunk and who got the motel room and still made pretty good money. After the first month I knew I belonged on the road.''

Burke thought not. Body to body with her, he fit her perfectly—and she him. Their hearts pulsed a synchronized beat. He inhaled, she exhaled, and they fed life-giving breath to each other. From shoulders to hips to arches side by side, they fit together. No two people could melt into one shape, one entity with such perfection if one of them belonged somewhere else.

Burke had only to convince Savannah of that.

"Oh, Savannah, you are stunning!" Christina exclaimed.

Yes, and stunned, Savannah thought as she stared at herself in the fitting-room mirror. Actually, it wasn't *a* mirror—no mere sliver of glass providing a one-dimensional view, this!—but six solid walls of mirrors, reflecting hundreds of Savannahs draped in shimmering black beads. And it wasn't exactly a fitting room, either, but a sumptuous hexagonal parlor, with mile-thick white carpeting and deep-pillowed sofas covered in peach silk. There were milk-glass ashtrays dotting petite marble tables, and a hostess who served tea and tiny cakes.

"Exquisite," Christina murmured.

"Yes," Savannah agreed. "Exquisite." Standing on a three-tiered pedestal in the center of the boutique's fitting room, she felt like a figurine atop a cake.

"With this dress the hair is worn up," the saleswoman noted. She stepped onto the podium, the top of her head level with Savannah's shoulder. "May I?"

Savannah shrugged and smiled. She didn't mind playing dress-up if they didn't mind wasting their time. She bent at the knees to assist the petite clerk loosely arranging her hair, securing it with pins fished out of a handy pocket. There'd been too many stores today, she thought with a tired sigh. Too many dresses. Gold lamé. Red marabou. Black lace. She was sure she'd find something that appealed to her if Christina would give her a chance to wander. Please, let this be the last boutique within a fifty-mile radius, she prayed.

"There," the pleased clerk announced. "See what you think."

Savannah straightened and stared. The gown bared one arm and shoulder and clung clear down to her ankles. Infinitesimal black beads on tissue-thin fabric shimmered like wet ebony and whispered when she moved. The tiniest of light-catching rhinestones edged the diagonal neckline, slashed hem and wrist of the one sleeve.

The woman she'd become took Savannah's breath away. What she saw in the mirror was all that a skinny girl in a Kansas prairie orphanage had once dreamed of becoming. Tall and straight, with a set of curves that dipped and swerved where they were supposed to dip and swerve. Silky hair and a pretty face. Wearing a knockout dress that was brand-spanking new...even if it was for only twenty minutes. Yet it wasn't style or elegance or even beauty Savannah marveled at. It was the woman, the proud-shouldered, clear-eyed, confident woman.

"It's you, Savannah," Christina said.

*Yes*, Savannah thought, *it's me.*

"We'll take it," Christina informed the clerk.

"No, we won't," Savannah countered. "Unless, Christina, you'd like to try it on."

"But the dress looks perfect on you."

"It *looks* perfect, yes. But it feels wrong." She stepped down and gave her back to the amiable assistant to have the zipper let down. "It was a kick to put on, but it really is a dress meant for standing on pedestals."

"Savannah." Christina discreetly lowered her voice. "Is it the price?"

"No...well...what is the price?"

The saleswoman nimbly located the little white tag secreted inside the gown and flipped it over.

"Good God," Savannah muttered. "For that much money I could replace the tires on my truck—all eighteen of them."

The saleswoman gaped at Savannah's comment before remembering herself and departing with the dress draped over her arm. Laughing, Savannah stepped into her skirt. Absurd to think of anyone spending that much money for a bolt of cloth and five pounds of crushed glass.

"Let me buy the dress for you, Savannah."

Savannah shoved her head through the neck opening of a loosely woven pumpkin-colored sweater and spent more time than necessary smoothing her hair.

"Oh, stop fussing, Savannah, and turn around. You needn't feel insulted. If I were stupid enough to think you a charity case, I'd at least have the good sense to offer you something more sensible than an evening gown."

Knowing what Christina said was true, Savannah pushed away the resentment. Where had the confident woman she'd just seen gone? *Don't lose it, Savannah, or this special friend.* "I appreciate your offer," she told Christina with sincerity as she went in search of her shoes. "But I'd buy the dress myself if I really wanted it. I'm fairly well-heeled financially. I've been working nonstop for eight years, and I've no one but myself to support."

"Then?"

Savannah managed to find both shoes, though she couldn't imagine how they'd lost themselves at opposite ends of the room. Standing, she looped her arm through Christina's, pulling her out of the fitting room and toward the street door. "First, I have no use for the dress. What would I do with it after the party? Hang it in my sleeper-cab closet and Windex it once a week? Second, the dress looks great, but it feels wrong. It's just not a dress a girl has fun in, unless she's got a thing for standing around on pedestals."

"If you say so." Christina sighed and checked her wristwatch. "We've been at it nearly five hours, and we still haven't found you a dress. Not one you've taken to, anyway."

Savannah glanced up and down the street. "You remember that second or third place we were at? The one where they put me in that tent of pink feathers?"

"Yes." Christina frowned. "The...dress...didn't do much for you."

"To say the least. But if you could get me back to that street, I saw a little shop close by that just might have what I'm looking for."

An hour later, Savannah had her outfit. Much to Christina's astonishment, she'd found one half in a dusty little secondhand shop and the other in a punk rock store blasting heavy metal music onto the street.

## Chapter Eight

Savannah sat before her dressing-table mirror, chin planted in her palm, eyes fixed on her reflection. The scent of flowers drifted about her. Not the delicate whiff of roses from outside but the heady perfume of orchids and gardenias wafting up from the rooms below. The caterer had transformed Weatherby's efficient kitchen into a madhouse of egotistical chefs and gastronomical delights. Musicians were tuning their instruments in the stone foyer. Soon cars would pull up the drive, the doorbell begin ringing.

Gray tones for eyeshadow? Savannah speculated. Or earth shades? Leaning forward for a closer study, she wondered when her skin had last been exposed to so much sun. Not since she'd been a barefoot child, she thought. She hadn't the sort of complexion that toasted up bronze. Rather she looked as if she'd taken a dip in a vat of honey. "Pinks, I think."

Decided, she swirled a brush over a cake of pale powder and blew off loose dust before applying the first gossamer layer to her eyelids. By the time she finished she'd blended as many as six or seven shades, and no single one would be discernible. Though she usually forgot to bother with makeup, she was quite adept at it when she remembered. Thanks to Mrs. Wilmington-Parkinson, she added silently. She suddenly realized she hadn't thought of the woman in years.

Savannah had been fifteen, disillusioned and defiant. The last thing she'd been interested in was another foster home—not that anyone had bothered to consult her about it. She'd found herself packed and put into a car within forty minutes of Beasley's having sent for her. Forty minutes later the capped and gloved driver was letting Savannah out on a tree-lined street in the center of town, in front of a square brick home where lace curtains hung in the windows. The chauffeur lifted her bag from the trunk and motioned her through the front door.

"I am Mrs. Wilmington-Parkinson," an imperious voice announced from the living room. Savannah let it guide her, then gave the lilac-scented room a long, considering survey, blatantly ignoring the woman. Few people, she'd discovered, could stand being the last, therefore the least important, object in a room to receive attention. And so Savannah took her time looking at the prismed lampshades, the starched doilies protecting oiled woods, the two Siamese cats curled into each other and asleep in a patch of sunlight on the flower-patterned rug. After she'd looked everything over twice, Savannah deigned to turn her eyes on the elderly woman sitting militarily straight in a high-backed chair.

She was a large woman, big boned and solid. She wore a fitted serge dress the same shade of pewter-grey as her hair, a brooch at her throat and orthopedic shoes. Her hands were overlapped and resting on the brass knob of a walking cane.

"So you're the most difficult one they've got, hmm?"

Savannah narrowed her eyes on this new foster mother of hers. It was the strangest opening line she'd ever heard.

She was used to gushingly optimistic promises of how happy she was going to be or uncertain stutterings of "I'll show you to your room."

"They didn't tell you anything about me, did they?" the woman demanded.

"No."

"And you'll have been too belligerent to ask." She hadn't invited Savannah to sit, and Savannah realized she wasn't going to. "The home sends me their hard cases. Girls, teenagers. I'm too old to chase after youngsters. I never go out there myself; can't imagine you kids appreciate being sized up like sale items in a bargain basement. Doesn't matter to me what you look like. I've never sent a girl back, and none has asked to leave once she was here. This will be your last foster home. You'll stay until you come of age. When you go, I'll send for another." She nodded, as if satisfied with a meeting going as planned. "You'll like it here, eventually."

Savannah thought she'd yet to be shown a reason she might.

"You'll call me Mrs. Wilmington-Parkinson. Not Mrs. Wilmington, not Mrs. Parkinson. I will call you Savannah and not by a nickname. Do you have one?"

"Some people call me Van."

"And do you answer to it?"

Haughtily, Savannah raised one eyebrow. "No."

"Good for you." A gleam of approval touched the wizened brown eyes. "Someone blessed you with an unforgettable name. Don't let anyone mess with it. Is Jones your family name, or were you a foundling?"

Aghast, Savannah took a step back. Whatever warmth the woman's frank compliment had encouraged slid beneath ice.

Mrs. Wilmington-Parkinson gave the floor two thumps with her cane. "Answer me. If it's none of my business, say so."

"It's none of your business."

"There. Though I already know the answer; your file was read to me. Get used to questions, Savannah. You'll be asked them all your life. Some will be necessary; most will be for no good reason. Don't let slack-witted snoops embarrass you. Stare them down, cut them off or learn to be glib. Don't back away." Using her cane for leverage, Mrs. Wilmington-Parkinson stood. "So now we've met. I'll take you to your room. You'll keep it clean. Strip the bed on Monday and Thursday..."

Savannah had expected the woman to limp. But though it cost her in effort, Mrs. Wilmington-Parkinson exited the room with a steady, unfaltering gait. She turned at the foot of the stairs to give her ward one more thorough review. "I see they still can't seem to fit the kids to the clothes out there."

Savannah's hands curled into fists, catching some of the horrid plaid skirt she wore.

"Bothers you, does it? Well, I'm not going to tell you it shouldn't. A girl doesn't want to be stared at for short-comings forced on her by another. God will have given you enough of your own. You've been looked over and passed up most of your life, usually on first appearances alone. The next time someone gives you a skirt too short, hike it up another inch. You've got the legs for it. If people are going to stare, Savannah, and if their staring is going to intimidate you, then *you* decide what they'll stare at. Take what control you can of your life." She paused. Another survey, this time of hair, face, eyes. "One day you'll realize it isn't an imagined flaw they stare at."

She turned and started up the stairs with Savannah following three steps behind. "Tomorrow I'll take you for new clothes. Nothing fancy, but they'll fit. You'll get a weekly allowance until your sixteenth birthday, then you'll get an after-school job. I don't like my girls to work the first year; there's too much else to learn. You'll budget your money and be responsible for buying personal items. I'll give you a list..."

To a fifteen-year-old girl makeup was an important personal item. Mrs. Wilmington-Parkinson hadn't provided Savannah with any, nor was it on the list. Savannah scrimped with her allowance for two months and then walked to the corner drugstore. Untutored in skin tones or subtlety, she randomly purchased foundation, lipstick, blush and eyeshadow. The foundation had a bronzy orange base, the lipstick was a blue-red and the eyeshadow leaned to green. That she looked a bit brilliant when she finished she chalked up to being unfamiliar with her new look.

No mention was made of her exotic face at dinner, and Savannah assumed she'd done a passable job of it. Two hours later there was a knock on her bedroom door. Mrs. Wilmington-Parkinson entered and set a ten-pound shopping bag on Savannah's bed. Inside the pink paper sack was a treasure trove of makeup—pots, tubes, creams, powders—in a rainbow of shades.

"Lock yourself in the bathroom," her stoic guardian said, "and paint yourself to your heart's content. Experiment, mix colors, pile on layers, look as silly and ridiculous as you please in private. You'll know it's time to come out when you've managed to look as if you're wearing no color at all." With the thud of her cane pacing her strides, Mrs. Wilmington-Parkinson walked back to the door. From the threshold, she delivered her final bit of advice on the subject. "You should look as if you've been out walking on a brisk autumn day. Your eyes should sparkle. Your cheeks should be rosy. Your mouth should look as if Mr. Clark Gable has just kissed it."

Mrs. Wilmington-Parkinson died seven months later. It had, as the old woman had promised, been Savannah's last foster home. Savannah hadn't bothered speaking with Mr. Glass, who wouldn't approve a request for a glass of water without first checking his book of rules and regulations; she'd gone straight to Beasley. No more foster homes, Savannah had informed her. It was the first time she had spoken up for herself. It was Mrs. Wilmington-Parkinson who'd taught her she had the right.

Ten years later, Savannah dabbed her lips with coral-pink gloss, then blotted away the shine, leaving only the faint blush of stain. She considered her mouth and approved. "Mr. Clark Gable couldn't have done better himself."

Letting her robe slip from her shoulders, she stood. Naked except for a scrap of lace passing for panties, she gave herself an all-over spray of fragrance. It wasn't until she turned from the mirror that she felt the nerves churn in her stomach. Situations like tonight's were precisely the sort of thing she handled badly. And what she handled badly she made a point of avoiding. She could think of nothing less desirable than being put on display before a crowd of curious strangers. If they looked too closely, would she know what they wanted or expected of her? If they shrugged and turned away, would she know why they'd found her lacking?

One on one, Savannah stood up to the best of them. But in a roomful of people, whether a family gathered at the dinner table or a high school assembly hall—a glamorous party in Napa!—Savannah thought only of escape.

Don't be so arrogant, she told herself as she stepped into her skirt. They aren't coming to see you. These are Burke's friends, Claude's and Christina's friends. Friends. An exclusive, impenetrable association of others. Their choice to let you in or freeze you out. Their privilege to measure and reject. Though they would come tonight for Burke, guests of the Juliennes, Savannah was a stranger, a new face...a curiosity.

Shutting her eyes, she reached inside for her armor, her mantle of ice that froze them out first. She knew even as she groped for it that she wasn't going to find it. She'd had to take it off in the vineyards to let the past get in. Vulnerable. Distractedly taking up the white gardenia she'd snitched earlier from one of the living room arrangements, Savannah knew she'd never felt more vulnerable in her life.

Whoever these people were, she wanted their acceptance. They were Burke's friends, and she wanted to fit in. That was another overwhelming reality to deal with. Burke mattered, much more than he should. And Savannah wanted his approval—not to mold and shape herself into what she thought might please him, but to be herself and know the woman she was brought him satisfaction.

"This is going to be one hell of a night," she muttered, unsure whether she wanted to cry or throw something. She gazed into the mirror to decide where in her hair she'd pin the gardenia. Instead of her own reflection she saw a little girl there, a skinny little five-year-old in an oversize coat and a floppy felt hat looking lost and bewildered. She was so clear, so real, that Savannah nearly reached out to touch her. But it was the little girl who put out a hand and brought to Savannah the proud, confident woman she'd met in another mirror yesterday. Together they stood there, daring Savannah to let them down.

It isn't real confidence if it can't stand the test, they seemed to say. And then they faded. Savannah reached for a hairpin to attach to the gardenia and saw that her fingers trembled. She envisioned doors and highways and escape. But she wouldn't disappoint them. Or herself. The time for running away was past.

"Fitzhugh!" Burke's voice echoed in the stone stairwell beyond her door, and Savannah stopped in the act of pinning the gardenia. "Damn your scrawny little neck! I'll wring it with my bare hands if I get within strangling distance. *Fitzhugh!*"

Savannah opened her door and looked out. His back to her, Burke stood at the balcony rail bellowing down into the foyer. "She's already gone to her quarters, Burke. What in the world are you shouting for?"

He spun around and Savannah's breath caught. *Handsome* hardly did him justice. *Devastating* came close, but even that seemed too tame for how powerfully magnificent he looked. He was sleek, sophisticated. He wore formal black tie as if he were born to it. His jacket was basic elegance, no satin or velvet trim. Onyx studs closed his tiny-pleated shirt.

Leaving the rail, he flicked a finger at the short dangling tails of his tie, a gesture of frustration. "I can't do these damn things so they don't fall apart in ten minutes. Fitzhugh's tossed out my clip-on bow tie. Again. *She* doesn't approve. I'd snuck a few back from France, and the old biddy must have thrown them out when she unpacked my bags."

"Good for her." Chuckling, Savannah left her bedroom. "A grown man shouldn't wear a clip-on tie. Would you like me to do it for you?"

Burke watched her move into the upper hall, which was lit only by overflow from the chandelier hanging deep in the stairwell. With the lights from her bedroom glowing behind her, she was a vision in white lawn and lace. A Victorian virgin in yards of skirt ending a few inches short of her ankles. A sultry Southern belle in a snug corset-styled chemise with impudently narrow shoulder straps and tiny pearl buttons down the front. Her raven hair was piled casually on top of her head. Soft, undisciplined wisps framed her face, and stray tendrils trailed at the nape of her neck. Burke thought she looked as Scarlett O'Hara might have, caught in her petticoats, fresh from her bed and a quick tumble.

"Hold this for me." She handed him a flower and a hairpin, then began with his tie.

Her scent enveloped him. Jasmine, tinged with gardenia. She fashioned a new knot, her tongue darting out to dampen her top lip. Burke made a sound in his throat that was half sigh, half groan. She stilled, and he watched her thick, dark lashes slowly sweep up as her gaze rose from the tie at his throat to linger at his mouth before meeting his eyes. Transfixed by her gray irises deepening to smoke, Burke cradled her cheek, the gardenia petals caressing her skin.

Savannah's heart thudded in her breast. Her pulse raced. His warm breath fanned over her lips, searing the faint sheen of moisture she'd placed there. Her fingers fumbled, and the half-completed bow fell apart.

"Be still," she murmured huskily. "I'll never get this right if you keep moving."

"I didn't move." Captivated, Burke drew the flower down the side of her face, skimmed it along her jaw. "I swear to God, I'm not even breathing."

But he was, unsteadily. His quick, shallow gasps were a taste on her tongue, an intoxicant that made her feel warm and light-headed. She shivered, then frowned in concentration while her trembling hands worked at his tie.

"Where did you want the flower?" he asked.

With a smile, she glanced up. "In my hair."

"Anywhere in particular?"

"No. Wherever you think it looks best." Intimacy. Savannah felt the velvet cloak of intimacy wrap around them. She standing there fixing his tie, Burke pinning a flower in her hair, as if they were a couple who performed personal favors for each other every day...as if they were a couple.

In no hurry, Burke tried the gardenia at the top of her head, then moved it to just behind her ear. Finally, he nestled it high and to one side in the raven cloud so that the waxy white petals barely brushed her temple. "You're beautiful."

Savannah closed her eyes to better savor those words, more contented than she believed possible. If he thought her beautiful, then she was. When had she come to trust him so much? When had her natural inclination to doubt vanished? "Thank you." Pinching the bow's loops between her thumbs and forefingers, she tugged to tighten the knot. "There. That should do nicely."

"So will this." Dragging her closer, Burke took her mouth. She didn't hesitate but surged with him, toward him. If she'd struggled, he would have fought to conquer; but she surrendered willingly. He'd planned to stroke if she stiffened, but she melted. He stroked anyway. *His. But not his... yet.*

Senses swimming, Savannah clasped him to her. Beneath her hands and the rich fabric of his jacket he was lean and hard. Bunched muscles, firm flesh. But his mouth—she could linger forever rediscovering the exquisite softness of his mouth. Music began, sweetly singing strings rendering a melody meant to accompany the joining of lovers. Savannah smelled the gardenia in her hair and the musky scent of Burke's skin. She felt the radiant heat of his body and the subtly arousing friction of his tux on her bare skin. Her mind emptied of thought to make room for more and more sensations. Pleasure was lazy and thick as it moved through her, like honey. Desire sped, like brandy in the blood.

Fingers spread, Burke ran a hand down her back, luxuriating in the warm-water silkiness of her skin. More—he wanted, *needed* more of her. With a murmur to his moan, Savannah shifted in his arms. Creating a space between them, she made a woman's request for the caress of a man's hand. His palm curved to her breast, taut and throbbing with the urgent pounding of her heart. With his thumb he skimmed the plump flesh just above her bodice, her skin smooth and heated. Did she realize he loved her? Couldn't she feel it? Sense it? Releasing her mouth warred with his every instinct, demanded his total effort.

When the kiss ended, Savannah rested her head on his shoulder. For a moment she had been mindless, her grip on sanity lost. For a moment she had been ablaze, her contact with reality seared to ash. Whirl and burn. Violent storms and hot sun. She was a woman who'd always craved both. In the midst of that moment she'd realized— no, she'd *decided*—that Burke was a man she wouldn't walk away from. Her decision. This was what she had been waiting for, what she had needed. Not to be coerced, cajoled or overcome, but to choose, fervently, eagerly, freely.

Burke held her until she lifted her head from his shoulder and took a step back. One look in her eyes and he nearly hauled her across the hall and through her open bedroom door. She wouldn't have stopped him, he knew. There'd be no walls to break down, no resistance to overcome. For the first time he saw more than passion in her eyes; he saw desire.

"Burke?" Christina called up from the foot of the stairs. Burke answered his mother without taking his eyes from Savannah's. "You are the guest of honor, dear. You should be down here to greet people as they arrive."

Savannah's hand was taken. "Ready?" he asked.

*Never more so.* This was the man, she remembered, who'd once said, "You already satisfy me." Her knees no longer quaked. Her nerves had steadied. If there was still a trace of anxiety humming in her blood, that was good. Complacency on an unfamiliar road was foolish, dangerous. But she was ready to risk the journey.

Canvassing the foyer as she descended the stairs, Savannah was relieved to see only musicians. First arrivals had already been ushered to the living room, where portable bars serviced from every corner, and waiters roved with trays of hors d'oeuvres. The doorbell chimed as Savannah and Burke stepped off the bottom step. A formally attired Frank Weatherby admitted a swarm of new guests. An arm was draped over Burke's shoulder. Hand clasped, he was drawn into the midst of them. Savannah stepped back and nearly onto Claude's toes.

"My nose tells me food is close at hand," she whispered. "Suppose you could lead the way?"

Allowing her arm to be looped through Claude's, Savannah moved off. She couldn't have arranged it better if she'd choreographed it herself. She'd pique enough interest simply by being an unknown. Why add speculation to curiosity by making an entrance on Burke's arm? She appreciated this chance to ease into the evening. More, she needed a few moments to accustom herself to the knowledge that she would soon, very, very soon, take Burke as her lover.

"What's your pleasure?" Claude asked as he swept her toward a living-room corner.

Along the way Savannah helped herself to finger-size delicacies: chilled shrimp from one passing tray, marinated mushrooms from another. At the bar she glanced at the white-jacketed tender. "How's the house wine in this joint?"

Mouth twitching to smile, the barman tipped his head. "Superb, ma'am."

"How's the house wine, she asks," Claude muttered beside her.

Savannah grinned. "Something white, please."

Wineglass in hand, she turned to study the rapidly multiplying throng. A voluptuous young woman with the innate style to pull off both flash and sophistication dazzled a trio of avidly hopeful suitors. In direct contrast, a fresh-faced ingenue clung to the arm of her strikingly debonair escort, her eyes adoring the man who looked far too confident and experienced for one so artless. Does he know, Savannah wondered, that his date is impossibly in love with him? Four distinguished-looking men formed a huddle beside the French doors opening onto the gardens. The boyish gleams in their eyes and their frequent bursts of laughter suggested the swapping of slightly risqué, off-color jokes.

Exclusivity. It drifted in the air, as tangible as the perfume wafting from the flowers nestled in chandeliers and spilling from mantels. Excellence. As guests spilled from the cavernous living room into the quaint parlors off the gallery hall, the air thickened with the richer aromas of tobacco smoke and feminine fragrances. Exhilaration. The tinkling of crystal and laughter skipped across the muted din of voices as rooms turned into seas of flowing silks and shimmering satins.

Catching bits of conversation as she was led about and introduced in turn by Claude and Christina, Savannah decided everyone who was anyone in the region was here. Nearly every established wine house was represented, as well as the fashionable crowd from San Francisco's Nob Hill.

Sipping her wine, she smiled and nodded through yet another set of introductions. Joel and Marjorie Kent, both fair and fortyish, both a bit pompous. Joel showed Savannah the negligent party interest one extends to a stranger one doesn't anticipate meeting twice in the same lifetime. Marjorie was more effusive, working too hard at making Savannah feel welcome. That neither spurred her to bolt for the door boosted Savannah's confidence and drained the last bit of tension from her shoulders.

"A houseguest," Marjorie remarked, surprise evident in her voice. "How long have you known Christina and Julienne?"

Savannah had yet to get used to the fact that almost everyone called Claude by his last name. "About a year."

"Savannah was with us during the flood last winter," Claude interjected. "Single-handedly saved a few acres for us."

"Tragedy, that," Joel said. "Come through as well as you'd expected, Julienne?"

As Claude and Joel launched a discussion on disasters and recoveries, Savannah figured a backward step and a smooth about-face would allow her a discreet getaway. She'd noticed a platter of steaming quiche being set out on the buffet.

"Have you only just arrived?" Marjorie asked as Savannah shifted to take the first retreating step.

"No, I've been here over a week now." Savannah resettled her weight.

"My, you've planned quite a long visit."

"Actually, I hadn't planned any visit." Savannah smiled coolly. They might as well know straight off, she decided. She preferred they hear it from her, anyway. "My truck broke down last week when I delivered Claude's chemicals. It's undergoing repairs, and I'm stranded until it's fixed."

"Your truck?"

"Mmm. Differential gave out, and there's a delay getting a new ring and pinion gears."

Marjorie was still frowning her confusion when Joel choked on a swallow of his drink and began coughing. Without missing a beat, Savannah clapped him soundly on the back between his shoulder blades. "One of your ice cubes get away from you, Joel?"

"Oh, my," Marjorie breathed. "She's a truck driver...Joel, she's a truck driver. Why, Julienne, she's delightful."

Delightful? Behind her smile, Savannah gritted her teeth.

"And a fantastic hauler," Claude added, singing Savannah's praises and recommending her to Joel. Not once did he say she was in any way unsuitable. "If you ever decide to switch firms, Joel, give Neil Jones a call. I'll give his number to your secretary Monday. Ask for Savannah by name. You won't get better service."

When the Kents moved on Claude chuckled quietly. "You ignore Marjorie, Savannah. The rest of us do."

"Claude, have you been asking specifically for me all these months?" Wonder and gratitude roughened her voice.

"Have you ever known me to leave things to chance? The fate of my wines to just anybody?"

"I had no idea. Neil never told me."

Taking her hand, Claude walked her out to the gallery, which was beginning to run over with people. "You're a good little trucker, Savannah. I wouldn't have continued using you if you weren't."

Savannah rolled her eyes at him. "'A good little trucker?'"

"Mmm, and it will be a happy day when you're somebody's good little housewife."

Laughter sparkled in his eyes as Savannah narrowed her own. "Now, Claude, you haven't gone and cuffed a few eligibles to the living-room chairs, have you?"

"I might have," he returned. "If I didn't think Burke would break me in two for it."

The stem of Savannah's wineglass nearly broke when her fingers tightened on the fragile rod. Before she could formulate a response Christina glided up and carried her off to meet the next wave of arrivals.

*Does she see the way they watch her?* Arm stretched along a bar, Burke gazed through the crush at Savannah. Ed Zimmer had her trapped and seemingly engrossed. She looked so solemn that Burke figured it must be the tale of how Ed's platoon had drifted on rafts for five days on the Atlantic before being rescued. It was Savannah, Burke thought, who would shortly need rescuing. He would go for her soon, he decided. Dance with her. Hold her here in his home, among his family and friends. Move with her, melt to her.

But for now, he was enjoying watching her.

*She startles them, charms them, then leaves them astounded.* Burke remembered it well. Surrounded by satins and silks and sleek tuxedoes, she seduced with ruffles and white lace. With only a gardenia for adornment she made every woman who sparkled with diamonds and glimmered with gold look garish by comparison. Though she had the skin for precious gems, Burke decided. Sapphires. She was a woman meant to wear the frozen blue flames of sapphires.

"Is she the reason you haven't returned my calls?"

Shifting a quarter-turn, Burke smiled at Elaine Howser. "Good to see you, Elaine. Sorry about the calls. Catching up has been hell."

"Mm-hmm. So I should try again next week?" She raised a delicate blond brow. They had, Burke recalled, left the door open on a friendly flirtation when he'd left last year. There might have been an affair at the time if Elaine's divorce had been finalized. But it hadn't yet, and married women—even those married only by technicality—were against Burke's rules, particularly when their husbands were old college roommates.

"I believe next week is full."

Elaine's smile was easy, part good sport, part old friend. "Well, I can't say I blame you, Burke. She's luscious. She's got men regretting their wedding rings and women regretting they didn't think to dress like naughty brides."

Burke glanced again at Savannah. She'd divested herself of Zimmer and was caught between a cherrywood highboy and Mattie Harrison, grand dame of the party circuit. A naughty bride. Yes, Burke thought, she looked like innocence begging to be initiated. Savannah looked up then. The edges of the room slipped away, and Burke was aware only of the dark-smoke shade of her eyes.

"Oh, you've got it bad, my friend," Elaine went on, accepting a freshened drink from the bartender. "Stephen used to look at me like that. Made me feel like a melting mound of whipped cream set before a sugar-crazed diabetic." She gave a small, inelegant snort. "Then we got married."

"How is Stephen?" Burke asked, having caught little more of Elaine's words than that name.

Elaine laughed. "About as dumb-eyed stupid over some cute little brunette as you are over that truck driver."

At that Burke's eyes narrowed, sharpened.

"Oh, everyone knows. Gobbled it up over the caviar—with much more relish, I might add." Elaine shook her head. "It only adds to her mystique, you know. What's a diploma from Vassar against that? Darling, if I were you, I'd fetch her before Mattie confides more escapades of your lusty youth than you can talk yourself out of."

"No one throws a party like Christina," Savannah was informed by Mattie Harrison. The middle-aged woman was portly and powdered and stuffed into kelly-green taffeta. Olive-sized emeralds bobbed at her ears. Her hair was a most amazing shade of flaming orange. "Flowers flown in from the islands. Always the newest five-star caterer on the scene. And *always* something wickedly hush-hush in the air. This time a feud with Pisarro's. Luigi's at one end of the house when Julienne's at the other."

Savannah hadn't a clue what the woman was referring to, but she was fascinated nonetheless with the way the avaricious blue eyes ceaselessly scanned the room for interesting indiscretions while ruby lips spilled an unbroken stream of gossip.

"Rumor has it Luigi wouldn't be here if there'd been a graceful way to uninvite him. Knowing that, well, Luigi *had* to come. Oh, the Platts are here. And Susan's finally had her baby. It's because of Burke, you know."

Savannah blinked. "That Susan Platt's had her baby?"

"No, goodness no! That Luigi and Julienne aren't speaking. Something about Burke and Champagne. Speak of the devil...hello, Burke." Mattie offered a rouged cheek for Burke's kiss. "Welcome back, dear boy. I've been having a nice chat with your new young lady." Leaning closer, she dropped her voice to a conspiratorial murmur. "Never did think Elaine was for you." Straightening, she paused to nibble on a paté-spread cracker. "Very sweet girl."

"Elaine?" Burke questioned dryly.

Mattie sniffed. "Savannah. Elaine couldn't claim sweet on her sixteenth birthday...not that she'd wanted to. However, I approve."

"Of Savannah," Burke concluded. "Then you won't mind if I steal her away for a dance."

"Not at all." Mattie rolled her eyes as if it were they who were lingering and she being kept. Beringed hands flashing, she shooed them off. "Go, have a time of it."

Taken into Burke's arms, Savannah let him lead her in a waltz, relaxing against him instead of planning when to run and wishing she didn't have to. Yielding, she discovered, could bring immense pleasure when it was to the right man. Torture when it was in a public place. "Have you enjoyed catching up with old friends?" she asked, needing to redirect her thoughts.

"Mmm." Holding her, moving with her only whetted the longing Burke had thought to satisfy. "And I wish they'd go home now. I was otherwise engaged before they barged in, and having a much better time."

I know nothing of his friends, Savannah realized. Or of his life, really. She'd shared more of her past with him than she had with any other living soul, yet she knew virtually nothing of who he was, other than a vintner. "Who's Elaine?" She tipped her head back, her eyes serious with the question.

Burke's gaze narrowed suspiciously. "Why? What did Mattie say about me and Elaine?"

"Nothing." Suddenly the haughty ice queen, Savannah arched a delicate eyebrow. "What *might* she have said?"

"Nothing," he muttered, then pressed his cheek to her temple. Damned if he didn't feel as guilty as an unfaithful husband. "I've known Elaine since high school. We're good friends—" who flirted with having an affair "—but that's all. I introduced her to my college roommate one summer, and they married before the next term began. Just before I left for France they started divorce proceedings. I took Elaine out to dinner once or twice last year, and Mattie jumped to a wrong conclusion."

"Mmm. She seems to do that a lot. Apparently she's started a few rumors about us tonight."

"No, I started those," Burke murmured against her ear. "Though I trusted Mattie to spread them."

Resting her head on his shoulder, Savannah realized she didn't care what others might think because of what they heard or saw tonight. She knew what was in Burke's mind as well as in her own. No one else mattered.

They danced often throughout the evening. Once without exchanging a word, without finding any necessary. Once on the terrace, alone in the moonlight. Savannah invited the magic. She could have a bit of the fairy tale so long as she remembered it was only make-believe. So long as she remembered there were no happily-ever-after endings. This man was hers to take—for a night or a few days. No one was going to deprive her, she vowed, least of all herself.

* * *

The distant thud of the front door shutting behind the last straggler rebounded in the lofty stone foyer, echoed in Savannah's bedroom. From her window she watched a pair of taillights disappear down the drive. Palms pressed to the sill, she drank in the rose-scented night. The sky was a rare deep purple, graced with a crescent moon and a faint dusting of stars. The air was still, a warm caress. She heard the door at her back open and then close again gently.

"Savannah." Her name was a steamy, sultry night on his lips. He spoke it like a man so steeped in the heat that he'd been rendered incapable of seeking the relief of anything cooler.

She stayed as she was for several heartbeats. Like her first taste of freedom, this was a moment to cherish, to prolong and memorize. Her turn to savor before his to consume. Then, ready to begin the journey, she turned away from the window and toward Burke.

Neither of them spoke immediately. She looked at the wine bottle and two glasses he held in one hand, and smiled. He looked at the lit candles on the mantel, and smiled. She'd known Burke would come to her tonight. He hadn't asked if he could; she hadn't asked if he would. The words hadn't been necessary. All through the long evening, every brush of thighs while dancing, every clash of eyes across crowded rooms, had conveyed the promise that what had begun that first day at dawn would be brought to its inevitable conclusion this day at midnight.

Resistance had crumbled.

Patience had run out.

Burke sought her eyes across the room. Thin moonlight flowed through the windows, shifting with the interruption of shadows. Melting candle wax scented the air. Wavering flames played on her skin. "Waiting for me, Savannah?"

Still smiling, she took her first steps to him. She brought no past with her. There was no future to hold her back.

There was only now, this night, this man. "Wishing. I was wishing for you."

He held out a hand, looking as sleek and sophisticated as he had at seven o'clock that evening. His tie was still neatly knotted, although more than half the male guests had left the party with their collars already opened. Foolish of her to think of that at a time like this. Perhaps not so foolish. It seemed right somehow that Savannah would be the one to pull his tie apart, unleash the power instead of cede to it.

In the center of the room their fingertips met, curling together. Their lips joined without the rest of their bodies touching. Mouths briefly, barely pressed together.

He's so gentle, Savannah thought.

She's so fragile, Burke marveled.

Gray eyes lifted to him, open and wanting. Burke trailed the fingers of one hand down the side of her face, her throat and over her shoulder. Satin had never felt smoother, no woman sweeter. Circling her wrist, he brought her palm to his mouth and watched her jolt as he placed the kiss. She melted and whimpered.

Taking his face between her hands, Savannah gazed into his eyes. Those depthless black eyes that saw her better than she saw herself. "You'll be my first," she murmured.

Though he'd already been sure, her admission made him tremble. Innocence. A gift. A trust. Breakable, he thought and hoped he wouldn't forget before the night was over. Burke had never been a woman's first; he knew now he'd never wanted to matter that much to another life. Until tonight. Until Savannah. "You'll be my last," he vowed.

Savannah brushed the words away in her mind. Her life was full of sincere but broken promises, of best but unfulfilled intentions. *We'll be each other's for a while.* Knowing that, she wouldn't be hurt later. Knowing that, she would take what he offered her and be greedy about it. She would place no expectations on it or him.

"Is the wine for us?" she whispered huskily.

"Us," Burke repeated, discovering with the utterance of that simple two-letter word that he wanted every commitment it could be stretched around. Marriage. Stunned, he ran the thought through his mind again.

Savannah wanted no more wine to cloud her head or dim her senses. She wanted every nerve and cell in her body to be alive. "Could we save it for later?"

"All right." Burke crossed the room to the rosewood desk. He could have set the bottle and glasses down on the low coffee table less than a foot from where they'd stood, but he needed a moment to deal with the fear, the panic stirred by this new discovery.

She'll never go for it, he realized. Savannah would never willingly enter another institution. And marriage was the most socially respected, unquestionably conventional institution of them all. But then, Claude was never going to allow Juliennes to make Champagne, Burke remembered. Yet, in less than a week, the Chardonnays would be in the ground. So it would be with Savannah. Constructing the future was what Burke did best, and changing minds when it was necessary.

Savannah felt a shift in the air, in the balance and strength of emotions. Studying Burke for a clue to what had changed, she was stunned and touched to see that his hand trembled on the fluted crystal. Raising her eyes to his profile, she watched an unexpected tenderness soften his features. He wanted to be tender, she realized, because of her inexperience. An aching gratitude gripped her heart, but so did a twinge of regret.

As Burke turned he heard a faint rustle and soft thump. When he gazed at Savannah she stood half-naked and proudly quivering, her skirt a rumpled mound of white froth at her feet. The sharp spear of desire snatched his breath; it returned rasping a French profanity that managed to sound like worshipful poetry. Her slender legs seemed to reach clear to her waist, the high cut of her lace panties baring her hips. Naughty bride, Burke mused. Innocence begging. The glimpse of high, strappy heels when she stepped over her discarded skirt hinted of the decadent.

"You're not planning a tender seduction, are you, Burke?" If she'd been unsure of herself, the curve of his mouth into a sexy smile relieved her. "Did you think I'd need a soft hand and sweet kisses because I'm inexperienced?" She tugged at his tie, and it unraveled. Then she opened the button at his throat. Dragging her palms over him, she shoved his jacket from his shoulders. "Know me, Burke. Make love to the woman I am. I've never been one to float if I can fly. I'd rather sprint till I drop than linger along the way." When his arms were free again, she worked the onyx studs from his shirt, letting them fall to the floor. "I've always preferred the sky-wrenching storm to the soft summer shower."

Catching her at the waist, Burke bent her hips so they pressed hard against his. "You'll have your storm, Savannah." Because he was within an inch of taking her to the ground for a frenzied release, Burke forced himself to do something infinitely careful. He pulled a pin from her hair, and then another. "But first you'll have your summer shower. There's something to be said for quick, desperate passion, but I knew the first night I kissed you that you were a woman I would linger over."

Her hair was beginning to fall, one curl tumbling at a time; Savannah felt it whispering down onto her shoulders as Burke dropped hairpins to scatter among studs and cufflinks on the carpet. Lips pressed to his chest, she made sounds she thought resembled the words in her head.

Savannah's mindless mutterings sharpened the edge of Burke's needs. Lifting the hair he'd let loose, he placed his lips to the sensitive skin of her neck just below her ear. Jasmine. Whenever he thought of her, he would remember she was a cloud of jasmine faintly tinged with gardenia. Tasting her, he fed a hunger new and gnawing.

His mouth moved on her skin. He nipped softly at her shoulder. Savannah's own lips sped over his chest where she'd shoved open his shirt. His skin tasted of salt and sun,

although she couldn't think when he'd been near either.
His scent was earthy, rich and dark, something to drink in
with her eyes closed. Reaching around him, she freed the
clip at the back of his cummerbund.

With her hands racing frantically over him, Burke
crushed her closer. He tunneled into her hair with both
hands, bringing her head back. Her eyes were open, her
lips parted. He covered her mouth, not so tender, not so
soft. Pulling away, he turned her head to taste her mouth
from another angle. Savannah shuddered and bent forward, hip to hip with him. Her arms reached up his back.
Her fingers curled, and she filled her fists with his shirt,
clinging to him as his teeth pressed and his tongue plundered. She was spinning away into a world faster and more
thrilling than any she'd traveled. No one, nothing, had
ever brought her to this. Almost from the first day, she'd
known Burke could.

Her moan yanked Burke from the edge of devouring
her. She was shuddering when he had yet to feel her shiver.
She was groaning when he wanted to hear her gasp.

Confusion swam in Savannah's brain when Burke
stepped away from her. She felt empty, robbed of something vital. She felt cold, her heated flesh insulted by the
cooler air of evening. And then she was lifted into his
arms—a romantic, she remembered—and carried to the
bed Fitzhugh had turned down earlier in the evening.

Had she ever wanted anyone, anything, as much as she
wanted him at this moment? He hovered above her, his
eyes taking her in. Had she ever felt more desirable? More
worthy?

Had he ever wanted anyone, anything, as much as he
wanted her at this moment? Her hair spilled luxuriously
over the pillow. Her breasts heaved beneath snug lace. So
many buttons. Such tiny buttons. Impatient to release her
passion, Burke didn't wait to fumble through opening all
of them. As inch by inch the lace loosened between her
breasts, his mouth sought her.

Savannah floated without knowing she could soar. She burned without knowing she could flame. "Love me," she cried in a desperate, wrenching whisper.

"I do." With his teeth, Burke tugged one narrow strap from her shoulder. He dragged his tongue over her skin, his face nudging aside lace. *I do.*

But it wasn't enough. Something too wide and empty in Savannah ached to be filled. "*Make* love to me."

He brought his head up and gazed into the swirling depths of her eyes. "I am, sweetheart." Then his lips sought her nipple and brushed softly over the hot, erect bead. "Oh, God, baby, I am."

Savannah gasped with surprise and wonder. Pleasure was a jolt, then a spreading heat. She hadn't known it existed. His tongue flicked at her nipple as his fingers worked magic on her other breast. Half-crazy with need, Savannah ran her hands over his shoulders, through his hair. "Now," she pleaded.

"Soon." He would give her more than writhing and release, Burke promised himself. She was someone starving, begging for a drop of sustenance when a feast awaited her. And in satisfying her hunger, he would have all of her. Every breath from her mouth would flow into his body. Every throb of her pulse would hammer at his flesh. Every inch of her skin would be a taste on his tongue.

Through the rush of blood in her ears, Savannah heard Burke moan. Not a groan of desperation but an admission of need. Drawing her nipple into his mouth, he suckled her. Tender, for her sake; insistent for his. No one had ever found fulfillment in Savannah. Whatever they had needed, she'd fallen short of providing. But he needed and was satisfied just in the taste of her.

His mouth explored and spread heat; his fingers journeyed and removed clothes. Tugging the swatch of lace from her hips, he drew back and looked at her. If, for only a moment, her instinct had been to shrink away, the adoration in his eyes made Savannah relax and stretch.

Sprawled naked beneath him, she saw he was still dressed. His shirt hung open, and she reached to touch the tensed, dark flesh. But he caught her wrist before her fingertips met skin and moved her arm onto the pillow over her head.

"Lie still." He moved down her body, lips and fingers whispering over her. At her feet he began the journey back up. He raked his teeth over the arch of her foot. "There's so much more to give you." His mouth opened on the inside of her knee. "Be greedy, Savannah." The light rasp of his beard on her thigh made her gasp, shiver. "Good," he murmured.

And then she was mindless as his fingers found her, opened her, as his mouth took her. She reached out, grasping blindly. As if he'd known she would, he caught her hands and pinned them to the mattress. His lips nuzzled; his tongue plunged. The first wave of pleasure swelled. The next lifted Savannah higher. And then she was swept away.

Her body was lax, her skin moist. By inches, Burke eased away from her until he stood at the side of the bed removing his clothes, dizzy with the scent of her that clung to him.

Through a luxuriant fog, Savannah watched him undress. *I wanted to do that.* But she couldn't move, could only watch. Magnificent, she thought. He's magnificent. Powerful. Naked, he should have seemed vulnerable. But his lean, bunched strength had never been more evident.

With both hands she reached for him. With open arms she gathered him close. He tangled his hands in her hair as she ran hers over his body. He plundered her mouth as he prepared to take and make her his. This, he vowed with his last lucid thought, this she will never forget. This will be impossible for her to one day tuck away in her safe little box of memories. This, she will never walk away from.

Whole. It came to Savannah in one blinding revelation as Burke entered her. There was a quick wrench, an insignificant price.

And then they were lost, but lost together.

## Chapter Nine

For a time that had no measure—minutes? hours?—they lay just that way, his body covering hers, both of them spent but for the urgency to breathe. Burke held her, and she him, both of them still but for tiny pulsing tremors.

When Savannah opened her eyes, the candlelit room seemed as mist-clouded as her mind. Gradually vision and wit returned. Who would have thought abandon could be so reckless, pleasure so complete? She'd imagined that passion at its fullest force would have a volcanic power. But she'd never guessed how raw and primitive the need could be, or that need alone made demands to give and take more than the physical.

Her arms fell heavily away as Burke eased his weight from her. Without a word, he rolled onto his side and gathered her close.

Again they drifted in a timeless space. With her back curved to his chest Savannah felt inexplicably sated by the total drain of mind and body. She felt, too, an exhilaration of spirit even as she languorously floated in the co-

coon of Burke's warmth. She was just deciding she could stay this way forever when he carefully eased his arm from under her head. She fought the urge to pull him back, her fingers digging into her pillow as he slid away from her and out of bed. Biting down on her bottom lip, she prevented the whispered plea for him to stay.

Rounding the bed, Burke strolled into her line of vision. Gloriously naked, he approached the rosewood desk. It wasn't until Savannah saw him uncork the wine that she realized he wasn't leaving. Through the fan of her lashes, she gazed at his lean, powerful body. She had touched him, tasted him, in one mindless throe raked her nails over him, but she hadn't really had a chance to look long and hard at him. Candlelight flickered over his bronzed flesh, and she thought him magnificent: the strongly sculpted shoulders, the trim torso and flat belly, the unexpectedly stunning beauty of male skin tautly stretched over long hip bones.

Mental images of their lovemaking flashed through her mind. Second thoughts and misgivings raced after them. Dear God, there were no depths to her Burke hadn't delved into and savaged, no secret shadows he hadn't churned up. Savannah remembered that she'd wanted him to, pleaded with him, driven him to take... and then take more. And she had given... given until she was empty and then strangely made whole by him.

Regret. It descended on her with an avalanche of other emotions: joy, longing, vulnerability, fear.

Burke returned with two brimming glasses. With tears threatening, Savannah untangled the sheet and piled pillows against the headboard. She hadn't counted on emotions. They'd always been hers to control. She'd thought she could give herself up to passion without losing possession of her heart in the bargain. It's going to hurt, she realized. When he was no longer in her life, the ache of need was going to be a throb of agony.

"Savannah?" Burke murmured as she accepted a glass with a trembling hand. Had he seen something in her eyes? The fear? The regret?

Determined to force her feelings down, she smiled. "To a coming home," she toasted as their glasses clinked together.

"To home," Burke said. They sipped, their eyes meeting over crystal rims. Home, Burke thought. Being with Savannah had felt precisely like finding home. He touched his lips to her shoulder, marveling anew at the rich texture. "You have incredible skin. Smooth, warm and so, so soft. I could spend hours just touching."

"I think you did," she said, striving to strike a note of casual amusement.

Burke's smile slipped as a frown knit his brow. "Are you sore, Savannah? Did I hurt you?"

His concern for her filled her with an aching tenderness. "No, I'm fine." She laughed softly as he tucked her under his arm. "I'm better than fine." Propped on pillows beside him, she rested her head on his shoulder. His hand was spread low on her hip, his thumb making slow, arousing circles. "Is it always like that?"

No, Burke thought, it had never been like that. "It can be, when the right man makes love with the right woman."

Savannah felt his heartbeat, just there beneath her right shoulder blade. She felt his warm, moist breath sifting over her face. Much as she wanted to twine her fingers in his hair, she kept them wrapped around her glass. She wouldn't cling to him, she vowed. She wouldn't attach herself and have to be pried away. But, oh, God, it was going to be so hard not to hold on. Harder yet to walk away.

"What?" Burke asked of her long, shuddering sigh. Her hair was soft and fragrant under his chin, soothing to his skin. He'd never lost himself so completely in a woman or found so much sweetness in intimacy. "Why the sigh?"

She hated the lie even as she formulated it. But it was for both their sakes. He didn't know how pitifully desperate she could be when she couldn't let go. He didn't know that she could claw and cry and beg for more chances.

"You'll have to leave soon." Against her back his chest muscles tensed, and she knew he was prepared to argue. "You're not going to sleep with me, Burke. Fitzhugh can't find that your bed hasn't been slept in."

"Is that so?" He set his glass on the bedside table. Rolling toward her, he took her glass and set that one on the floor. "Do you think Fitzhugh has never found my bed empty in the morning?" Wrapping long-boned fingers around her trim calf, he pulled her from the mound of pillows so that he had her lying flat beneath him. "Do you think she gives a damn where I sleep? Or that she'd dare ask me with whom?"

"She wouldn't have to ask," Savannah pointed out dryly. She wanted to resist him, but his hands were clever and knew her too well. Her skin, still tender and sensitive, thrilled to the friction of his legs moving down her. With featherlight forays he began rediscovering all the places that had made her tremble. "This bed looks as if a pair of wrestlers used it for a championship bout."

Taking his mouth from her shoulder, Burke gave negligent attention to the bed and its surroundings. Two of her four pillows were on the floor. Only a corner of the satin quilt clung tenaciously to the edge of the mattress. The sheet had been loosened all around, becoming only a twisted strip of linen barely covering his hips.

"Considering the work we've given her with this bed, it seems highly inconsiderate of us to give her another." He nibbled at her mouth as he trailed a finger down her side, skimming the slender ribs, delicate hips and long length of leg. He hadn't had enough of her. He thought he might never have enough of her.

With her blood beginning to run hot, her mind beginning to spin, Savannah pushed in vain at his chest. "You won't sleep here, Burke," she insisted. She might never recover what she'd lost to him an hour ago, but she could keep and protect whatever was left. She wouldn't sleep with him, she vowed. She wouldn't risk being in that vulnerable, unguarded state with him, when she might curl herself around him and cling.

Frustration coiled in Burke's stomach where fresh desire had sprung. The combination threatened patience and temper. He realized that with her penchant for secrets and privacy she'd find it difficult to face others, even closemouthed Fitzhugh, with a knowledge she wasn't ready to face herself. But whether or not Savannah could admit it, she'd opened more than her body to him—she'd opened her heart, and he had firmly, irrevocably planted himself inside.

Even so, Burke felt her recede. The urge to grab her back was intense, the sting of hurt acute and unexpected. To assuage it, he instinctively sought comfort where he knew he would find it at its sweetest. "We've hours till dawn," he murmured, his lips skimming down to her breast. "Three or four, at least."

If he'd used his advantage of physical prowess to overcome her, Savannah would have fought him. Instead he overpowered her by needily nuzzling at her breast. Sinking quickly, she curved a hand to the back of his neck as he suckled. A little while longer, she thought. But then he would have to go.

And a little while after that, so would she.

In an uncommon state of frustration and indecision, Burke flipped his lighter over and over on his desk. The steady tapping sound in the otherwise quiet office didn't help his edginess. Yet he seemed compelled to keep up the irritating habit.

Whatever course Burke had thought an affair with Savannah might take, the path they'd started down two days ago hadn't even been in the running. Once they'd become lovers, he'd assumed things would be different between them. *They* would be different. And so they were, he thought wryly, though not in ways that held out much hope. But he and Savannah were different, all right. He was sinking deeper and deeper into love, while she was constantly clawing her away out of it.

What now? Burke took out a cigarette and put the lighter to use, then went back to making it cartwheel between his thumb and fingertip. He needed a plan...he'd settle for half an idea. If he'd thought she'd find it impossible to walk away from a night of mindless passion, it was only because he'd forgotten that nothing was impossible for Savannah. She'd lost her virginity at midnight and been cool and composed at breakfast.

Savannah, polite! Burke hadn't thought it possible. If there'd been walls to smash down, ice to melt... But how the hell did a man get past starch and etiquette? Hauling her over the top of the table and into his lap had occurred to him. Instead he'd taken what satisfaction he could in watching her nibble delicate bites of sausage when he knew she was dying to dig into her meal with relish.

On a growl, Burke tossed the gold lighter down and rose to pace the ice-blue carpet. It wasn't like him to move without a destination. Unproductive motion was wasted energy. Proved, he told himself now, by the fact that he'd paced his office on the average of twice an hour for the last four and had yet to produce a solution. Dammit! What good was pacing if you couldn't hear your feet count the yards? Was this how Savannah felt? he wondered. Was this what it meant to churn and stew with pent-up emotions until you thought you'd go mad with them?

Mad. He was half-mad with loving her. Burke pushed open the sliding glass door, then shoved his hands into his pockets. Fresh air and the warbling of birds breezily swirled into his office. He'd gone to her bedroom last night deciding to propose marriage. She'd acted so damn strange all day, looking at him but looking right through him. Thinking she wanted time to herself in which to balance a lover with her life, he'd intended giving it to her. Until the fear that if he didn't possess her, commit her, he would wake to find her gone, had driven him out of his room and down the dark halls. Until the need to have her soft and warm against him had carried him through her door and to the side of her bed.

He hadn't expected to find her asleep. Next to her cheek, her hand had been curled into a loose fist. Vulnerable and fragile. Tenderness for her had overridden need as he'd leaned over her. Gently, so as not to startle her, he'd traced her exquisite features. On a sigh, she'd opened her eyes. Before he could say the words he'd planned, her arms were around him, and he was sliding under the quilt with her, bringing her to lazy arousal, watching her wake fully. She'd surfaced slowly, struggling through the honey-thick depths of sleep and desire. Layers peeling away, she'd gone from submission to passion to aggression. When it was over and both could move again, she'd once again insisted Burke return to his own room.

Confused and angry all over again, Burke dragged a hand through his hair. One look in her eyes, at the underlying fear, and he'd swallowed back the proposal. If he'd been convinced that telling her he loved her that night at the stables would have her packed and on the road by midnight, he'd been just as convinced last night that if he'd so much as hinted at marriage, she'd have skipped the packing altogether. He'd realized last night that, as much as he might bring her pleasure, he was also a threat. Someone she'd loved, Burke thought, or someone she'd thought loved her, had left a scar beneath which Savannah's heart lay.

With a vicious oath, he flicked his cigarette toward the gardens. How much more time did he have? A week, if Jackson got her truck parts quickly. Two at the most. Then again, she could hop on a plane today.

With one part of his mind he heard the click of the intercom and automatically started back to his desk.

"Yes, Cynthia."

"I've put your call through to Neil Jones. He's on line one."

Savannah's brother, he thought as he lifted the receiver and tapped into line one. Then he wondered if he hadn't manufactured a reason to call the man. "Neil, Burke Julienne here. Julienne Winery. You're accustomed to dealing with my father, Claude, as I've been out of the country the past year. He has only good words to say about your company."

"Compliments are always accepted." The voice, Burke thought, was that of a large man. Also a cautious one. "We've got you scheduled for a coast-to-coast next week. Is this a confirmation, or have you got something else?"

"Something else. And on short notice, I'm afraid. I have four thousand vine cuttings from France arriving at the San Francisco port early Thursday morning. I'll need them delivered to Napa."

"Special handling?"

"It's a short trip, so, no, nothing special. Closed box, but with enough ventilation to keep the heat down."

"I can probably set you up. I'd like to have a look at the scheduling before I commit. Can I get back to you . . . say in the next hour or so?"

"That'll be fine."

In the silence that followed Burke assumed they were both wondering how best to approach the obvious subject of his sister.

"How is Savannah?" Neil finally asked.

Burke heard concern in the other man's voice and felt an instant sympathy for him. "She's fine, Neil. Working some things out," he added. Another silence, not as much uncomfortable as noticeable. "She speaks of you—speaks well of you, I mean." Burke didn't usually grope clumsily for words, yet it happened with unsettling frequency with the Joneses. "I was with her after the two of you talked on the phone last week."

Burke heard the scrape of a match and Neil pulling deeply on a cigarette. "We don't argue often," he commented. "She tell you about it?"

"About the call and the things you'd said to her, yes. Only some of what might have led up to it. She felt bad. Has she called you back yet?"

"No, but she will in her own time. I don't know how well you've gotten to know my sister; it usually doesn't take people too long to figure out you can't expect her to go in the direction you point."

"That much, at least, I've learned about her. And that I'm in love with her." He hadn't planned to say it, though he couldn't regret having done so. Still, it had been so abruptly out of context that he didn't wonder at the soft male laughter he heard over the wires.

"I'd sort of guessed that," Neil Jones said. It surprised Burke initially. He'd never thought himself a particularly easy man to read. Then he remembered another phone call, one a few years back with a business associate. The conversation had drifted to Amy, and Burke had known immediately. There was a special pitch to a man's voice when he talked about the woman he loved, a unique way he had of saying her name.

"And Savannah?" Neil asked. "Is she in love with you?"

"If she is, she isn't saying. She keeps a lot to herself."

"Anything I can do to help?"

"I'll take your offer as a vote of confidence. I appreciate it." It was tempting, Burke thought. It would be simple to tell Neil what he knew of Savannah's past and ask him to fill in the holes. If it were facts Burke needed, he might have asked Neil for them. But it was Savannah's trust he wanted. "Whatever she's holding back, Neil, I think it ought to come from her."

"You'll give her my best?" Neil said in a quiet tone.

"Yes, I will."

"I'll get back to you shortly on the haul."

Savannah sat on the knoll where she'd napped after her first tour of the vineyards. It was one of those fresh, lovely days one came to expect hereabouts. There'd been ten of them in a row now, except for one afternoon shower. The uninterrupted string of cloudless blue skies and earth-scented breezes should have begun to bore her. One of the joys of her job was being able to start out in a snowstorm and park on a hot, dusty desert. In under thirty hours she could go from New York's brilliant autumn to Florida's swaying palm trees. Yet, to date, she hadn't craved snow or palm trees.

Drawing her knees to her chest, she gazed out over the Zinfandel fields, where only a skeleton crew of pickers remained. The Pinot Noirs had come ripe; the Cabernets would in the next day or two. Savannah had believed she'd stay in the fields and be a part of the process for as long as her stint at the winery lasted. But she'd been restless in the vineyard this morning, unable to drum up enthusiasm for picking grapes or chatting with the laborers. Its magic was gone. It had served its purpose and no longer beckoned.

What precisely had its purpose been? she asked herself as she lay back on the cool, prickly grass. To find a cherished past and make it real again? To find the joyful pleasure she'd remembered feeling as a child? Neither had been there for the finding. She felt like a small-town girl, burned-out by the big city, who'd returned to what she remembered as the gentle pace of home, only to discover that what she'd remembered as quaint might actually be backward. Viewed through the eyes of maturity and experience, what had seemed carefree had too many disturbing earmarks of neglect.

Shutting her eyes, she listened to the leaves rustle. Was this, then, what she'd been running from? The terrible possibility that at no time in her life had she been cared for? That she had never been truly, truly loved? Not even as a young child? Or was it the more disturbing probability that she *had* been loved but that it simply hadn't made any difference?

Love, she thought as her mind began to drift. You couldn't count on it. If you were smart, you didn't give in to it. But what did you do if you found yourself falling head over heels into it? And was she, Savannah wondered, falling into love?

Unconsciousness hovered at the edge of her brain, like a fog on the horizon about to roll out its blanket. She'd been deprived of too much sleep in the last forty-eight hours. Burke. Folding her arms behind her head, she frowned, remembering how easily, willingly she'd drawn him to her last night.

It had been much too pleasant to wake and find she was already pliant and throbbing. Much too natural to fold back the quilt and make room for him. It wasn't as if she were accustomed to opening her eyes to find a lean, hard body hovering over her in bed, or a wide palm softly abrading her breast. Yet she hadn't felt the least bit disoriented as she'd slowly awakened. She had lost her senses, her control and her freedom to passion. But she remembered also breathing easier in the aftermath, when she'd been able to recover each of them.

The joy... she hadn't expected to feel such joy when intimately joined to Burke. It was wonderful, glowing, addictive. Oh, God, *was* she falling in love?

Drowsiness thickened, and she gave in to it. Dreamless, she slept.

When she awoke it was to the tickle of a breeze playing over her face. Before opening her eyes, she stretched. *He's here.* With her arms flung over her head and the tips of her fingers reaching, she caught his scent and smiled. When she opened her eyes, she saw him crouched down beside her, wearing a three-piece suit as richly dark brown as his sable hair.

Such a bold face, she thought, and reached up to trace his features as he so often did to her. As she let her fingertip travel the aggressive slash of his brows, his eyes closed, and she lightly swept over his thick lashes. It was the first time she'd noticed they were tipped with gold. He seemed different when his piercing black eyes weren't searing through the many layers to her soul. Not better, not worse. Just different.

As he allowed her to look her fill, Savannah detailed his face. Strength, precision, intelligence. It was all there. And that thrilling promise of passion. While she appreciated the patrician attractiveness of his smooth brow and bluntly angled jaw, her fascination had always been for his mouth, hinting of sweet, hot magic. Lingering over its long fullness with her eyes, Savannah wet her own lips with her tongue.

When her heart skipped into an erratic beat, she let her hand fall to his shoulder, to his flexed thigh, to the grass. "Hi," she murmured. "What are you doing out of your office in the middle of the day?"

"It was after five when I headed up here." Burke took her hand and pulled her up from the ground. She tumbled forward, throwing her arms around his neck.

"Is it that late? I've been asleep for hours." Rising on her toes she gave him her mouth, the kiss long and weakening.

Crushing her to his chest, Burke took his hand down the length of her. She was unresisting, generous. She laughed giddily, breathlessly against his lips before she drew away. Looking into her eyes, he found emotions in contrast to the sound of her laughter. He saw yearning and caution.

Savannah turned and let him link their hands as they moved toward the house. It had felt too good to give that time. Not to take anything at all, but to give everything. She had wanted nothing more from the press of their mouths than to pour herself into him.

Burke sensed her thoughts as surely as if she'd said them out loud. If it frightened her to find she responded to him before she'd considered the risks or its wisdom, then they were making steps in the right direction. "I spoke with Neil today."

She whirled unexpectedly. "Why?"

Burke couldn't mistake her tone for anything but the cold anger and resentment that it was. So, he was getting too close. "Do you object?"

"That would depend on your reason."

She dug her heels into the soft earth, but he tugged her along, anyway. They would play this scene his way, he decided. No walls. He'd noticed Savannah wasn't as skilled a brick-builder when she was on the move. "Am I supposed to check with you now before I make phone calls? The woman who doesn't impose restrictions on others?"

"If they are to my brother, yes," she huffed, as much from anger as from keeping up with his long strides. "If the two of you talked about me...if you called him just to... Well, *did* the two of you talk about me?"

"It seems only logical that if a woman's brother and her lover talk on the phone, the woman will be mentioned."

"You told him?" Because they were on the porch and Savannah didn't want this discussion to continue into the house, where a whole audience would no doubt gather, she looped her free arm around a stone pillar. Burke nearly yanked the other out of its socket before finally stopping and turning to face her. "Did you tell Neil we were lovers?"

Not in exactly those words, Burke thought. "I called him about a job. He asked how you were. I told you you were fine." He watched her relax, hands, shoulders, mouth, loosening one by one. Her personal space still uninvaded...she thought.

"The Reserves to New York," she said. "I knew about them. I'm the scheduled driver."

"No, it was another job. Cuttings in San Francisco." He waited, determined not to let her off easy.

"I suppose I overreacted."

"I suppose you did."

Why had she felt suddenly that Burke had had no right to...to... What? Question Neil? Why would he? Why did she think he might? He won't stay outside the safe zone. She didn't know if she even had a safe zone anymore.

Because she'd dropped her head to frown at the ground, Burke tipped her chin up. "You should call him, Savannah."

She sighed. "I know. I've waited because...because I owe him an apology, and I don't quite know how to say it." Burke ran his fingers through her hair in that lazy, idle way she loved.

" 'I'm sorry' usually suffices."

"Only for people to whom life is that simple."

"Nothing is simple, Savannah." Catching a handful of her hair, he turned her eyes back to his. "Not life, not people, not even apologies. They might be clear or straightforward, but that isn't the same as simple."

We're drifting away from Neil, Savannah realized, and toward us. "I'd rather things could be simple. If not simple, at least easy."

"Then they'd be boring." He turned them toward the front door. "The first two things I'd decided about you, Savannah, were that you were never boring nor the least bit easy."

She grinned as they entered the house and she caught the scent of roasting lamb. "How very astute of you."

Eyes closed, Savannah basked in the hot bathwater. Who'd have thought a shopping spree with Christina could take more out of a person than clearing an acre of grapes under Ramirez's watchful eye? They'd begun as the first store opened and heard the click of the lock on the door of the last store as they'd left.

There were rules to Christina's shopping, Savannah discovered. Window gazing was forbidden. So was veering off the preplanned route. If Savannah had ever wondered from which of his parents Burke had inherited his ambitiously organized mind, she knew now it had to have been his mother.

She sighed and wiggled her toes under the water. Her poor, aching burning feet.

Burke waited in the doorway for a minute or two, enjoying the sight of Savannah up to her neck in bubbles. Her hair was pinned up. The steam had crystallized into fragile beads clinging to the tip of each trailing curl. Her face was flushed from the heat and shiny with moisture, reminding Burke of how she looked in those first moments after climax. On a sigh, she sank deeper in the water. He crossed the room, his footsteps muffled by the seafoam green carpet.

"Soaking off a tough day?"

Savannah's eyes flew open. Burke, a glass of chilled white wine in each hand, stood beside the tub. Though she was modestly hidden beneath mounds of froth, she felt self-conscious. Bathing was intimate, personal. Because they were having an affair didn't give him the right to walk into her bathroom unannounced or without permission.

Reproach was on the tip of her tongue. Then she saw by the look in his eyes that he was expecting precisely that sort of reaction from her. She hated to be predictable. And so she smiled. "I never knew shopping could be such hard work."

As he sat on the edge of the marble tub, he offered one of the dripping glasses. Wondering if she was really going to put up with him sticking around, she hesitated before lifting a sudsy hand from the water.

"You tagged along with Mom on her day in town." She wasn't comfortable, Burke thought. He'd trespassed on a part of her life she hadn't chosen to make available to him. He felt like a man prying at a stubborn door, steadily increasing the force of his weight. "She approaches them like a corporate buy-out."

Savannah held a swallow of wine on her tongue as she watched Burke casually slip a bar of soap from the dish into his palm. She gulped the wine down as he skimmed the fragrant cake across her wet shoulder. "What do you think you're doing?"

"Seducing you in your bathtub."

He let the slick soap and the tips of his fingers skim along her skin even with the water line. "You'll ruin your shirt," Savannah cautioned. "Silk, isn't it?"

As if to prove to her how little he cared about the shirt, Burke placed the soap between her breasts and glided it on a straight, plunging path to her navel, his silk sleeve elbow-deep in sudsy water. Savannah let her gaze travel slowly up that arm while flutters danced in her stomach beneath his hand. When she met his eyes she saw the challenge.

"Aren't you going to rust your cufflink or something?"

He smiled, admiring her sharp tongue when he knew her brain was turning to putty. "If the cufflink rusts, I'll take both it and the shirt to the jeweler who charged me per ounce for the gold."

He leaned closer, his tie dipping a good two or three inches under the bubbles. "Apparently you don't give a damn for a single thing you're wearing."

"Apparently." He brushed her lips with his. The steam doubled, tripled the strength of her scent.

"In that case..." Savannah stood without a word of warning. Clumps of bubbles oozed down her gleaming, wet skin. Burke had automatically risen at the same time she did. Now she stepped out of the tub and wrapped her arms around his neck, pressing her drenched body against his neatly suited length. "You won't mind if I do this."

"Not one bit," he murmured before lifting her off her feet and carrying her into the bedroom.

Savannah threw open the door to Burke's outer office and strode through the dove-gray anteroom.

"Good morning, Ms. Jones," Cynthia said as she turned away from her typewriter. "I'm afraid you can't—"

Ignoring the woman, Savannah reached for the knob to the second door.

"Ms. Jones, you can't—"

The rest of Cynthia's voice was lost behind the door's closing. Savannah registered Burke's frown of disapproval as she crossed this office as well. He was tipped back in his chair, involved in a telephone conversation. Before she was halfway into the room he tossed out a hand meant to stop her. When she kept coming, his disapproval darkened into an ominous scowl.

"Something's come up, Ed," he said, leaning toward his desk. "Can I put you on hold for a minute?"

Savannah came to a halt before his desk at the same moment Burke fingered the hold button on the phone console. "I need—"

He cut her off abruptly. "Savannah, you cannot barge in here unexpected and unannounced."

Momentarily stunned, Savannah pulled back a bit. She whirled, considered the shut door and then turned back to Burke. The eyebrow she raised when she wanted to rebuff with cool haughtiness was climbing into a high arch. "It appears I just have."

With six acres of Gamay grapes hanging in the balance, Burke had no patience to match wits with her. "Well, you won't do it again," he ground out. "I work in this office. I have Ed Zimmer on the line, and I am trying to wrap up a crucial piece of business." He'd steadily risen from his chair, his jaw clenched tight enough to bunch muscles on either side of his face. Unsettled at having lost his temper, he raked his fingers through his hair and sucked in a deep breath. Calmer, he gestured at the door. "Now, go out and check my schedule with Cynthia. I'll see you later."

"Dismissed! Do you think you can simply wave a hand and dismiss me? Maybe I'll do the same when you come tapping at my door tonight!" Seething, Savannah narrowed her eyes on him. She was in no mood for protocol, had no time to check with Cynthia and she'd sooner go to hell than see Burke by appointment. "I don't give a damn for your business talk or Ed Zimmer's grapes! I need a doctor. And I'm not making an appointment with you to find one."

Belatedly, Burke noticed her face was unnaturally white. She seemed to vibrate where she stood. He was sure his own face whitened with the drain of blood from his brain. "What's wrong with you?"

"Me? Nothing. Do I look as if something's wrong with me?"

Relief washed down the fear and left anger in its wake. "Will you get to the point, then? I have no time to go searching for what you mean underneath what you say."

Fury like no other she could remember burned inside Savannah as she leaned over his desk. "The point is this: I ... need ... a ... doctor."

Keeping his eyes on her, Burke lifted the receiver and touched the blinking button. "Ed? I've something here I have to attend to. Can we get together later?" Her eyes were huge. It was the first time Burke had ever seen her truly terrified. "I'm not sure how long. Yes, I'm sure it will be sometime today. Goodbye."

Savannah forced calmness into her voice when he dropped the phone receiver to its cradle. "I need a doctor. I don't know of any here. If you will give me the name of your family doctor, I'll call him myself."

"If you don't need a doctor, who does?"

Her eyes flared. Her hands curled, crumpling Burke's notes that had been beneath them on the desk. "What difference does it make? Do I need permission to need a doctor?"

Burke flinched. It was back—the disdain, the resentment. He made himself be patient. "If someone has a head injury, I wouldn't call an obstetrician, would I? So why don't you just tell me what's wrong?"

Working hard to stay calm when what she wanted to do was grab him by both lapels and shake him, Savannah stepped back and walked to the window wall. "Nina's baby is worse."

"Nina's baby." He should have known. "You won't want to take him to my doctor then. Jeremy Driscoll doesn't—"

"Treat Mexicans?" she said sharply.

It was the first time Burke had ever felt like slapping her. They'd been circling each other too long, neither knowing what to do with the pressure that seemed to constantly build. If she needed to pick a fight in order to spark the explosion, Burke decided she was doing one hell of a good job of it. "Be careful, Savannah," he warned very quietly. "You're starting to sound like a bitch."

"I don't care." She started for him but stopped after three steps and dug her fingertips at her eyes. "He's going to die if someone doesn't help him. He's going to die."

Even as Burke understood her anguish, he wondered if she would ever, could ever, be as devoted to a man as she was to that baby. "Then he needs a baby doctor, doesn't he?"

He doesn't mean to be callous by being reasonable at a time like this, Savannah told herself. He is simply handling things as he always handles them: with his head first. "No." She let her hands drop. "He needs a hospital. *I* need a doctor who will admit him. Any kind of doctor, I don't care. A dermatologist as long as he's got M.D. after his name."

Still standing, Burke reached for the phone. "Cynthia, get me Jeremy Driscoll. I'll hold. And then write out the directions to his office for Savannah."

On legs that dragged, Savannah went to the sofa, where she sat with her head in her hands. Neither of them spoke. It seemed forever before Burke said, "Jeremy, Burke Julienne. Good. Look, I'm sending a friend of mine over, her name's Savannah Jones...yes, you probably did meet her Saturday. Mmm, she is. She's bringing a sick baby with her. Seems to think he'll need hospitalization... Thanks."

Savannah waited until she heard the receiver rock into its cradle before standing. "You didn't tell him his patient was the child of one of your laborers."

"It won't matter to Jeremy. Tell Nina his fee will be nominal. He'll bill the winery, and she can pay when and if."

"I'll pay the bill."

"Suit yourself."

He watched her walk to the door. "Savannah."

Lifting her chin, Savannah turned.

"You'll need a car. Take mine." He pulled the keys from his pocket and tossed them. Savannah snatched them neatly from midair.

She looked down at the keys in her palm. He was angry at her. And he probably had every right to be. But this was something he didn't understand, couldn't understand. How it was to be helpless, to have to ask for help, knowing you might not even be listened to, let alone given what you needed. He didn't know what it was to be powerless.

On a sigh, she raised her head. "Thank you."

He considered her a moment. Had the wall between them ever been higher, thicker? "You'd better go."

## Chapter Ten

Weary, Savannah depended on the mahogany banister for support, literally dragging herself up the curving stairs. It was ten o'clock in the morning. It felt like midnight. An hour ago she'd been in Burke's office; it felt as if a week had passed.

She'd parked his car at the front door, though she probably should have gone straight to the winery. Eventually she'd have to face him. No, soon, she corrected. First she needed a few minutes to regroup and figure out what she could possibly say that would explain her behavior. She couldn't even hope to excuse it.

After entering her bedroom, she quietly closed the door. For just a moment she rested her brow against the cool wood. It had drained her to deal with so many emotions in so short a time. First fear and worry, then anger, resentment. And now remorse. Emotions. Life had been much simpler without them. Everything had been simpler when people had been only pedestrians she watched out for on the road. It had also been emptier, she admitted.

Turning, she set her purse and the car keys on the mantel. It was then she noticed Burke in the fireside chair. He was asleep. Slumped low in the plump apricot-colored cushions, his feet, with ankles crossed, were propped on a low marble table. Dropping to her knees, Savannah gazed at him with all the love in her eyes she'd so far managed to keep concealed, if not contained.

The perfect triangular point of a starched handkerchief jutted from the breast pocket of his navy-blue jacket. His vest was neatly buttoned, she noted fondly. He hadn't even loosened his tie. One hand was curled into a fist and propped his head up. The other rested on the chair arm, palm up and open. Gently, Savannah laid her head down on his lap and closed her eyes.

What was she going to do with all the love inside her? Would she be able to squeeze it into a compact package for locking away? Was it something she could transpose into music and give up to the moon? By next week, perhaps as early as tomorrow, Jackson would have called, and she'd be on her way. Never to return. That much she had come to realize and accept: she would never again come back here.

*Oh, God, one more thing to run from.*

She woke to the soft settling of his hand on her head. His voice still carried the deep huskiness of sleep. "I know two people who ought to get more sleep at night."

Though she opened her eyes and smiled, Savannah left her head on his lap for a while longer. "If a certain gentleman didn't keep visiting a certain lady's bedroom at midnight, they might."

"How's the baby?" he asked in a low, concerned voice.

"Pneumonia. He's in intensive care, but they're pretty sure he'll make it."

"Intensive care," he repeated. "Pretty sick kid."

"Yeah. But he's going to get the best—no charity wards, no State-assigned doctors. I like your Jeremy Driscoll, Burke. He's called in an excellent specialist. I've instructed the hospital to bill me."

Strand by strand, Burke let her hair sift through his fingers. "Why don't you let the winery take care—"

"No." Savannah sat back and shook her head. She knew harvest pickers didn't get any sort of benefits, let alone medical coverage. She wouldn't have Burke doing for one of them what he couldn't do for the rest. And she wouldn't be deprived. She had yet to understand it, but Savannah wanted the gift of someone to take care of, even for this short period of time. "I'm seeing to this kid. This boy is going to have a *person*—not a winery or any other sort of institution—taking care of him."

"All right, Savannah."

Already braced to do battle, she let the tension go in one long, cleansing breath. "Burke, about the things I said in your office—I'm sorry."

He studied her in silence. Feeling a strange pang, she recognized sadness in him. "Savannah, was it so hard for you to ask something of me?"

"I hadn't thought so at first. If I had, I wouldn't have gone to you at all. Then you told me to go through Cynthia, and—"

"Savannah," he murmured.

"No, don't apologize. I didn't mean that as reproach." She stopped and took a breath. "If there was something we wanted or needed at the orphanage, we had to see a Mr. Glass. Unless you could afford to wait a month for the appointment, you learned how to get past his secretary. Even when you did get to him, he rarely granted a request. By the time you finished answering his endless string of whys, he'd refuse you, referring to something or other in his little book of rules. I promised myself then that the day would come that I'd never have to ask for anything I couldn't get for myself. Never have to answer why. That I needed would be reason enough to get." Rather than meet his eyes, she gazed down. "It wasn't fair to turn on you that way. You had every right to behave as you did. I had none to be so vicious and—"

He hushed her with a fingertip to her lips. "It's okay. In certain situations people say and do things they wouldn't normally. I understand, Savannah."

Catching his hand, she turned his palm up and placed a kiss there. "You're a good man, Burke Julienne."

It was, Burke realized, the first compliment she'd ever paid him. "How does your schedule look for the next couple of days?"

Intrigued by the question, Savannah cocked her head to one side. "You know me and schedules. I keep mine as loose as possible." She followed the track of his eyes as they shifted away from her face and saw an open suitcase on her bed that she hadn't noticed before. "You're going somewhere?"

"San Francisco. There's a shipment arriving from France—the one I called Neil about. I want to be at the port when its unloaded. I thought we'd go together, take a few days for ourselves."

"San Francisco." A few days with Burke. And a few nights. It would mean lowering more of her defenses, Savannah thought. She'd be sleeping and waking with him, sharing a hundred new intimacies. Letting the idea settle a moment in her mind, she discovered she wanted all she could have of him, every memory and moment possible, to store up and take with her when she left. "Just the two of us?"

Burke smiled at the anticipation shining from her eyes. "Unless you'd like to bring Fitzhugh along to do the packing and unpacking."

"No." Grinning, Savannah planted her chin on his chest. "Will we have breakfast in bed?"

"Mmm. With Champagne, if you'd like."

"When do we leave?"

"As soon as you're packed. There's room in my bag. Throw in something special. Tomorrow we'll have a night on the town."

Three hours later, Savannah was arranging her nylons beside Burke's socks in a dresser drawer at the Mark Hopkins hotel. Foolish, she thought. It was foolish to get romantic about nylons cozied up next to socks. Just as it was foolish to keep wandering into the bathroom to smile at the sight of his toothbrush set out beside hers on the vanity, then to the closet to grin at his suits snugly pressed against her dresses.

"Dinner reservations are for eight," Burke said, hanging up the bedside phone. "That gives us six or seven hours to fill." Taking her into his arms, he nuzzled her neck. "What would you like to do with them?"

"Go to Chinatown?" Savannah laughed as Burke backed her up to the bed and tumbled her down.

"Yeah?" He rained kisses over her face. Her blouse fell open under his hands.

"Mmm, yeah." She peeled his shirt off, dragging her hands over his chest, shoulders and down his arms. "I feel like shopping. Trinkets for my nephews. A dress for tomorrow night."

He swept her skirt down her legs and off the bed. His fingertip lingered as it made the journey back up, starting on the top of her foot and ending at the high cut of her bikini panties. Her stomach muscles quivered when he dipped inside the lacy border. "There are closer boutiques I could take you to."

"No. No chic perfume-scented boutiques." Clumsy with desperation, Savannah fumbled to unbuckle his belt and loosen his slacks. "No proper, whispering clerks." She raised her arms to assist Burke in pulling her teddy over her head. "Chinatown is alive, exciting—lots of ancient traditions, tons more decadence."

His mouth, open and greedy, raced over her shoulder, down her throat, up her arms. Tasting, savoring, moving on. "Chinatown it is." He skimmed her panties off, removing her last bit of clothing. "Shall I call a cab?"

Savannah took his briefs down his legs along with his slacks. "Didn't we leave your car in the parking lot?"

Naked. At last, simultaneous gasps seemed to say. Sunlight poured through the windows, submerging them in a pool of airy gold where they lay on the bed they hadn't bothered to pull the covers from. Savannah lay on her back. Burke was propped on an elbow beside her. Each looked their fill at the other, learning for the first time by broad daylight flesh they'd memorized by wavering candle flames and a moon's ethereal shower.

Eventually hands followed eyes. Thumbs, featherlight and tracing. Palms, spread open and pressing. Fingertips racing to arouse.

"My God," Burke murmured. "You are beautiful." Fanned out on the light-colored spread, her flowing raven hair intensified the fragility of her face. She was losing her tan, honey turning to cream. Her skin loved the sunlight, taking it in and giving it back with a glow. "Perfect."

Feeling a freedom, a wickedness she'd never allowed herself in a house where Burke's parents also slept, Savannah shoved Burke onto his back. Hovering, she raked her fingernails down his chest, gently, carefully, ever so slowly. He shuddered and groaned. Power. Savannah was heady with it. The power to make his strong, hard body quiver with a touch. To cause his organized mind to swim in chaos.

"I've never seduced you," she said just before dragging her tongue over his bottom lip.

"This isn't called seduction," Burke muttered as the blood pounded through his head.

"No?" Savannah nipped at the lip she'd moistened, then let it slide free of her teeth. "What's it called?"

"Savagery." Gripping her bottom, Burke brought her hips down hard against his. He sucked air between his teeth to breathe.

"Seduction or savagery, call it what you like. The rules are that you can't touch." She circled his wrists and moved his hands over his head as he'd once done to her.

"Rules?" She looked wanton, Burke thought, with her cloud-soft hair tumbling wildly about her face, with her skin flushing to rose as arousal burned through her. "Have you suddenly decided to set rules for yourself, Savannah?"

"No, the rules are for you. You can't touch. You can't move unless I tell you to. You have to lie right there and be still." She lowered herself so that her nipples barely brushed his chest and her lips just touched his ear. "While I get to do as I please."

She had him half-mad in less than a minute and kept him that way for what seemed an eternity.

Holding herself away from him, she sculpted his face like an artist learning her subject. With her fingertips she traced the bold slash of eyebrows, the aristocratic cut of cheekbones. Skin abraded by the gentle rasp of his beard was soon soothed by the velvet warmth of his lips. Eyes fastened on his mouth, Savannah slipped a finger past his teeth to take up a duel with his tongue. As she withdrew it, Burke bit down to hold her captive.

"No biting," she warned in a smoky, desire-filled voice. "Against the rules."

"No biting," he conceded as he folded his arms behind his head. "Just so you remember I'll give back as good as I get."

"I will." Fitting her knee between his legs, Savannah smiled down at him. "Though when it's your turn I doubt you'll be in any condition to remember your own name."

The ends of her hair touched him first as she lowered her lips to his chest. Her mouth whispered over him; her nails raked behind. Her tongue made hot, wet forays, searing his skin. Her hands stroked and teased until his muscles were knotted with need. God, he'd never known there could be such pleasure in prolonged torture.

At first Savannah's pulse had raced with an adrenaline-fed excitement, as it might at the start of any bold venture for which she hadn't the experience. Now her blood thudded as she held back her own urgency and lingered over him. He was so taut beneath her hands, so hot against her skin. His taste was pungently male and intoxicatingly personal. The only sounds in the room were of their unsynchronized breathing. His sharp and raspy. Hers long and deep as she went on taking him into herself through all her senses.

Burke was mindless. No woman had ever stripped him of reason, of thought. His hands were in her hair when control snapped. She was beneath him in a move so quick and sudden it stole breath.

For a suspended second their eyes locked. Savannah rose at the hips at the same moment Burke sank down to enter her. One. It seemed to sigh from them in unison before the world spun out from under them.


Savannah would not be talked out of Chinatown. She adored the green, red and gold world where dragons twined around the posts of streetlamps shaped like pagodas. She loved the confusion and cacophony and crush of people. As she surged through the human sea, she decided it had been worth the bargain Burke had forced: one afternoon in Chinatown for one symphony performance tomorrow night.

"Did you know it was always like this?" she tossed back at Burke as she wended her way down a narrow street lined with tradesmen hawking every sort of souvenir to tourists. "Two in the morning, three, it's nearly this crowded."

"I've lived outside San Francisco all my life," Burke reminded her. "I know about Chinatown."

"Oh, yeah?" She dropped back to wind her arm through his. "See that phone booth over there? What's the translation of the Chinese lettering?"

"I said I knew Chinatown, not how to read Chinese." In truth, he had to admit her enthusiasm was infectious. He was beginning to see Chinatown as he never had before. "It probably says telephone booth."

"Nope. Electric Voice House." She laughed and pulled him around a corner. "Isn't that wonderful?"

"How do you know that's what it says?"

"I asked an old Chinese man once. Oh, stop." Savannah sniffed, then turned to retrace her steps. "Egg rolls. Hot and fresh."

"You can't want an egg roll." But Burke was already reaching for his wallet.

"Just one," Savannah promised as she stepped up to the carryout counter of the cramped and dimly lit restaurant.

"It's been just one of something from every restaurant we've passed. Do you know how many there are in this twenty-block section of town?" Burke's change was still being counted out when Savannah sank her teeth into the crunchy dough.

"Didn't you want one?" she asked once they were on the street again.

"No. I don't know what you're doing tonight, but I'm having dinner at the Top of the Mark. In less than two hours, in fact."

"You're being practical again," Savannah said. But when she looked at him she approved of how lazy and comfortable he looked. For him, at least. His sleeves were rolled back at the cuffs, his hands casually stuffed in his pockets. He walked with a loose ranginess Savannah couldn't remember seeing before. As if he had nowhere in particular to go, nothing of the utmost importance to accomplish.

He'd forgotten what it was like to take a day and spend it without purpose. He hadn't even taken the time in France to do any of the sightseeing expected of Americans in Europe. When Savannah had finished her egg roll and tossed her napkin into a pagoda-styled wastebasket, Burke hooked an arm around her shoulders. The last time he'd been in Chinatown he'd cursed the congestion and sworn never to come back. Now he discovered that if you weren't late for an appointment, the onslaught to the senses could be pleasantly stimulating.

"We're almost there." Savannah beamed up at him.

He raised an eyebrow as he gazed down. "I didn't know you had a destination."

"I've always got a destination. I might change it as I go along. It's possible I won't know what it is till I get there. But it's only when you stand still that you haven't got a place where you'll wind up."

She tilted her head and gazed at him, as if expecting him to either agree or disagree. Burke smiled noncommittally. "I'll have to work at that one." He tugged her quickly to one side, out of the path of a bicyclist who didn't look as if he planned to veer from his path. "This place we're almost at—do you know what it is, or is it simply where we wind up?"

"Mmm, the herbalists' shops. Chinese are the best herbalists in the world. You name it, they can mix a brew to fix it." And then she was ducking through a narrow doorway and into a room of exotic smells and musical Far East accents. Burke stood back and watched her. Curious and quick to smile. How had he lived so many years without that in his life? She understood the Chinese culture and paid respect to it by letting the old man go on and on about the magic of a particular ginseng species long after his own son had tired of the man's soliloquy.

At the end of the old man's sales pitch, Savannah stubbornly shook her head. "No, no ginseng. *Jasmine.* White flower, grows on a vine."

"Ah, ah see. You nervous girl? Powder for tea?"

"No, I'm not a nervous girl. No powder, no tea. Oil. Jasmine oil."

"Ahh, oil." Burke noticed a change in the old man's inflection. "Good erotica," he murmured. "You want almond oil, too? Mix two and rub on skin, takes away frigidity."

Hearing Burke's chuckle behind her, Savannah snuck him a glance over her shoulder. "What do you think? Should I get a little almond oil?"

"It could be interesting," he murmured in a voice that was a velvet caress. "If it doesn't kill me."

Her smile was slow in coming and very private when it arrived. Then she turned back to the old herbalist. "No almond. The jasmine will do just fine."

The jasmine did better than fine. It saturated Burke's senses and numbed him to everything but the woman sitting beside him at the Opera House. She wore a dress she'd bought as they'd fought their way out of Chinatown the day before. From the frog-closing at her throat to the narrow hem slit to bare a length of slender leg, the slate-gray silk clung to her like a layer of smoke. Burke could think of little but sliding it away from her skin.

Ten minutes into the program Savannah felt the whisper of Burke's lips at her ear. "Are you bored?" he murmured.

She smiled and shook her head. He nodded and smiled back. In fact, Savannah was surprised to discover she was actually enjoying the music. She'd always preferred playing to listening, performer to audience. But tonight Mozart moved her. Restful yet stirring. Where before it had always been her own emotions she'd heard humming in the music, now she identified those of the composer. Appreciation and enjoyment centered on what she was able to absorb rather than on what she could expel.

"Are you sure you wouldn't prefer leaving?"

This time Savannah slid him a look. Since she'd warned him she might wind up pacing the lobby if she suddenly found it impossible to sit still for hours on end, she thought it sweet of him to be concerned. Particularly since *he* was the patron of the arts, so to speak, and *she* was not.

"No, I'm enjoying it," she whispered back. "The strings are quite good, if the opinion of a partly accomplished cellist means anything to you."

Another ten minutes passed before Savannah noticed Burke's thumb distractedly running up and down the arm of his chair. Sneaking him a glance, she saw that his eyes were on the ceiling, as if he'd found the antics of a crawling fly more entertaining than the music.

"Burke, are you bored?"

"To death."

The giggle was out before Savannah could stop it. It drew enough attention that those sitting closest to them heard quite distinctly Burke's next words.

"I'm wishing the damn thing were over so that I could take you home and make love to you."

There were several giggles then, along with one or two snorts. Burke and Savannah managed to hold in their own laughter until they'd left their seats with as much dignity as possible and were on the street rushing to Burke's car.

* * *

The harbor smelled of salty air and fish. The bustle here was industrious, what there was of it. Most of the long piers were no longer used; the roads were crumbling from disrepair. Though it had once ranked as one of the busiest ports on the coast, San Francisco's waterfront was in a sad state of decline.

Savannah leaned back against the truck cab's front end, catching up on the latest with Remus Taylor. A few yards away Burke personally oversaw the raising of his shipping container from the hold of the oceangoing freighter.

"Neil sends regards," Remus told Savannah, then spat a stream of tobacco juice onto the pavement. He was a bear of a man, with a bright red ponytail hanging down to the middle of his back and a wild auburn beard spreading over a good deal of his chest. He was also as gentle as a pussycat.

"Tell him I'll see him soon," Savannah said, head thrown all the way back as she watched a container dangling from a long-armed crane swing through the air. "I can't imagine I'll be laid up much longer."

"Could be you'll no sooner get on the road than you'll be getting off again."

Savannah dropped her head and frowned at Remus. "What do you mean I'll be getting off again?"

"There's talk of a nationwide strike by independent haulers. Deadline's in forty-eight hours. From what comes over the CB it don't look to me like they'll reach an agreement at the tables in time."

"Strike? But there hasn't been a strike in years...not in all the years I've been driving, in fact. The whole country will come to a standstill, Remus. No one's going to let that happen."

"Hell, Savannah, where you been? Haven't you read the papers? Turned on the news?"

No, she hadn't. It was as if she'd left the world altogether these past weeks. Completely isolated and cut off.

"Did I hear you mention a strike?" Satisfied with the unloading, Burke approached them.

"It's in the wind," Remus said. "Don't like 'em myself, but a lot of the boys are itching for it. And a lot of 'em will be nasty if it comes about. Something about a strike brings out the worst in some people."

More time, was Burke's first thought. His only thought. Savannah could get her truck back any day now but if she couldn't work, then why should she leave Napa? Where would she go?

Savannah kicked at a rut of loosened concrete, wondering at the uneasiness she felt. This talk of a strike made her nervous, though she couldn't quite put her finger on why. And then she thought of Neil, of what the financial hardship could do to his business when he was only just now getting it off the ground. And the others, the community of haulers of which she was a part. They'd all be in for hard times.

"There can't be a strike," she said, looking away from the coastline and down the road leading to the highway heading east. "There just can't."

Burke heard the thin chord of anxiety in her voice and felt the first twinge of fear in his chest.

Savannah relaxed in Burke's plush leather chair, her feet irreverently propped on his desk. Her felt hat dangled from a sandaled toe. She glanced over at the wicker hamper she'd brought with her and thought that if Burke didn't return soon she'd lose her willpower and give in to the tempting smells.

He came through the door then, his head bowed as he shuffled through a handful of mail. When he looked up and saw her, Savannah basked in the quick surprise followed by pleasure that always lit his eyes when he gazed at her, making her feel uniquely special.

"Cynthia didn't mention you were waiting," Burke said as he tossed the mail to the desk with sudden disinterest.

"Cynthia didn't know I was waiting." With a sly smile, Savannah pointed to the open garden door. "I knocked first," she defended when he gave her a narrow look.

"You ought to keep it locked if you don't want anyone coming through *unexpected* and *unannounced*."

Rounding the desk, Burke lifted the hat from her toes in a signal for her to place her feet on the floor, where they belonged. He leaned one hip on the mahogany desk and considered her. "Cynthia isn't some sort of dragon lady. Why the hell does she intimidate you so?"

"Intimidate?" Savannah bolted from the chair to stand eye to eye with him. "*Intimidate!* She does nothing of the sort."

"I see. And you don't go to great and creative lengths to avoid her, either."

"Sure I do, but it has nothing to do with being intimidated by her. I don't come here to see Cynthia. I come here to see you. If I'm going to Atlanta from Philadelphia, why should I go through Chicago first?"

Unconvinced, Burke shook his head. "For an analogy, Savannah, that is very poor. Why don't you try thinking of Cynthia as a weight station on the highway? A nuisance to pull over, but simpler in the long run than upsetting the authorities."

Savannah scowled. Not only did she hate being bested in an argument, but his analogy had been more apropos than hers. "I'll see what I can do."

Chuckling, Burke pulled her closer, fitting her hips between his open legs. He took her mouth in a long, debilitating kiss, bending her head back so that her lips were under his in a symbolic submission Savannah had begun to develop a longing for. Even as her body yielded to his touch she was heady with the knowledge that she, and she alone, could tear free the tethers on this man's control. She had the power to create a storm of passion in the center of this calm and ordered room.

Letting his lips glide to her cheek and then temple, Burke noticed the hamper from over the top of her head. "What have we here?"

"Lunch, if you're free. Weatherby fixed it for us."

"Great! I'll clear the desk, and you can set it out."

"No, not here," Savannah countered. "I thought we'd go off by ourselves and get lost for a while."

It shouldn't have appealed to Burke. He'd already been away from the office two days this week. He had afternoon meetings to prepare for. "Where did you have in mind?"

"I don't know." She waved a hand toward the windows. "You've got miles of land out there; you must know of a secluded place where we can shake out a blanket for an hour or so."

Burke knew exactly the place. And, he thought, it was high time he showed it to her. "You've got a deal." Taking his arm from around her waist, he leaned toward the phone console. Before he could press the intercom button, Savannah's hand was closing on his wrist.

"Don't," she murmured in a wicked whisper. "Don't tell Cynthia."

"She has to know that I've gone and when I'll be back."

"Why?"

Why, indeed? Burke asked himself. "She's expecting to walk in here in another fifteen minutes to take dictation."

Her lowering lashes tempted and dared. "Then if we snuck out the garden door, she might think you'd vanished into thin air."

Burke chuckled. "You'd get a kick out of that, wouldn't you? Throwing my ultraefficient Cynthia into a state of confusion." Her eyes asked him if he ever did anything for the sheer fun of it. They almost seemed to plead with him to do it just this once for the hell of it. "All right. We'll go without a word."

It wasn't until he'd agreed that Savannah realized she hadn't expected him to. At best she might have gotten him to sprawl out on the floor, a pseudo-picnic. "Just one more thing," she said. Before he realized her intent, she had his jacket off and was draping it across the back of his chair. "There. That should really confuse her."

With Burke carrying the hamper, they left through the garden door, shutting it behind them. "This way," he directed and led her along the sides of buildings to the back corner of the parking lot where the Jeep was parked. Fifteen minutes later he braked in a gentle ravine cutting through two soft, grassy slopes.

Savannah followed him around the base of one hill until he finally set the hamper down. Coming up beside him, she took a slow, sweeping look at the most glorious view she had ever seen in her life. Miles and miles of lush land, very little of it turned to vineyards. In one little corner of the panoramic scene sat the winery buildings. There were glens here, and woods. There were birds sailing and swooping overhead and furry creatures hopping through the long grass.

"This is it," Savannah murmured. "This is where you'll build your house."

Absorbing the peace and breathing space he was always able to find here, Burke instinctively loosened his tie and slipped his collar button free. "I picture a house with lots of glass, so open it leaves you no choice but to treat the valley as an integral part of every room. The back of the house." He turned to where level land met the elevation of a hill, around which stood a cool stand of oaks. "I see it cutting right into the earth. That's where I'd put the wine cellar."

Savannah let the vision take shape in her mind as she unpacked the hamper and set out the lunch the cook had prepared for them. Burke stretched out on the blanket beside her and helped himself to a cold chicken leg and a plastic cup filled with white wine. "Is that Weatherby's apple pie?"

Savannah chuckled. "She said you'd be pleased."

As they nibbled on cold finger foods washed down with wine, Burke talked of the new cuttings. He was hopeful about the Chardonnay vines and his plans for Champagne, confident Claude would eventually, if grudgingly, accept this next step for Julienne's.

The sun was warm, the breeze soft. Savannah angled her head back and closed her eyes, loving the rich, fertile scents of mulch from the woods and wild flowers in the fields.

"Tell me more about the house," she said. "Have you told your parents?"

"No. It's early yet. I haven't even settled on floor plans. Claude's edgy enough over the Champagne."

"Picked out the architect?"

"Mm-hmm. I had a message that he called while we were away. Apparently he came out to walk the plot and is ready for our first meeting." Gazing around, Burke realized he wasn't a bit prepared to talk designs yet. To him, the house was a mood more than an image. He knew the feel he wanted to create but none of the specifics.

Pushing himself up, he walked to the edge of the woods where fieldstones were strewn about. Taking up a hefty rock in each hand, he started pacing off long strides. "Help me out, Savannah. What do you think about putting the front door right about here?"

Shading her eyes with one hand, she considered where he stood. "Depends. One story or two? Where's the road going to be?"

"Road's up there." He gestured to a point left of the woods. "One-story house," he decided on the spur of the moment, instinctively knowing it was the right choice. "No jutting monoliths. Just a nice roomy sprawl."

"Well, if it were my choice, I'd move the door to that side of the house, closer to the road. The spot you're standing at is your best view. You'd have to open your front door and stand on the porch to see it."

"You're right." Burke paced off land, moving closer to where he visualized the road would cut in.

"Hey," Savannah called. "Where are you going?"

Right about then he stopped and set the rocks on the ground, roughly five feet apart. "Front door," he announced and moved to the edge of the woods for two more rocks.

Savannah swept a glance over the distance. "That's *some* sprawl. How big a house are you planning?"

"Big. Lots of space. Master bedroom here, on a corner with views in two directions." Before actually marking off

the size of the room, Burke looked behind him to see Savannah, rocks in hand and getting into the spirit.

"Wrong corner for a bedroom," she said. "That side
faces east. You'll have the sun in your face about six
o'clock every morning. If you put it in the west corner,
you'll have the sunset every night instead."

Burke nodded. "Bedroom in the west corner."

"Kitchen in the east," Savannah decided.

Rocks in hand, they passed each other. A few minutes
later they had the first two rooms of the house marked off.
Soon there were too many stones to know what any of
them were supposed to designate, and so Savannah stuck
twigs in the ground. To the twigs she tied strips of shred-
ded paper napkins where she'd written room names.

"Four bathrooms, Burke," she called out, laughing.
"You've got four bathrooms but no closets."

Burke surveyed the rock and twig strewn land. "No
closets," he muttered. "Of course we need closets."

Savannah stilled, not realizing precisely why at first.
We? *We* need closets? He didn't notice that she'd stopped
moving, that she stood frozen in place, holding a pair of
bent twigs in her hands as he located a spot for a coat
closet near the front door.

"And linens," Burke said, heading back to her end of
the imaginary house. "With four bedrooms, you'll need a
good-size linen closet convenient to this wing."

"Who needs a linen closet?" Savannah was slowly
backing away. "*I* don't need a linen closet."

Burke knew in that moment why he hadn't visualized the
house before today, why he hadn't been ready to sit down
with an architect. This wasn't his house but their house.
This was *their* house, and he'd wanted Savannah's input.

"Your linen closet," Burke said, walking toward her at
the same careful pace as she backed away. "Your bedroom. Your kitchen and bathrooms and closets. Our
house, Savannah."

"No." She stopped, throwing up a hand to make him
stop, too. "No."

"Yes. I love you, Savannah." His heart was beating too fast; his breathing wasn't quite steady. "I love you."

"No." Savannah dropped the twigs and clapped her hands over her ears. She wouldn't hear those words. She wouldn't, not ever again, make the mistake of believing those words. "No."

"Yes!" Burke shouted. In three long strides he had her by her shoulders. "I love you. *Have* loved you for quite some time. How could you not have known? Not have seen? I love you. I want to marry you."

Fear. Savannah was filling up with so much fear that it threatened to smother her. Burke had hauled her onto her toes. His hands gripped her so tightly that she could feel the imprint of his fingers clear to her bones. But all she really thought about was the fear. "I won't marry you, Burke. I *can't* marry you."

"You love me, Savannah." Burke shook her, as if he could knock loose the words he needed to hear. "Look me in the eye and tell me you don't love me. Tell me, damn you."

She cried out, not so much from the pain of his brutal hold but from the anguish of ripping those words from her heart in order to give them to him. "I love you."

*But it changes nothing*, her eyes said.

Her cry forced Burke to see that he was hurting her. He stared at his hands, at how deep in her flesh they were digging. If he didn't let go of her now, didn't step away quickly, he might very well break her in two. "Don't run," he said as he gradually loosened his grip. "Stay and talk to me, Savannah," he pleaded as he took one, two, then three steps back from her. "Just don't run."

## Chapter Eleven

*Don't run.*

Savannah nodded, promising. A numb calm settled around her. It felt, she thought, like death. But she wouldn't run. She'd known all along that she wouldn't be able to when the time came. It couldn't be her choice to vanish in the middle of the night as Amy used to. Burke didn't deserve that twice in one lifetime. There'd be no freedom to pick up and take off because the need was driving her, the trap closing. When you loved, you lost freedom.

Burke struggled against fury and tucked his hands safely into his pants pockets. Once there, he balled them into fists and struggled against the frustration. "*Home* isn't a word you trust," he began. "I understand that. Your experiences with them have been less than ideal. I'm sorry for that, Savannah."

Wide gray eyes as unrevealing as slate stared at him. She was listening, Burke decided. But she was being very careful to keep what she was feeling inside from showing. If her defenses were that weakened, he thought, if she had to be that diligent with control, then he just might have a chance to get through.

"You've never mentioned foster homes," he said, looking for signs of having hit a target. "I suspect that in addition to the orphanage there were probably foster homes that didn't work out. It's only natural you'd build a protective barrier against hopes that you'd one day have a home of your own, a place where you belonged." God, he felt as if he was talking to the birds for all the good it was doing. "Savannah, those people didn't love you!" His anger surfaced, meant for all the faceless *thems* who had done this to her, and, by virtue of that, were now doing it to him. "Love makes all the difference. Doesn't Neil love his wife, his children? Can you conceive of his ever leaving them? Do you think for a minute he'd ever shut you out of his life? If your parents hadn't died, Savannah, if—"

"My parents didn't die," she said in a cool, emotionless voice.

Caught unaware, Burke paused a moment. "You told me they'd died," he said in confusion.

"No, I didn't. I told you I'd lost them when I was five years old."

And then he knew. Before she said the next words, Burke knew what he was going to hear. If there'd been a way, by miracle or magic, to reach into her life and alter that moment from her past, Burke thought he might have traded his soul to the devil to bring it about.

"My father left us in Georgia," she said, staring at him through the blankest eyes Burke had ever seen in a living human being. "In a gas station. Neil and I were in the bathroom with our mother, having our weekly sink bath. When we came out he was pulling away. Mom let out this terrible scream and went running after him. It was a very old car, rusty, noisy, noxious. When he gunned the accelerator a cloud of foul black exhaust spewed out, into my mother's face...some of it into mine and Neil's. My dad's hat flew out the window." Her eyes shifted to where the tattered felt lay beside their picnic things. Her mouth curved wryly. "It's all I have left of either of them."

Then she turned her back on Burke and walked to the pale gray rock that marked the cornerstone of the master bedroom. "We started walking down the gravel shoulder. I don't know how long our mother cried and whimpered and bemoaned our fate. Hours, I guess. Miles. It was dark before she thought to go through her pockets for money. She found a bill—twenty dollars, I think. He'd left with our clothes, our money, our food. We slept in the woods that night and most of the nights that came after. After a few days my mother came up with a plan...or a goal, a dream, whatever you want to call it. We were going to California."

She glanced over her shoulder at Burke. "California," she said again in a voice curdled with bitterness. "Where the sun always shines and we'd never be cold. Where we'd be movie stars—or she'd marry one—and we'd be rich. When I remember her, I remember a woman who was very patient with the curve balls life had thrown her, but I also remember her as having always been weary, worn-out and weary. I don't know how such a tired-out soul thought she'd get herself and two kids from Georgia to California on twenty dollars and a dream."

Some of her protective calm was slipping away. Savannah kicked at the stone and accepted that it was too late to stop what had begun. "A big dream, a twenty-dollar bill and a mother's love will get you from Georgia to Kansas. It was a hot summer day when my father left us in that gas station. There was a snowstorm when my mother left us on a street corner."

Behind her Burke breathed a curse. Had he shouted the expletive he couldn't have filled it with more frustrated rage.

"She didn't even take us to the authorities herself. She left it to Neil. She put dad's hat on my head to keep the snow off and sort of straightened my clothes, the way mothers do when they want you to make a good impression. She told Neil to take hold of my hand and walk me two blocks up the road to the police station and tell them we had no family. She said they'd find one for us. That we'd have regular parents and a real home."

Without warning, Savannah's eyes filled. And she began to pace, keeping always to the interior of the imaginary house they'd built. "I was so scared. I tried to run down the street after her." Tears coursed down her cheeks. "She yelled back at Neil not to let go . . . and then she ran. *Ran.* I hung on to Neil so tight that sometimes he'd have to pry my fingers loose to get circulation back into his hand. But he never let go of me. Not once in the police station. Only when he had to in the hospital where they took us next. Not later in the courthouse. It was dark by the time a car took us out to the youth home. All these adults were grouped around us, trying to talk me into letting go of him.

"Neil finally asked them if he could take me to the girls' dormitory himself. I suppose after what I'd been through none of them wanted to have to physically pry us apart, so they agreed. There were twelve beds, six on each side of the room. Someone had laid out a nightgown on the one empty cot. The other girls were asleep, so Neil whispered quietly to me as he helped me change. I don't remember everything he said. Promises that we'd stick together. That no matter what, he'd always take care of me. I believed him. He looked so big to me, so much older. I had to believe in someone, didn't I?" A sob tore from her chest. "God, he was just a boy. He looked so tall to me. His voice always seemed so sure. But he was eleven years old and scared to death himself. I see kids that age now, and I'm stunned by what he had to take on."

Savannah wiped the tears from her face. There was more. It wouldn't be held back. The rhythm of her pacing quickened. "Foster homes," she said. "Yeah, there were foster homes." Her voiced was hard and ungiving. Burke remembered it that way once before. *"It never ceases to amaze me how many people think they know where children belong."*

"In the beginning, when people came out to look us over, I'd try to act invisible. Keep my head down, never do anything that made me more noticeable than the others. I was terrified of being chosen. What if our mother came back? I believed she would. I just knew she had to be missing us as much as we were missing her. What if she came back and we were gone to another family?"

Burke felt a wave of pity and anger. He paced with her, keeping to her side, careful not to get too close too quickly.

"After a while, I gave up believing she'd come. Then I *wanted* to be picked. I wanted clothes that were mine, a bedroom that was mine, parents that were mine. My first home was with the Mulroneys. Martha—Mrs. Mulroney—wanted to make me the next Shirley Temple and herself rich. She was the first to tell me why I hadn't been picked before. Neil and I were unadoptable." She laughed, a hard, humorless sound. "Because my mother couldn't stick around long enough to properly sign us over, we were unadoptable."

In the master bedroom corner, where the words had first begun to pour, Savannah came to a halt. "Martha Mulroney took pictures of me: with my hair in pigtails and in sausage curls, inside in my pajamas, outside on a swing. She mailed them to agents all over the country. While she waited for them to come knocking on her door, she put me into dancing classes and singing classes, elocution and charm schools. I squalled when I sang. Forget poise—I was all knees and elbows. But I liked dance class. Tap."

Burke touched her, gently. Hands on her shoulders, thumbs moving soothingly at her throat. She didn't draw away, though he couldn't swear she was aware of him at all.

"Give me a pair of tap shoes, put me in a room with mirrors on all four walls and I was in heaven." She sighed unevenly. "When New York, Chicago and L.A. didn't pound on the Mulroneys' door to sign me up, Martha sent me back. Or maybe it was a hard year for wheat farmers and they just couldn't afford to keep me. I don't know. They never bothered to tell me why. She kept the tap shoes...took them out of my suitcase. Said they cost enough that she could get something back for her money at a secondhand store. Frankly, I think she kept them, hoping they'd fit the next kid."

Burke couldn't imagine people so heartless. "They couldn't have all been that bad."

"No, I'm sure they weren't. I didn't give them too many chances after that. When I got back to the orphanage, Neil was gone. To a farmer. God, how Neil hated farming. I remembered thinking that he'd promised he wouldn't let anything keep us apart. It was a few years before I realized we never had much to say about our lives. He was back a few months later, and we sort of made a pact then that any time they sent one or the other of us somewhere, we'd be so difficult, so obnoxiously impossible, we'd get ourselves sent right back."

With a thumb under her chin, Burke tipped her face up. "Now Neil has a home and a family. Are you going to cheat yourself of the same? It's what you've wanted, hoped for all your life. It's here with me. Us, Savannah. This is home."

"No." She shook her head, trying to pull free of his arms. "That's all Neil ever wanted. His own. His own place, his own family, one nobody could come along and take back from him. I'm not like that, Burke. It didn't leave me wanting the same. I can't...I can't take the chance anymore. It's not in me."

Acting on a frustrated impulse, an instinctive fear, Burke yanked her back against him. He crushed his mouth to hers, demanding from her. And when she stopped resisting, he demanded more. His hands raced over her as he kept their mouths fused. Savannah took the kiss and the punishment. Oh, God, what had she done to him? To them? She tasted the faint tinge of blood rise in the tissues behind her teeth. She felt the strength of his arms nearly break her in two as he tried to bring her closer than two bodies were ever meant to be. Her quiet groan was a protest to the pain in her heart.

Reason slammed back into Burke. Her hands were twisted in his hair, hard and gripping, pulling his head back. Still he churned with the need to have her, to keep her. She wasn't part of his life—she *was* his life. Mouths open, inches apart and gasping, they seemed to snatch the breath from each other. Forcing himself to see her, Burke gazed down, at her eyes, her mouth. Her lips were swollen—from one kiss? Only one kiss? Oh, God, what was he doing to her? To them?

With unwavering eyes, Savannah watched his features change as emotions registered. She saw disgust for himself spread and push at other feelings. No, she wouldn't leave him with that, too. She made a small coaxing sound in her throat, then forced back the eyes he tried to tear away. *He hurts.* She let her fingers loosen in his hair, her palms urging his head down and his mouth to hers again. *He needs.* She had so little to give him. This, Savannah decided as she pulled him to the ground with her, this she could give him. *Oh, God, I'm sorry.*

Clothes were peeled away, his hands not necessarily tender or careful. They were rough with each other, as if they had to force feelings past numbness. Kisses were hungry. Hands rushed. There seemed so much to take and so little time to take it in.

Hands tangled in her hair, Burke positioned her mouth for his repeated onslaughts. Savannah saw and tasted his desperation. She understood the rough urgency, the furious hunger. He clawed at her and clung. With each press of his body to hers, he begged for more chances. Savannah knew—knew the terrors and wants... as well as the futility. Dear God, how could she have done to another person what had been done to her?

When Burke took her he lost himself. Savannah gasped and then gave, holding nothing back. He was drowning in her, sinking deeper than the mind could fathom. She was opened and filled with him, one last time. Body to body, mouth to mouth, they fused a union so utterly complete that they seemed to be a single heart beating.

* * *

Burke braced himself in the shower. Hands flattened to the sweating tiles, he held his head under the pummeling spray. He couldn't remember the last time he'd had quite this bad a hangover. He couldn't remember the last time he'd needed quite so badly to get rip-roaring drunk.

So you went out and got drunk. Now what? What in hell was he supposed to do next? How did a man wipe twenty years of pain from a woman's life in only two weeks? He didn't. It was that clear and that simple. Burke needed more time. And so did Savannah. At least the secrets were out. He knew what he was up against. He knew where her scars were and who had put them there.

Damn, but things weren't quite so black and white anymore. Burke was lost in this murky gray world of husbands skipping out on wives, of mothers abandoning children. Hell, it was no wonder Savannah had to paint it over in her own colors.

Time, he thought again as he shut off the water. He'd been granted more of it last night at midnight. A reprieve. Toweling himself dry, he recalled having toasted the announcement of a nationwide independent haulers' strike with a double Scotch. Tossing the balled-up towel at the hamper, he left the bathroom to dress.

He'd stepped into his slacks, his shirt dangling from his fingers, when he heard sounds drifting through his window. He knew those sounds. Letting the shirt fall to the floor, he whirled and crossed the room.

The blue and silver truck caught and splashed back the morning sun. Julienne employees were carrying cases of wine from the storage shed to the trailer. Savannah, clipboard in hand, was tallying the count and occasionally tossing out an order. Propped beside the driver's door was her cello.

Savannah checked the trailer herself after the last case was loaded. Satisfied that everything was strapped down and secured, she swung the long doors shut and locked them. She turned the clipboard for a signature. Done, she walked back to the cab and tossed the clipboard through the open window. The tears welled in her eyes.

No, she would not cry. Not now. Later. Tonight, tomorrow. When she crossed the Rockies, she promised herself, playing the old game. She'd let herself cry as soon as she crossed the Rockies. Then she'd start again, making herself hold them back again until she reached Omaha, then Chicago. On and on, until the urge had finally been controlled and the emotions deadened.

Spinning on her heels, she started toward the house. There was just Burke to say goodbye to. But then she sensed him. Coming to a halt, she let her eyes slowly lift to the window where Burke, bare-chested, his hair disheveled and damp, glared down at her.

"What are you doing, Savannah?"

She waited until the employees had left the yard and they were alone. "The wines have to be in New York by the end of the week. It's important, Burke. To Claude. To Julienne's."

"The hell with the wines! You can't do this?"

"I have to, Burke." She clenched her teeth, the only bit of strength she could seem to find.

"There's a strike, for God's sake." She could be hurt. Good God, she could be killed! "You can't haul during a strike. Dammit, Savannah, you can't do this!"

"I'll be all right, Burke." Because the tears were building, she stopped to clear her throat. "I've predated the shipping invoice for yesterday. There'll be some tolerance for haulers already en-route when the strike was called. I'll have a few tricky miles till I put enough distance between me and Napa." It had been word of the strike at midnight that had made up Savannah's mind. The door that had been closing had clicked shut with the news. To Savannah it sounded like the word *stuck*.

"Give it a chance, Savannah. Give us some time to try. Running away has never been an answer."

"The choice isn't always between right and wrong. Sometimes it's between the lesser of two wrongs. Will you say goodbye to me, Burke?"

Pain. He was in more pain than he knew existed in the world. "Goodbye."

"Won't you come down here and say it?" Without knowing she did so, Savannah worried her hat in her hands, running it around and around by its brim.

Could he? Be that close and not hold her? Hold her but not keep her? "No, Savannah, I won't come down."

She nodded, understanding. "It's for the best, Burke," she said, backing up and away. "It's better this way. If I didn't go now, I would have eventually. There's less hurt if I do it now, before... before..."

Burke backed away from the window when she turned and shoved the hat onto her head. Numb except for a steadily growing ache in his chest he didn't yet know would become agony, he turned in his bedroom.

As the sound of her engine roared to life, Claude rushed through Burke's door, fumbling to tie a robe at his waist. For a moment they stared at each other. It was like slipping back in time. They'd done this before.

Burke watched his father's eyes skim past him to the window, then back to face him. "You're not letting her go, are you? Stop her!"

Burke shook his head. "It's what she wants."

"Wants! What *she* wants? She's in love with you. Any fool can see it. You're in love with her."

My God, Burke thought, I'm going to fall apart. I'm not going to handle this. "She doesn't want this life. She doesn't want me as much as she wants her freedom."

"Hell, if you don't stop her, I will." Claude spun around. Before he could take his first step, Burke grabbed his shoulder. Burke had never in his life laid a hand on his father; the one he laid on him now would brook no argument.

"No, you won't. I hope to God we've learned that much with Amy." Claude whitened, flinching at the mention of Amy's name. Burke didn't want to inflict pain unnecessarily, but this had to be done, had to be said. "Bringing her back didn't keep her. It made her feel like our prisoner. And so we lost her forever. Savannah will never stay here unless it's what *she* wants, what *she* chooses."

"Girl doesn't know what she wants," Claude muttered angrily. "She's ruining two lives."

"That's her right!" Burke shouted. God, he didn't want to go through this right now. He wanted only to go somewhere and collapse, never feel anything again as long as he lived. "The only chance I've got of getting her back is to let her go. Can you understand that? She's got to come back on her own. She's got to want to be here, with me. If I go after her, she'll run to the ends of the earth to get away."

Burke watched his father age before his eyes. He's thinking of Amy, of how much we might have been responsible for. Claude looked down at the floor, tiredly tucked his hands into the deep pockets of his robe, then turned for the door. On the threshold, he turned back once. "You really think she'll be back?"

"I have to think it. I have to," Burke said, his voice roughening. "If I didn't, I'd go mad."

There was snow in the Rockies. Enough that Savannah couldn't once afford to let her concentration rest for a minute. She told herself she was grateful for the early fall storm. She didn't have the time to think of Burke. Her eyes were too busy keeping track of the road to shed tears. Neither did she marvel at the exquisite shapes of the crystalline flakes as they plopped on her windshield and printed themselves for the millisecond of a wiper blade's swipe. She barely noticed the wonderland beauty of snow building soft down pillows along the ground.

Near Cheyenne the weather heated. So did tempers— ments. There were reports of highway ambushes to find strikebreaking truckers. Savannah pulled into truck stops late at night, filling her tires with air so they'd sit up higher, as if the trailer were empty, working under the cloak of darkness. She was up again before dawn to let them down. She drove with a constant eye on her rearview mirror, knowing her trailer was riding too heavy and steady on the highway. If her body felt as lifeless as a chunk of concrete, she told herself it was nerves.

In Omaha she did something she'd never done before on the road. She sat on her cab's step and played her cello where she was pulled in for the night in a truck stop parking lot. It wasn't a need she'd ever had when she was on the move, with somewhere to go. She wondered how it was she could feel trapped when she was on the wide-open road right smack-dab in the middle of the country. She decided it had to be the closeness of emotions from the other drivers. Most were on their way home. Last job, last paycheck for a while. Sometimes the tension was so thick that Savannah thought it'd take a truck just to get through it.

Outside Chicago, she nearly turned off the interstate to spend a day with Neil. She could have a hell of a time getting back out of the city with a load, though. If her heart seemed swollen enough to explode in her chest, she told herself it was because she missed her brother and his family. She almost never thought of Burke anymore...she told herself.

The restlessness began in Cleveland. She couldn't sleep. The walls of the sleeper-cabin seemed to close in around her. She started wearing her clothes to bed; sometimes she couldn't wait to get dressed before leaping outside, for there seemed to be no air at all in the cab. She'd walk up and down the truck stop lots, each one emptier than the one before. Who could sleep when engines didn't roar in and out? Who could sleep without exhaust fumes?

She cried the night she arrived in New York. She drove only a few miles out of the city and up the coast after unloading the wines before she found a rest stop where she could climb onto her bunk and cry. She deserved a good weep, she decided. She'd never gone from one coast to the other under worse circumstances. When the strike was over it would be better. Not better, fine! She'd put a whole country between them. How much farther apart could two people get?

When she stepped out of her truck in the morning, she discovered she was close enough to the Atlantic shore to smell it in the air and taste it on her tongue. Walking over a high shoulder, she caught a glimpse of it.

Hands in pockets, Savannah walked down to the beach to where the surf foamed as it rushed back down the sand. The wind tore at her hair as she watched the sun rise higher and spread red dye across the horizon.

*"You're going to find yourself at the edge of the earth one day, and the past still right there behind you. Where the hell do you think you'll run to then?"*

"He called this morning," Neil said, stepping into the small family room he'd built onto the house himself three summers ago. "Asked for you."

Savannah shook her head. "No." It wasn't necessary to say Burke's name. They both knew who Neil meant. Shifting her sleeping nephew in her arms, she pressed a kiss to his baby-warm skin.

"Okay, I'll send Anderson, then." Neil lowered himself to the sofa beside Savannah, then leaned forward to smile at his sleeping son. "Looks like an angel, hmm? Like to tan his hide this morning. Dumped a whole bottle of oil on the kitchen floor."

"I think they're supposed to do things like that," Savannah said with a smile.

Terry came in then, giving a disgusted sigh when she saw Danny curled up on Savannah's lap. "You know I'll have to rock him every night for weeks when you're gone."

"I couldn't help myself." Savannah shifted Danny to Terry's arms.

"So have some of your own to spoil," Terry suggested as she left the room.

"Well, Savannah?" Neil laid one of his wide hands on her knee. Wherever he planned to take this conversation, he was apparently ready to stop her from walking away from him. "What about a family of your own?"

"It's never been what I wanted, Neil. You know that."

"Bull," he tossed back. "I don't think he'll call again, Savannah." She felt the tips of his fingers tighten on her knee. "He didn't say it, but there was a weariness there in his voice."

"Don't, Neil. I don't want to hear that he hurts." Savannah shut her eyes and pressed her thumb and finger to them. "It's bad enough being without him."

"Then what the hell are you doing here?" Neil roared at her. "You're not working. Strike's been over ten days, and you've only taken two short hauls. I love you, little sis, but I've got news for you: If you're thinking about making a permanent home here, think again."

"I know it's a nuisance. Of course I'm not thinking of staying much longer."

"Hell, you're no nuisance. But I won't have you start hiding out at your age. And we're going to be needing more room in about seven months."

It was a moment before Savannah realized exactly what Neil meant. "A baby? Another baby? Oh, Neil." She threw her arms around him as the tears sprang up. "I'm so happy for you."

"Yeah." There was a gentle roughness in his voice. "It's what I always dreamed of, sis. My own home, my own family. It's turned out pretty good." They were quiet together for a while. "Savannah, do you ever wonder where they are?"

She clutched more tightly at his shirt. It was time she and Neil talked about them, really talked about them. Then maybe they could finally be put in the past. "Yeah. A lot. I wonder if they married or had more kids. Sometimes I wonder if they've died and we didn't even know it. Your Danny looks so much like Dad. Doesn't he, Neil?" She let the tears fall silently. "Do you hate them?"

"Sometimes. Most of the time, I guess." He folded her slender hand in his bigger one. "But now and then I realize they couldn't handle their own lives; they may have done us a big favor not trying to handle ours."

"No, I don't believe that!" Savannah pulled away from him. "If they'd loved us, either one of them, they'd never have done it. They couldn't have."

"Savannah." Neil sighed and tore a hand through his hair. "I remember her face that last night. I think it was the hardest thing she ever had to do. I think she felt she had no other choice."

"She could have tried for one more day, Neil? Just one more day?" Savannah's voice trailed off. Burke had asked the same of her, hadn't he? For her to give them a chance.

"I'm not saying she was right, Savannah. I'm saying she didn't mean it to turn out wrong. She probably thought we would get adopted, wind up in wonderful homes. Dad had been tough on her for a long time. I remember the fights, her crying at night. You remember him when he wanted to play. After Dad left, Mom didn't have much to keep her going. She wanted to do right by us." Neil patted her knee just before standing. "She did what she thought was best."

But she was wrong, Savannah thought. You didn't abandon someone you loved. No matter what your reason.

## Chapter Twelve

Burke steadily worked his way through the mail Cynthia had opened and separated. A neglected cigarette burned in the ashtray, sending up a column of white smoke. He set aside two letters for dictated answers and reviewed three invoices in a row before slipping them into a file for the accounting department. The rest, he decided, would require telephone correspondence. Noticing the cigarette, Burke stubbed it out. Minutes later he would be lighting another.

"Burke?"

Wearily, he leaned back in his chair and rubbed thumb and forefinger over the bridge of his nose. "Yes, Cynthia." He smoked too much; he didn't sleep enough.

"You asked to be notified when Jones Hauling arrived." Burke automatically tensed. "Shipping just called. Truck pulled in five minutes ago."

His hand fell away from his brow, then curled into a fist. "All right, thanks."

A month. Burke stood and flexed his hands before shoving them into his pockets. Four of the longest, most wretched weeks of his life. Would they be over today? Was it sensible to hope?

It was time to find out, he decided, and he walked into the anteroom. With a glance at Cynthia, he said, "I'll be in the yard for a few minutes. I should return shortly."

He moved down the brightly lit hall that was the spine connecting the separate winery buildings. It would take him to the tunnels, and the tunnels to the yard.

He hadn't had a word from Savannah in all this time. Not even to let him know she'd arrived safely in New York. He'd had to wait for the shipping confirmation to arrive by return mail. When he'd finally read her name for himself he'd slumped in his chair, weakened with relief. Then he'd crushed the damned invoice in his fist.

For too many days that followed, Burke had felt the cold, cold anger. At Savannah. For what she'd thrown away. For doing to him, to them, exactly what her mother had done to her twenty years ago. And now? he asked himself. Was he as cold? As angry?

How long did it take to recover from loving someone with every bone in your body? Did one ever recover? How long did the pain last?

He'd been so sure she'd come back. He'd believed in her—and she'd let him down. Would she let him down again today? He'd asked Neil, one more time, to send her out. Damn woman didn't even have a phone!

Burke lit a cigarette and dragged deeply. She hadn't come the last two trips. If she wasn't in the yard today, Burke would not ask for her again. Hearing the echo of his footsteps in the dank tunnel, he remembered the day he'd brought Savannah here, and then to the cellars. God, why did he torture himself with the memories?

Burke followed the sunlit path, feeling as anxious as a teenage boy expecting to be stood up. Suppose, he mused, he walked into the yard and she *was* there? Then what? Suppose she was her cool, haughty self again?

There was activity in the yard. A forklift murmured around, unloading crates. Burke glanced around, seeing only his own employees at first. Then he saw a tall, lanky blond man, a stranger. Burke was pointed out to him, and he came forward with a clipboard in hand. *She's not coming back.* It wasn't conviction as much as fear that put the thought into his head.

"You Burke Julienne?" the man asked. "Jones Hauling. I need a signature."

Without noticing the pen the driver offered, Burke automatically slid his own from his inside pocket. He scrawled his signature, handed back the clipboard and turned for the path, all without saying a word.

*She's not coming back.* It was a mocking chant all the way back to his office. He said nothing when he passed Cynthia's desk. She looked up and shook her head, her habitual signal there'd been no calls or visitors in his absence.

He was three steps inside his office before something nagged at his senses. Jasmine. A thick, mind-stripping cloud of jasmine. Muscle by muscle, his body drew tight. He felt his jaw clenching, his spine straightening. Sometimes he imagined that scent at night and woke from a dream reaching for her, only to find her gone. Slowly, Burke lifted his head.

She was curled up in his leather chair almost the same as the first day. Her legs were crossed Indian-fashion, her arms loosely folded. Her face was hidden behind the felt hat pulled low on her brow. He didn't have to see her eyes to know they would be closed. She was no longer a stranger to him. He knew she slept by the curl of her hand, the rise and fall of her chest, the precise beat of her pulse.

He walked closer. When she didn't move, he crouched down to sit on his heels. Shadows. He saw the shadows of strain beneath her eyes. Shifting his gaze, he saw her cello propped against the wall near the open garden door.

He needed a moment. Rising, he walked to the windows and stared out. There was a logical conclusion that could be drawn, he decided. He had only to find the pieces.

There was a truck in the yard. It wasn't Savannah's truck, and it already had a driver. Her truck could be out of commission again. So why was there a cello leaning against the wall? Because she never left the cello with the truck.

Savannah woke just as he stood and walked away. Her heart had started thudding; fear pinned her to the seat. Why had he walked away? The Burke of last month wouldn't have. But he wasn't that man anymore, a small voice accused her. You've changed him. You've taught him love couldn't be counted on.

Unable to wait another moment to know if he still loved her, Savannah opened her mouth to say his name. Then she noticed, really noticed, his profile. He looked so tired. No, not tired, lifeless.

They moved in the same moment—Burke turned, Savannah stood—and froze. It was instinctive for Savannah to pull on her ice in order to meet his eyes and face what might or might not be there. Burke looked for the smoke that would have told him she'd come back. He saw slate instead.

"Your truck out of commission again, Savannah?" God, she was lovely, and he wanted to reach out now and touch her.

"No, no, the truck's fine...just fine." She couldn't have lost him, not when it was her turn to have her own. "I sold the truck." She waited, but all he did was arch one dark eyebrow. "There I was on the same old highways, seeing the same cities and towns and people that I've been seeing for years. And it was just one more institution. A whole lot bigger, and without walls. But it was still a...a place where I was stuck...and alone...."

*She's come back.* If Burke hadn't moved yet, if his features were frozen in place, it was because he was taking in that one delirious truth. Savannah had come home.

"I can't be alone, Burke." Tears gathered, and she tried to blink them dry. "I can't be without you. Will you have me back? Please, will you—"

And then she was in his arms. Where she belonged. His mouth was on hers. Savannah moaned to the gruff sound from Burke's throat as each seemed to need this moment to satisfy a gnawing hunger.

"Savannah," he murmured.

She melted to the sound of her name on his lips. "Will you kiss me again?" She plunged her hands into his hair. "And then again?"

His mouth covered hers, and she swayed. The kiss was long and deep. "Savannah." Burke framed her face with his hands, tipping it up until he saw the swirling smoke. "Why? Why did you change your mind?"

Quivering with the sheer joy of being able to love without fear, Savannah rested her head on his shoulder. "Besides the fact that I was miserable without you?" She nuzzled his neck, taking in the familiar musky scent of him. "The best days of my life were those first years, when I had love and laughter, the sun on my face and smell of earth on my hands. That's here, with you. Freedom is... freedom isn't picking up and leaving when I feel like it; it's knowing that I have the choice to go if I need to." She captured his face with her hands. "You'd let me, wouldn't you, Burke? If I had to leave, you wouldn't stop me?"

Burke knew what his answer would be, though it hurt to realize she might have come back only for a little while. "You're free to go whenever and wherever you choose, Savannah."

"Good." Tossing her head back, she laughed. "'Cause Neil and Terry expect another baby in the spring. And I'm to be godmother... again."

On a sigh, Burke dropped his brow to rest on the top of her head. "Chicago."

"Hey," Savannah said. "You didn't think I meant I wanted to flit all over the country? Uh-uh. Don't think for a minute you're going to get rid of me that easily." She was backing away, dragging him along by the hand. At the couch, she flopped down and brought him tumbling down on top of her.

Before the softness of her body stripped his mind of thought, Burke held her chin and commanded her eyes. "You'll marry me, Savannah?"

She breathed in and savored this moment. "You've got me for a lifetime. And there's a fifth generation of Juliennes to have yet."

\*   \*   \*   \*   \*

*...and now an exciting short story
from Silhouette Books.*

\*

**HEATHER GRAHAM POZZESSERE**

# Shadows on the Nile

### CHAPTER ONE

Alex could tell that the woman was very nervous. Her fingers were wound tightly about the arm rests, and she had been staring straight ahead since the flight began. Who was she? Why was she flying alone? Why to Egypt? She was a small woman, fine-boned, with classical features and porcelain skin. Her hair was golden blond, and she had blue-gray eyes that were slightly tilted at the corners, giving her a sensual and exotic appeal.

And she smelled divine. He had been sitting there, glancing through the flight magazine, and her scent had reached him, filling him like something rushing through his bloodstream, and before he had looked at her he had known that she would be beautiful.

John was frowning at him. His gaze clearly said that this was not the time for Alex to become interested in a woman. Alex lowered his head, grinning. Nuts to John. He was the one who had made the reservations so late that there was already another passenger between them in their row. Alex couldn't have remained silent anyway; he was certain that he could ease the flight for her. Besides, he had to know her name, had to see if her eyes would turn silver when she smiled. Even though he should, he couldn't ignore her.

"Alex," John said warningly.

Maybe John was wrong, Alex thought. Maybe this was precisely the right time for him to get involved. A woman would be the perfect shield, in case anyone was interested in his business in Cairo.

The two men should have been sitting next to each other, Jillian decided. She didn't know why she had wound up sandwiched between the two of them, but she couldn't do a thing about it. Frankly, she was far too nervous to do much of anything.

"It's really not so bad," a voice said sympathetically. It came from her right. It was the younger of the two men, the one next to the window. "How about a drink? That might help."

Jillian took a deep, steadying breath, then managed to answer. "Yes . . . please. Thank you."

His fingers curled over hers. Long, very strong fingers, nicely tanned. She had noticed him when she had taken her seat—he was difficult not to notice. There was an arresting quality about him. He had a certain look: high-powered, confident, self-reliant. He was medium tall and medium built, with shoulders that nicely filled out his suit jacket, dark brown eyes, and sandy hair that seemed to defy any effort at combing it. And he had a wonderful voice, deep and compelling. It broke through her fear and actually soothed her. Or perhaps it was the warmth of his hand over hers that did it.

"Your first trip to Egypt?" he asked. She managed a brief nod, but was saved from having to comment when the stewardess came by. Her companion ordered her a white wine, then began to converse with her quite normally, as if unaware that her fear of flying had nearly rendered her speechless. He asked her what she did for a living, and she heard herself tell him that she was a music teacher at a junior college. He responded easily to everything she said, his voice warm and concerned each time he asked another question. She didn't think; she simply answered him, because flying had become easier the moment he touched her. She even told him that she was a widow, that her husband had been killed in a car accident four years ago, and that she was here now to fulfill a long-held dream, because she had always longed to see the pyramids, the Nile and all the ancient wonders Egypt held.

She had loved her husband, Alex thought, watching as pain briefly darkened her eyes. Her voice held a thread of sadness when she mentioned her husband's name. Out of nowhere, he wondered how it would feel to be loved by such a woman.

Alex noticed that even John was listening, commenting on things now and then. How interesting, Alex thought, looking across at his friend and associate.

The stewardess came with the wine. Alex took it for her, chatting casually with the woman as he paid. Charmer, Jillian thought ruefully. She flushed, realizing that it was his charm that had led her to tell him so much about her life.

Her fingers trembled when she took the wineglass. "I'm sorry," she murmured. "I don't really like to fly."

Alex—he had introduced himself as Alex, but without telling her his last name—laughed and said that was the understatement of the year. He pointed out the window to the clear blue sky—an omen of good things to come, he said—then assured her that the airline had an excellent safety record. His friend, the older man with the haggard, world-weary face, eventually introduced himself as John. He joked and tried to reassure her, too, and eventually their efforts paid off. Once she felt a little calmer, she offered to move, so they could converse without her in the way.

Alex tightened his fingers around hers, and she felt the startling warmth in his eyes. His gaze was appreciative and sensual, without being insulting. She felt a rush of sweet heat swirl within her, and she realized with surprise that it was excitement, that she was enjoying his company the way a woman enjoyed the company of a man who attracted her. She had thought she would never feel that way again.

"I wouldn't move for all the gold in ancient Egypt," he said with a grin, "and I doubt that John would, either." He touched her cheek. "I might lose track of you, and I don't even know your name."

"Jillian," she said, meeting his eyes. "Jillian Jacoby."

He repeated her name softly, as if to commit it to memory, then went on to talk about Cairo, the pyramids at Giza, the Valley of the Kings, and the beauty of the nights when the sun set over the desert in a riot of blazing red.

And then the plane was landing. To her amazement, the flight had ended. Once she was on solid ground again, Jillian realized that Alex knew all sorts of things about her, while she didn't know a thing about him or John—not even their full names.

They went through customs together. Jillian was immediately fascinated, in love with the colorful atmosphere of Cairo, and not at all dismayed by the waiting and the bureaucracy. When they finally reached the street she fell head over heels in love with the exotic land. The heat shimmered in the air, and taxi drivers in long burnooses lined up for fares. She could hear the soft singsong of their language, and she was thrilled to realize that the dream she had harbored for so long was finally coming true.

She didn't realize that two men had followed them from the airport to the street. Alex, however, did. He saw the men behind him, and his jaw tightened as he nodded to John to stay put and hurried after Jillian.

"Where are you staying?" he asked her.

"The Hilton," she told him, pleased at his interest. Maybe her dream was going to turn out to have some unexpected aspects.

He whistled for a taxi. Then, as the driver opened the door, Jillian looked up to find Alex staring at her. She felt . . . something. A fleeting magic raced along her spine, as if she knew what he was about to do. Knew, and should have protested, but couldn't.

Alex slipped his arm around her. One hand fell to her waist, the other cupped her nape, and he kissed her. His mouth was hot, his touch firm, persuasive. She was filled with heat; she trembled . . . and then she broke away at last, staring at him, the look in her eyes more eloquent than any words. Confused, she turned away and stepped into the taxi. As soon as she was seated she turned to stare after him, but he was already gone, a part of the crowd.

She touched her lips as the taxi sped toward the heart of the city. She shouldn't have allowed the kiss; she barely knew him. But she couldn't forget him.

She was still thinking about him when she reached the Hilton. She checked in quickly, but she was too late to acquire a guide for the day. The manager suggested that she stop by the Kahil bazaar, not far from the hotel. She dropped her bags in her room, then took another taxi to the bazaar. Once again she was enchanted. She loved everything: the noise, the people, the donkey carts that blocked the narrow streets, the shops with their beaded entryways and beautiful wares in silver and stone, copper and brass. Old men smoking water pipes sat on mats drinking tea, while younger men shouted out their wares from stalls and doorways. Jillian began walking slowly, trying to take it all in. She was occasionally jostled, but she kept her hand on her purse and sidestepped quickly. She was just congratulating herself on her competence when she was suddenly dragged into an alley by two Arabs swaddled in burnooses.

"What—" she gasped, but then her voice suddenly fled. The alley was empty and shadowed, and night was coming. One man had a scar on his cheek, and held a long, curved knife; the other carried a switchblade.

"Where is it?" the first demanded.

"Where is what?" she asked frantically.

The one with the scar compressed his lips grimly. He set his knife against her cheek, then stroked the flat side down to her throat. She could feel the deadly coolness of the steel blade.

"Where is it? Tell me now!"

Her knees were trembling, and she tried to find the breath to speak. Suddenly she noticed a shadow emerging from the darkness behind her attackers. She gasped, stunned, as the man drew nearer. It was Alex.

Alex . . . silent, stealthy, his features taut and grim. Her heart seemed to stop. Had he come to her rescue? Or was he allied with her attackers, there to threaten, even destroy, her?

* * * * *

*Watch for Chapter Two of SHADOWS ON THE NILE coming next month—only in Silhouette Intimate Moments.*

**Take 4 Silhouette Romance novels & a surprise gift**

# FREE

Then preview 6 brand-new Silhouette Romance novels—delivered to your door as soon as they come off the presses! If you decide to keep them, pay just $1.95* each, *with no shipping, handling or other charges of any kind!*

Each month, you'll meet lively young heroines and share in their thrilling escapes, trials and triumphs . . . virile men you'll find as attractive and irresistible as the heroines do . . . and colorful supporting characters you'll feel you've always known.

Start with 4 Silhouette Romance novels and a surprise gift absolutely FREE. They're yours to keep without obligation. You can always return a shipment and cancel at any time.

Simply fill out and return the coupon today!

*$1.70 each plus 69¢ postage and handling per shipment in Canada.

## *Silhouette* ❦ *Romance*®

---

### Clip and mail to: Silhouette Books

**In U.S.:**
901 Fuhrmann Blvd.
P.O. Box 9013
Buffalo, NY 14240-9013

**In Canada:**
P.O. Box 609
Fort Erie, Ontario
L2A 5X3

**YES!** Please rush me 4 FREE Silhouette Romance novels and my free surprise gift. Then send me 6 new Silhouette Romance novels to preview each month as soon as they come off the presses. Bill me at the low price of $1.95* each with no shipping, handling or other hidden costs. There is no minimum number of books I must purchase. I can always return a shipment and cancel at any time. Even if I never buy another book from Silhouette Romance, the 4 free novels and the surprise gift are mine to keep forever.

*$1.70 each plus 69¢ postage and handling per shipment in Canada.

215 BPL BP7F

| | | |
|---|---|---|
| Name | (please print) | |
| Address | | Apt. |
| City | State/Prov. | Zip/Postal Code |

This offer is limited to one order per household and not valid to present subscribers. Price is subject to change.

SilR-SUB-1D

# ATTRACTIVE, SPACE SAVING BOOK RACK

Display your most prized novels on this handsome and sturdy book rack. The hand-rubbed walnut finish will blend into your library decor with quiet elegance, providing a practical organizer for your favorite hard-or soft-covered books.

*Only $9.95*

**Approximately 16" x 8" when assembled**

**Assembles in seconds!**

To order, rush your name, address and zip code, along with a check or money order for $10.70* ($9.95 plus 75¢ postage and handling) payable to *Silhouette Books*.

Silhouette Books
Book Rack Offer
901 Fuhrmann Blvd.
P.O. Box 1396
Buffalo, NY 14269-1396

*Offer not available in Canada.*

*New York and Iowa residents add appropriate sales tax.

BKR-2A

# Silhouette Special Edition

# COMING NEXT MONTH

**#415 TIME AFTER TIME—Billie Green**
Airline executives Leah French and Paul Gregory had a cool, professional relationship. Then the dreams began, dreams that carried them out of time, to faraway lands and into each other's arms.

**#416 FOOLS RUSH IN—Ginna Gray**
In tracing her missing twin, Erin Blaine's first find was dashing Max Delany, her sister's supposed beloved. Dodging gunmen and double-crossers, Max and Erin sought clues...and stumbled onto unwanted desire.

**#417 WHITE NIGHTS—Dee Norman**
Whether racing down ski slopes or chasing the chills in a hot tub, Jennifer Ericson couldn't seem to avoid hostile financier Travis MacKay. Though he suspected her of pursuing him, she was really only running from love.

**#418 TORN ASUNDER—Celeste Hamilton**
Years ago Alexa Thorpe, the boss's daughter, and Ty Duncan, the laborer's son, fell in forbidden love, but family objections and deceptions drove them apart. By tackling their history, could they succeed in sharing a future?

**#419 SUMMER RAIN—Lisa Jackson**
Widowed Ainsley Hughes reluctantly brought her troubled son to her father's ranch, only to find the Circle S failing...and aloof Trent McCullough in charge. She'd once loved Trent's fire, but could she trust his iciness now?

**#420 LESSONS IN LOVING—Bay Matthews**
Bachelor Mitch Bishop had much to learn about parenting, and special ed teacher Jamie Carr was the perfect instructor. But in the school of love, both adults faltered on their ABC's.

# AVAILABLE THIS MONTH

**#409 A CERTAIN SMILE**
Lynda Trent
**#410 FINAL VERDICT**
Pat Warren
**#411 THUNDERSTRUCK**
Pamela Toth

**#412 RUN AWAY HOME**
Marianne Shock
**#413 A NATURAL WOMAN**
Caitlin Cross
**#414 BELONGING**
Dixie Browning